A GRAVE SEARCH

Previously published Worldwide Mystery title by
WENDY ROBERTS

A GRAVE CALLING

A GRAVE SEARCH

WENDY ROBERTS

W🌐RLDWIDE®

TORONTO • NEW YORK • LONDON
AMSTERDAM • PARIS • SYDNEY • HAMBURG
STOCKHOLM • ATHENS • TOKYO • MILAN
MADRID • WARSAW • BUDAPEST • AUCKLAND

Recycling programs
for this product may
not exist in your area.

A Grave Search

A Worldwide Mystery/January 2019

First published by Carina Press

ISBN-13: 978-1-335-45526-0

Copyright © 2018 by Wendy Roberts

Carina Press acknowledges the editorial services of Deborah Nemeth

This book is dedicated to you, gentle reader. Thank you for the privilege of continuing to tell my stories.

ONE

The first time I found a body I thought it was a fluke. If I'd known that it would become my entire life, I would've let those remains stay buried. Finding corpses is not a job for the damaged or broken and I am both of those things.

Who would ever think that using divining rods to turn up deceased loved ones could be a lucrative business?

Just as I was about to click on the email icon on my laptop, a cold wet nose pressed against my bare thigh.

"Leave me alone, Wookie, I'm working here."

My protests fell on the deaf ears of my Rottweiler, who punctuated his desire for affection with a long, sloppy lick from my ankle to knee.

"You are so-o-o gross," I complained as I got to my feet.

When a hundred-thirty-pound dog wants your attention, it's best to just give in. The second I was away from my kitchen table he ran over to his basket of toys, snagged a tennis ball and bounded excitedly to the patio doors that led out to my backyard.

The moment I stepped from the air-conditioned house to the patio a wave of damp heat slopped over me, and sweat dotted my brow and dampened my armpits.

"Jesus," I muttered, wiping my forehead and bending to pick up the ball Wookie dropped at my feet.

Ninety degrees with equally high humidity wasn't normal weather for Washington in July. This was more like vacationing in Hades.

Wookie seemed oblivious to the weather as he charged into the backfield and looked back at me expectantly. I threw the ball with as much effort as I could muster and he bounded after to retrieve it and then returned it covered in slobber for another toss.

I made a face at the dripping ball but tossed it again anyway. I wished I could throw the ball as far as my neighbor's house two acres away, just to wear Wookie out. He lost the ball in the tall grass and, while he searched, I walked the back concrete patio, pausing to yank a few scorched weeds that persisted in the cracks.

When we were both panting, tongues hanging out and thirsty for the air-conditioned comforts of my small ranch house, I ushered Wookie inside then walked around the side of the house to water my sun-scorched flower planters.

I sprayed the sorry petunias with their droopy heads and yellowed leaves until they sat in muddy puddles.

Deadheading…watering…weeding…fertilizing. It was my first attempt at the domesticity of planting flowers and I was thinking my last. My therapist told me gardening could be therapeutic but I was beginning to suspect my thumb was more the shade of black root rot than green.

As I wrapped the watering hose back around the reel, I heard the sound of a car in my driveway. I turned, hoping to see Garrett pulling up for an impromptu visit but I didn't recognize the red BMW convertible that parked behind my newer Jeep Cherokee. I hesitated with my hand still on the spray nozzle of the hose. My fingers itched for my shotgun left behind in another place and time.

I walked forward, dragging the hose with me. I was willing to turn the nozzle on and fully soak the sixty-something coiffed woman climbing out of the car if she gave me any trouble.

"Julie Hall?" she called out. There was an accent, something mixed European that accompanied her pale Nordic skin and svelte body.

"State your name and business," I shouted back. The shout was unnecessary since she was now less than a couple feet from me.

Wookie took up watchdog duties inside the house, barking as if he wanted to eat his way through the drywall and chomp on BMW lady's pantsuited butt.

"Ebba Johansson." The woman stuck out her hand.

She wasn't drunk but she'd definitely had at least one drink. The scent on her breath wasn't muted by her musky perfume. It wafted over to me, permeated my sinuses and the desire for an icy cold glass of Moscato nearly caused my knees to buckle. I rubbed my hands on the side of my denim shorts.

The fabric is rough around the seams but soft because it's worn from years of wear.

I focused on that one sensation, a grounding exercise my psychiatrist taught me. It was stupid. But it worked.

Since I didn't accept her offered hand, Ms. Ebba Johansson let it drop to her side.

The name and face were familiar but I knew we'd never met. She must've seen the question written on my face.

"I've been emailing you about my daughter, Ava."

Right. The kidnap case that flooded all forms of media. The pretty twenty-five-year-old was last seen a couple months ago getting into a car with her ex-boyfriend. Ebba Johansson received a ransom note and was prepared to pay the hundred thousand requested but something went wrong. When she arrived at the instructed location without telling the cops, as the kidnapper instructed, her daughter wasn't there. She dropped the money and waited but Ava never showed even after the hidden bag of cash was taken. When she finally did call the police all they found at the remote, forested campsite was a sticky puddle of blood large enough to indicate the girl was not coming back.

"How did you find my house?" I demanded.

I'd taken pains to make sure my home stayed secret. There was no link to the address on the Divine Reunions website. I had no friends. No family. Okay, that made me sound pathetic. But I did have a hunky FBI boyfriend who'd die before spilling my location and that made up for all the rest.

"If you'll just give me a few minutes of your time," the woman said, stepping closer and holding up an eight-by-ten glossy picture of the pretty blonde face that had blanketed TV news for months.

"Just like I said in my email reply, I can't help you find your daughter."

"Why?" she demanded.

There were a dozen reasons. The first two of those reasons had to do with location. The campground where the blood was found had been searched by experts and volunteers for weeks and if there was a body out there, they would've found it. The second reason had to do with the fact that she lived not far from my old trailer. I'd worked long and hard and paid Dr. Chen a ton of money to purge my head of the quicksand, sticky thoughts associated with the torture chamber formerly known as home. I was still dealing with that anguish and trauma, and had zero desire to open that old wound by stomping around the area searching for a body.

"I can't possibly search an entire county for your daughter and, even if I could, I don't have the time."

This was true. I had dozens of requests every day. Sadly, there were a ton of people who searched out www.DivineReunions.com and messaged me to help find the bones of their loved ones and bring them home.

"But even if you could just give it a try for a few days I'd be so grateful. You don't know what it's like… the not knowing."

I did know. That's what had me making a full-time job out of finding the dead.

I shook my head. "I'm sorry."

I turned to walk away and the woman put a pale, trembling hand on my arm.

"Denny said you'd help."

Her voice was hardly above a whisper but the name on her lips hit me like a scream and I flinched.

When I turned back around to face her she looked relieved. I let the name roll around in my head bringing me back to another time.

"How do you know Denny?" I tried to draw a correlation between this fancy-shmancy-looking white woman and my Native American ex-boyfriend.

"I run a spa inside the casino where he works." She unzipped the large white leather purse that hung from her shoulder and pulled out a neatly folded sheet of lined paper. When she handed me the page I shook it open and took a look.

Denny had sketched a picture of the two of us. He had a real gift as an artist and an offhand, easygoing talent that always surprised. The drawing of himself was in profile with his hands cupped over his mouth calling out. A bubble above his head said: *Hey! She's a stuffy old lady but she could use your help.*

In the drawing I was in the distance, walking away from him. I had bare feet and was wearing a skimpy flowered sundress that showed curves he knew personally. My hair was blowing around my shoulders and I appeared soft and vulnerable. He'd always drawn me prettier than I could ever be. He had sketched me with one hand raised over my shoulder offering him my middle finger in answer. It made my lips twitch into a smile in spite of myself. Everything from the scrub of grass and packed earth he drew around my feet to the distant clouds penciled on the horizon reminded me of home. For a fraction in time I ached for those days but then, quicker than a lion can spot a limp, that feeling was gone.

I refolded the paper and went to hand it back to her.

"No." She shook her head. "Keep it."

The drawing disappeared into the back pocket of my denim shorts.

"I resent the part where he called me stuffy," she said, her voice indignant and huffy. "And the old part."

We stood there wordlessly for a minute while I toyed with thoughts in my head.

"I know my daughter is dead, Ms. Hall. All I want is to bury her. Will you do it?" Ebba asked. "Please. Will you help bring my Ava home?"

I won't go back there. Ever. Not even for Denny. "I'll think about it and give you an answer in a few days."

She looked so relieved that it made me feel guilty for not giving her an immediate yes but if I had given her an immediate reply it would've been a fat no.

"I'll give you my phone number." She pulled out a violet business card and a pen, scrawled a number on the back of the card and handed it to me. "Ebba's Bliss spa number and my email are on the front and my personal cell number is on the back. Since all this happened I haven't been at any of my spas as much as I should be so try my cell phone first. You can call me anytime at all day or night."

I took the card and she thanked me emphatically before turning to walk back to her car.

"Just a sec." I followed her. "How did you find me, Ebba?"

She paused with the car door open and her face had a pinched look that told me she was considering offering me a lie but then it softened.

"Denny heard rumors you were living somewhere in east Snohomish County. He also told me you had a Rottweiler named Wookie." She nodded to the picture window where Wookie was still barking nonstop to protect me. "So…well… I visited vet offices until I found one that knew you." She looked oddly puffed up and proud. "I gave them a song and dance about having Wookie's sister as a pet and wanting to arrange a doggie playdate."

A small part of me was impressed by her persistence and ingenuity.

"Wow. As easy as that, huh?"

"It wasn't that easy. I must've visited a dozen veterinarians until I discovered yours."

I walked inside the house thinking that Ebba Johansson was a very smart woman and it made me feel decidedly unsafe, because there were a lot of people who were just as desperate to find the remains of their loved ones. Inside, Wookie wagged his entire body with delight that I hadn't been kidnapped while he was stuck inside.

"You're such a good boy. I know you wanted to chomp the ol' lady's butt." I rubbed the top of his head. "You'll have to settle for a treat instead."

I felt chilled as the air-conditioning evaporated the sheen of sweat on my body. Wookie followed me into the kitchen where I rewarded his loyalty with a liver treat. Calming myself wasn't as easy. I didn't like being tracked down.

I dropped Ebba's business card on my counter and pulled Denny's sketch from my back pocket. I unfolded it, smoothed the creases and admired the talent, then used a Pike Place magnet to stick it on the fridge.

I checked my cell for any messages I might've missed from Garrett but there weren't any. Not waking up with him hurt that tender achy spot in the center of my chest but I'd been the one who left his place to be on my own. I typed him a text describing Ebba Johansson's visit and how she tracked me down, knowing that it would irritate him as much as it did me. Even more. But then I deleted the message before hitting Send and sent him another.

Good morning, sexy. Followed by a kissy face emoji.

After I sent the text a reminder chimed on my phone.

I was late to do some skeleton mapping.

I grabbed my backpack that contained everything I needed for the job, even a can of bear spray Garrett insisted I keep close while hiking. I tossed in some water bottles as well. On my way out I pulled on a Mariners cap and promised Wookie I wouldn't be long.

The newer Jeep cruised like a Cadillac and the sound system blasted out my newest self-help book as the temperature control kept the interior cool but not cold.

"Nobody needs fancy doodads to get from A to B."

"Shaddup, Gramps."

I cranked the narrator's voice that played through the speakers so loud that the sound of someone giving soothing advice about PTSD was more like a battle cry.

An hour later I drove up the rutted dirt drive of a small dilapidated church built in the early nineteen hundreds. After much discussion, the local community had decided to renovate the old building. The plan was to lease it out as a daycare center and turn the quarter acre property out back into a community garden. The garden part was where I came in. One of the oldest town residents had contacted me to help map out the graveyard behind the church. Near as Old Abel could remember there'd been a couple families buried behind the church but nobody had been able to dig up records.

Any grave markers had long since been covered by earth and sod over the years and possibly disintegrated.

Abel was sitting in the shade on the steps of the church. A ninety-something-year-old black man who I knew by now would be playing Candy Crush on his phone.

"Haven't you beaten that game yet?" I climbed out of the Jeep and reached in the back seat for my pack.

"I don't think that's possible," he admitted, looking at me over the top of his readers.

I hooked my backpack over one shoulder and walked over to the church.

Abel slipped his phone and glasses into the front pocket of his shirt and groaned slightly as he got to his feet. "Man, it's hot as blazes out here."

"Yeah. Too hot," I agreed. "So hot the trees are whistling for dogs."

"I like that one." He added, "Hotter than a hooker in church."

"Hotter than the hinges on the gates of hell."

"You win." He wagged a finger at me. "It's the global warming." He took out a handkerchief and mopped his forehead. "It's gonna cook us in our own skin."

"Your grandson meeting us here?"

Abel nodded. "Wes should be along shortly but he does things in his own time so let's not wait on him."

We walked around to the back of the church. Massive cedars surrounded much of the property, which was banked by a dry creek on the left and the main road into town on the right. When Abel first contacted me through my site and sent me pictures of the churchyard I'd noticed that the area intended for the garden boasted knee-high weeds. Wading through that would've made my search harder so I was pleased to see Abel's grandson had mowed the area, as promised. Not that I couldn't shuffle through weeds like I had many times before.

The sun was scorching the top of my head as I pulled my ball cap down over my eyes. I wish we'd decided to do this earlier or later in the day when I wouldn't be frying out here.

"I'm going to walk the property in a grid. Wherever my rods determine there's a grave, I'm going to leave a flag. After that, your grandson can do a little digging to see if there are any grave markers that got buried."

"Wes is not going to be happy about digging up dirt in this hot weather." Abel chuckled. "But he'll be thrilled to finally get the go-ahead to get his guys in here and start the job for the garden."

Abel's grandson had a landscaping company and had been given the approval to dig up the land and install a ground sprinkler system for the future garden. With it already being late July it was too late to be planting veggies this year, but they'd prepare the plot. From what Abel had told me, his grandson was a lazy son of a gun who liked to give the grunt work to his underlings while he supervised, but he'd agreed to help us uncover any graves by hand before bringing in equipment.

Abel leaned against the building to take advantage of the shade and resumed the game on his phone. I opened my pack, took a long drink from a water bottle, then pulled out my divining rods. They were not the rods I'd been given as a child. Those had been given an unexpected retirement. The new ones worked just the same though, and the copper felt cool, light and reassuring in my hands.

"You do the devil's work because Satan is inside you."

I flinched as an imagined lash from Grandma's whip cut a deep groove into my back.

I took a deep breath and concentrated on the cool rods in my hands and the sun hot against my skin.

"Oh hell in a handbasket!" Abel grumped at his game, snapping me out of my exercise.

I laughed at him. "Just give up."

"Never," he mumbled with a determined set to his mouth.

I snagged the satchel that contained a dozen bright orange ten-inch marker flags on tiny aluminum poles. I pulled the canvas satchel over my head and the strap crossed over my body so the bag rested on my hip. While Abel continued crushing candies on his phone, I went to work.

Here goes nothing.

I was just beginning my walk when a pickup truck zoomed up the drive with a roar and a short, stout man about the same as my mid-twenties hopped out.

The paunchy man came over and hugged Abel.

"This is my grandson, Wes," Abel said.

"Hi ya," Wes said.

He had crooked teeth and an oily salesman smile that set me on edge. He was dressed a little too fine for a landscaper in freshly ironed khakis and a buttoned-down shirt. I walked over, transferred the rods to my left hand and gave Wes's thick, sweaty hand a shake.

"So-o-o…" Wes nodded to the quarter acre lot. "Gramps tells me ya going to find bodies using some sticks."

The nickname "Gramps" gave me a jolt that stung from my running-shoe-clad feet to the top of my Mariners cap.

My fingers clutched the canvas satchel at my hip.

The bag is smooth and cool and light and bumpy because of the flags inside and… My mind fumbled and kept going back to "Gramps."

"And Wes here will help with anything you need."

"I will indeed."

I was surprised at the offer because Abel had told me his grandson, and a lot of people in the town, thought the grave-dowsing idea was a stinky pile of crap. A money grab. Although I wasn't charging much. I figured Wes agreeing to help was more because he was just anxious to get on with the part of the job where he could install his sprinklers and make some cash of his own.

"Thanks. I don't need help with the search," I replied but then offered, "but if I find any unmarked graves, you can check if there are any buried markers."

His smile broadened in the kind of way that said there was no chance I was finding a damn thing with my little copper rods, but he'd be polite and humor both me and his grandfather.

Gramps.

Shit.

As I took my place on the right side of the lot, Wes went and got out a couple lawn chairs and a small cooler. He set Abel up with a lawn chair and a Coke in the small sliver of shade offered by the church and put his own lawn chair beside, snagging a beer for himself. Maybe Wes wasn't so bad.

I stuck the rods straight out in front of me and started my slow, steady walk up and down the lot in long rows. The L-shaped rods would cross if there was something to tell me. As I sometimes did while strolling and waiting for the dead to announce themselves, I thought up a random story. Abel and Wes were so different and maybe they weren't related at all. I devised a tale of secret love. Maybe Abel and his son were polygamists with a half dozen wives and Wes called six different women Mom. If that were the case, Abel would be running from woman to woman trying to get them all to help him beat the next level of Candy Crush. I laughed. My scenario wasn't going to win any awards for creativity but it kept my brain distracted.

"Want a Coke or a beer?"

Wes's shout startled me from my revelry. I was surprised to see I had already covered three-quarters of the lot.

My throat was dry and parched from the heat. I could imagine how good an ice-cold beer would taste right now. The liquid gold would slide over my tongue and hit the back of my throat and...

"I'm good," I called back, bending my head to the task at hand. "Thanks though!"

There was always the chance that Abel had been wrong. Maybe there'd never been bodies buried behind the old church. If that was the case, I'd cut my rate for him since I was sure he'd already taken flack for hiring me in the first place. A salty trail of sweat dribbled into my eye. I removed my cap, wiped my brow with the back of my hand and then tugged the hat down lower.

"Let's just get this done," I mumbled.

It was in the farthest left-hand corner of the lot when the rods first crossed. They crossed in a listless, lacka-daisical manner, which I'd come to learn was a sure sign of someone buried long ago. I took a few steps back and walked forward again to be sure of the spot, then pulled out my first flag, poking it into the grass. I could feel curious eyes burning into my back. Wes called out a comment to me but I didn't hear and didn't care. After a few more steps the rods crossed again. Slow, easy and languidly as if the long dead barely sighed in the announcement of their presence. I punctured the grass with another flag. By the time I was finished walking that final segment of the grid, I'd put out four flags.

My pack was on the ground just a couple feet from where Abel and Wes sat in their lawn chairs. I dropped my copper rods into the satchel on my hip, walked back and held up my hand to stop their questions while I pulled a now warm water bottle from my bag and drank long and deep until the bottle was empty.

"Oh gosh-all-Potomac!" Abel cried at his phone, then angrily stuffed the phone and readers back in his pocket and regarded me with a smile. "How'd you do?"

"Four graves," I said, panting a little as I dropped the empty water bottle on top of my bag. "How about you get out a shovel or spade so we can do a quick check for grave markers," I told Wes.

He rolled his eyes and finished off the beer in his hand.

"If Gramps here says you know graves, then that's

fine. We don't need to do nothing else. The part ya dropped your flags on is a small area of the lot." He waved to the corner where my bright orange marker flags punctuated the green. "Wa-a-ay in the back. No need to dig it up over there. I'll stake that area off and just dig up the rest for the garden."

"But we want to pay them due respect," Abel said gently. "If there are markers there they should be uncovered and—"

"For God's sakes, Gramps, if there are people buried there they've been gone so long nobody even cares."

Anger and a torrent of curse words burned the back of my throat and I clenched my teeth. Wes didn't get it and never would. A lot of people were like that. They didn't see the point of honoring the dead. They were the same people who would never lead an exhaustive search for the body of a loved one to bring them home for proper burial. I didn't need Wes to understand why it was important to his grandfather but I sure wasn't going to stand back and watch him disrespect Abel's wishes.

Wordlessly, I walked the dozen yards to Wes's pickup. In the bed of the truck there were gardening tools and I snagged a long-handled square-point shovel. With the tool hoisted over my shoulder I marched across the lot and suddenly Wes was on his feet.

"Never mind, I'll take care of it. You don't have to." The sour scent of hops and bad teeth wafted out of his mouth and into my nostrils.

"Shut up," I said through gritted teeth. My voice was just loud enough for Wes to hear but quiet enough that Abel could not.

The old man was on his feet and slowly walking over to join us.

I placed the tip of the shovel into the sod next to the first flag, kicking down the blade with the heel of my running shoe until it sank a couple inches down. I turned over a few inches of soil, the satchel on my hip bouncing with my movement and the dowsing rods inside poking me in the side. After I dug up a small patch, I moved a few inches over and did the same. It was on the third attempt that you could hear the distinct sound of metal on rock. I looked over my shoulder to Abel and nodded.

I carefully dug up an eight-inch-square section of topsoil then got down on my knees to clean off the hard, dry earth with my fingers to expose a twelve-inch rectangular gravestone. The name and date were so faded and worn I couldn't make them out but it didn't matter. I got to my feet, wiped my filthy fingers on my shorts and roughly handed the shovel to Wes.

"That's one down. Took me less than five minutes. Only three more to go. Think you can handle it?"

He complained under his breath as he turned his back to me and Abel and began to dig.

"Let's walk over to the shade so we can talk about your bill," Abel said with an easy tone that immediately tamped down the fury that had bubbled beneath the surface of my skin.

I stopped to get my bag and then we walked around the far side of the church, which was banked by the dry creek bed and trees that were over a hundred years old. We stood in the shade of the massive cedars that gave us enough of a break from the sun that the temperature dropped a dozen degrees.

"My grandson isn't exactly a rocket scientist but he's a good boy."

He wasn't a boy. He was a grown ass man with an attitude, and the *good* part was probably debatable too, but I smiled back, dropped the pack at my feet and leaned against the wooden church with a sigh.

"The heat makes me cranky," I admitted. Also the burning desire for booze that never really left. "When you wrote me, I quoted you a few hundred dollars but I've been out here less than an hour so let's just say you owe me one." I offered him my dirty hand to shake.

"Not necessary." Abel shook my hand and his head at the same time. "You performed a service, young lady, and you'll get paid for your work. You'll never make it in this world selling your skills short and giving your time away for free."

"Okay. I appreciate that. I'll email you the invoice later today and you can just send me an e-transfer when you get the chance." But I was already planning on giving him a discount since the work hadn't taken me as long as I'd expected.

"I'll be including your bill with the landscaping costs so the community will pay the whole works anyway." Abel patted my shoulder with a heavy hand and then strolled back to watch his grandson.

Full rate it is then. I hoisted my bag and headed to my Jeep parked at the front. A bright streak of sunlight pierced through the cedars and shone on something glinting in the grass. It was a toonie—a Canadian two-dollar coin that reminded me of working at the gas station near the border. That was fifteen months ago but felt like a lifetime.

When I bent to pick up the coin I felt a twitch of movement from the satchel, which had slid from my hip to my stomach. Slowly I straightened, pocketing the coin in the process. I placed my hand on the bag as it slid back to rest on my hip. Could've been my imagination.

When I took a step forward, the distinct quiver inside the satchel could not be ignored. I dropped my bag and got out my dowsing rods. Immediately both arms of the rods swung to my right. I followed in the direction they pointed. My throat was dry and my chest was tight. The steady hum coming from the rods and the magnetic pull tugged me like a fish on a line through the tall cedars. The level of vibration announced loud and clear that I was not headed toward some long-ago skeletal remains from the turn of the century. The attraction was too strong.

Pushing my way gently around a thatch of poky blackberry brambles, I stepped onto the small clearing and the rods began to cross. A wide sunbeam pierced the treetops to offer a spotlight onto the partially nude body of a gaunt, elderly man who lay sprawled and twisted on the dry creek bed.

Dust motes danced merrily in the ray of light around the man's head as flies buzzed in and out of his gaping mouth.

TWO

WHEN THE LOCAL LAW arrived I was sitting in my car blasting the air-conditioning and listening to the audio book. The officer was official, enthusiastic and seemed way out of her element. Apparently in this small town old men didn't usually wind up dead wearing only briefs and black knee socks. I could see the excitement dancing in her eyes even as she tried to keep a serious demeanor.

Everything seemed to take longer than usual, although I probably had far more experience about the *usual* police procedures when finding bodies. I didn't complain about time spent sitting in the hot sun waiting for the officer and those people who dealt with unexpected deaths to do their jobs. I got out of the Jeep and walked her around the scene, describing how I found the body. Surprisingly, she didn't raise a single eyebrow at the description. As if dowsing rods were a perfectly normal way to start an investigation.

Abel was helpful because he identified the elderly deceased as a local named Cornelius Dooley. Corny for short. Wes wasn't quite as helpful because he lost his lunch in the nearby bushes.

We waited while the officer did some checking and she came back and told us the senior home in town had reported Mr. Dooley missing first thing this morning and the consensus seemed to be that he'd wandered off in the middle of the night.

The officer who identified herself as Officer O'Keefe played with a strand of bottle-red hair that had escaped her ponytail as she told me, "Corny had the start of Alzheimer's. They said he'd been doing good though. Still living in the independent living side of the home rather than, you know, in the part that's more like a hospital. He hadn't wandered before. Was supposed to meet a friend for a beer last night but didn't show so that friend drank alone and went to check on him this morning."

During the space when she stopped talking I just nodded and shifted on my feet. Sweat had soaked the underarms of my T-shirt and I was getting antsy to leave. When Abel described why we were there she seemed to take it all in stride. I was surprised she hadn't asked for more information about the grave dowsing and how I'd stumbled on the body.

"Here's my contact information." I handed O'Keefe a business card even though she'd taken my information earlier. "I'm going to head back home but feel free to call me if you need anything."

I hoped she didn't call but she followed me to my car, chatting in my ear about the weather and how it was a good thing we found old Mr. Dooley before he lay there too long in this heat.

"I'll let you get back to work." I pressed the fob on my keyring to unlock the vehicle.

"I hear you're going to help find Ava Johansson."

My eyebrows went up. "Where on earth did you hear that?"

"People talk." She shrugged. "I was part of the early search crews that went out looking for her body. Most of us are keeping in touch on Facebook and some of the people are still going out on weekends, you know, to try and find her."

"Search groups have been looking for Ava for a couple months now. Why do you think they haven't been able to find her?"

"Maybe he took her somewhere else after he killed her there." She looked thoughtful. "Or maybe an animal dragged the body off. Lots of bears out that way and coyotes and all kinds of critters."

"They found blood there and that's how they determined it was the crime scene, right?"

She nodded. "Yup. Testing confirmed it was her. They figured it was just after her mom went up to do the ransom money handoff. Guess something went wrong and he killed her."

"Enough blood at the scene that there was no doubt she died?"

"It was raining on the day and so the evidence was a little diluted. The feds had their hand in the investigation and they confirmed there was too much blood on the ground for her to be anything but dead." She got out a pen and paper. "You want me to add you to our group online? You know, so you can ask all the other searchers questions?"

Oh heck no.

"Actually, I'm not looking for Ava. Her mother has asked but, honestly, I've got so many other—"

"Oh sure, you're busy, I get that." She smiled but the curve of her lips didn't quite meet her eyes and

I felt a little judged for not jumping on the find Ava bandwagon.

Once in my Jeep I was pulling out of the lot when Wes walked directly in front of my vehicle to get to his truck, forcing me to brake. He had his hand on Abel's elbow in a kindly gesture but the look he shot me over his shoulder was neither kind nor gentle. He was pissed.

Even though I blasted the a/c all the way home I still felt like a hot, smelly mess. I let Wookie out to pee on my petunias and the second he was back inside he sprawled on the cool tile in the kitchen, and I began stripping my clothes off on the way to the shower. One of the benefits of living alone was being able to leave a trail of clothing down the hall and being naked without a care. Although it would've been nice to end the striptease in the bedroom with Garrett.

The en suite shower in my new house was huge compared to the tiny one in my old trailer. Even though I'd been here six months, I still instinctively reached for my shampoo bottle on the floor before remembering this shower had a built-in shelf. With my hair slicked back and forehead leaning against the tile I hummed along to a song in my head and let the cooler water pound the back of my neck. I tried to clear the picture of an old dead man with flies buzzing out of his mouth.

I muttered under my breath, "Lord, when it's my time to go, let it be at a ripe old age but peacefully in my sleep and—"

The sentence stopped in my throat when I heard a sound and whirled around. Through the steamed shower doors I saw a figure standing there and began to scream.

The shower door was ripped open.

"It's me. It's just me," Garrett assured me. "I'm sorry. I was calling to you through the bathroom door and thought you heard me."

I put a hand to my pounding heart and forced a silly and relieved smile back at my FBI agent lover. The grin on my face could not strip away the terror that had gripped me only seconds before. I was shaking all over and my lower lip began to tremble.

"It's okay," Garrett said, stepping fully clothed into the shower. "It's okay."

He wrapped his arms around me and squeezed me tight under the spray until I stopped shaking in fear and, instead, shook with laughter at the sight of him in dress pants, shirt and tie soaked completely through. Still, he didn't let me go until the water began to run cold.

"This isn't a wet T-shirt contest," I guffawed and slapped his chest as I pushed him away. "What in the world are you doing?"

"I thought you'd like to see me dripping wet." He turned off the water and pulled my hair playfully as he bent to nibble my neck. "Hmm-m."

My body always responded to his no matter what my mind had to say about it, and within seconds we were in bed. Afterward, we lay in my bed toweled off and content in each other's arms. I cuddled into the crook of his arm and breathed against his bare chest.

"I've missed you."

I could almost feel him holding his tongue. He wanted to remind me that I was the one who moved out. That I bought this house without even telling him and then moved an hour away from his Seattle condo with hardly any notice. I would argue back that my psychiatrist encouraged me to get out on my own and I couldn't breathe with him protecting me to the point of suffocation. The words had already been said countless times both heatedly and tearfully. He'd stopped short of begging me to stay and I'd stopped just shy of breaking up with him.

"I've missed you too."

He kissed the top of my head and I released a contented sigh because we weren't going to have that argument today. We dozed wrapped in each other's arms until Wookie tried to join us and hogged the majority of the bed.

Garrett slipped into sweatpants and a Seahawks T-shirt he'd left behind from another visit and I pulled on clean shorts and a T-shirt. Together we gathered his wet clothes from the shower and wrung them out and draped them over the railing of my back patio to dry in the sun. I made tomato soup and he fried us grilled cheese sandwiches.

"I'm using the last of your bread and the last of your cheese. You need to go shopping." He rubbed the top of Wookie's head and said in a singsong voice, "Doesn't she, Wookie? Your momma needs to buy some food."

I smiled at the silly tone he only ever used for the dog. Then a thought entered my head. He'd probably used the same fun voice when talking to his five-year-old son before a drunk driver erased his wife and boy from the planet a few years ago. My heart hurt knowing how much grief he must still endure.

"Are you okay?" he asked, with a tilt of his head as he watched me.

I walked over carrying our soup bowls.

"I'm great." I mussed his damp hair that was showing more gray at the temples these days.

I fetched our sandwiches and cutlery and we sat at my small oak table to eat our simple meal with Wookie on the floor at our feet. I couldn't help but enjoy the domesticity of it.

"First time I met you at your trailer you were eating tomato soup," he remarked.

I brought a spoon to my mouth and slurped. The memory of him standing in the doorway of my trailer looking so serious filled my head. "I don't remember you screwing me in the shower though."

He threw back his head and howled with laughter.

God, how I'd missed that sound.

He leaned over and kissed me and then we ate the rest of our meal in silence. Garrett was doing the dishes afterward when he offhandedly asked, "When did you see Denny?"

He had his back to the fridge but he'd no doubt seen the sketch. The question had layers. The underlying questions were when did I see my ex-boyfriend, why hadn't I mentioned it, and how would this affect "us."

I took a tea towel from the drawer and bumped his hip good-naturedly with mine. "I didn't see him."

Part of me didn't want to tell him about Ebba Johansson's visit and how she tracked me down using Wookie. Telling him would unravel all those worries and old arguments about keeping me safe and how if I'd stayed living with him in his Seattle condo he would've been able to protect me.

Keep an eye on me.

Keep his thumb on me.

"Ebba Johansson popped in for a visit," I said coolly, putting the last of our few dishes in the cupboard.

"Ava Johansson's mother?" He was taken aback by that. With his arms folded he leaned against the counter.

"Yes."

"As in the Ava Johansson who was kidnapped and murdered by her ex-boyfriend?"

"Yes."

"The Ava Johansson whose name and face was in all the papers the last couple months and whose body was never found?"

The look on his face showed his mind was flipping through every single detail he knew about the case.

I swatted him with the dish towel. "Are you going to let me finish?"

He grabbed the towel and used it to pull me close for a kiss that ended with him tickling my ribs and me pinching him hard until he let me go.

"Finish your story," he said.

So I gave him the CliffsNotes version of Ebba's visit and her desire to have me search for Ava's body. His face was impassive until I got to the part where the woman brought the sketch from Denny because, apparently, she runs the spa in the casino and my name came up.

"And just like that when the topic of conversation becomes you, Denny immediately gives up where you live?" He blew an angry puff of breath through his lips and pressed his palm to his forehead. "Wait a second; you never told anyone up there your new location, right?"

"Up there" being the small town that cozied up to the Canadian border. "Up there" being where I'd been raised in savage and cruel circumstances. Abandoned by my mother. Abused by my grandmother. And then... Gramps.

"Who would I tell?" I shrugged. "I don't talk to anyone there."

"So if Denny didn't know where you live then how—?"

"People talk. There were, I guess, rumors about the general location and Ebba Johansson, well, she got creative."

He wasn't going to let me get away with being vague. It was one of the biggest drawbacks to talking to someone in his line of work. He wasn't just nosy by personality; it was the exact trait that fed his motivation and drove him to excel as a federal agent.

After a pause, during which he drilled holes into me with those questioning eyes and I tried to find a way to soften it, I finally just gave in and filled in the blanks about how Ebba Johansson had found me through Wookie's vet.

"I'm going to kill your vet," he growled. "Have they never heard of patient confidentiality?"

"Isn't that more of a human doctor thing?" I joked.

He drained the dishwater, strangled the life out of the wet dishrag and tossed the cloth angrily into the corner of the sink. "If she can find you, *anyone* can."

The anger vibrated off him in waves. He kept it

under control because FBI agents specialized in control and because he always coddled, softened and cushioned his words when he talked to me as if any rise in anger would cause me to freak out and get so crazy I'd need to be zipped off to the loony bin. I should appreciate the fact that he was so kind and gentle with me but the truth was that it was a form of Bubble Wrap that made me want to explode.

He pulled me into a tight hug and Wookie immediately joined us, nudging his large Rotty head between our thighs to either pull us apart or somehow join in.

"I'm not blaming you." Garrett breathed the words onto the top of my head but the truth was that was *exactly* what he was doing.

"Look, what's done is done." I untangled myself from his hug and went to the cupboard to get a chew bone for Wookie. "I'll have a word with the vet."

"And obviously you're not going to take on this job of finding Ava Johansson, right? I mean, if law enforcement agencies all over Washington State couldn't find her body…"

"Then I couldn't either?" I raised my eyebrows at him in feigned amusement.

It was a ridiculous thought considering he had recruited me himself to find the dead when the FBI and local law failed.

Wookie snagged the bone from my hand and jogged over to his bed to begin the serious task of gnawing it to a nub.

"If anyone could find her body, you could. Obviously." He backed down. "I just don't think—"

"You don't think it would be safe for me to be out

looking for the body of a girl in such a high-profile case when her killer is still on the loose? I know and I get that." I fingered my damp hair in exasperation. "I haven't decided yet if I'll take the job. I told her I'd think about it. It's not like I need the work. Emails keep pouring in. Hey, if you'd like, there's a body that needs finding just outside of Portland. We could make a weekend of it."

He wordlessly went to the fridge and poured us each a glass of iced tea and we sat back down at the table.

"Look, I know you'd love it if all I did was cemetery dowsing for the graves of people who've been gone a hundred years or more." I put my hand on his. "But I don't ask you to not go looking for bad guys, right?"

I took a drink from the cold tea, and as the taste hit the back of my throat my recipe for a Long Island Iced Tea immediately sprang to mind. A perfect concoction of gin, rum, tequila, vodka, triple sec and Coke.

"You were thirsty." Garrett stared at the glass in my hand. It was completely empty.

Three hundred twenty-nine.

"So I had that gig this morning behind the old church. The one I mentioned before?" I washed out my iced tea glass and put it on the rack to air-dry. "And it didn't exactly go as planned."

"Really?"

I told him about Abel and his love of Candy Crush and we shared a laugh at me finding the old grave marker and Wes having to admit his grandfather and I were right. Then I shared about poor old Corny Dooley in the dried-up creek wearing nothing but boxers and knee socks.

"Who did you say the officer was at the scene?"

"I didn't say." I frowned because he was no longer interested in our conversation. He was staring hard at his phone. "Officer O'Keefe."

"Don't know him."

"Her."

He nodded and got to his feet. "Sorry. I have to go."

There was no use in asking why because it was FBI work and he wasn't about to share those details with me.

Garrett gathered his damp clothes from the back deck, snagged a bag for them from under my sink and then kissed me goodbye.

"I wish you could stay."

Wookie and I walked him to his car.

"I wish I could too." He pulled me close and gave me the kind of kiss that made me wish we still lived together so that when he got home I'd feel his body spooning mine in the middle of the night.

He opened his door and climbed behind the wheel. "You're going to tell Ebba Johansson that you're not going to search for her daughter's body, right? At least tell her you'll help only once Ronald Low is found and locked up. I don't want you to get in the middle of an active investigation."

"You are not the boss of me, Mr. FBI." I gave his shoulder a shove but he didn't look amused. "Look, I told her I'd think about it." I shrugged. "So that's what I'm going to do."

His face was pinched in a frown of disapproval as he started the car, and I watched as he reversed down my long drive and then pulled away. Wookie was sniffing intently at a sun-browned shrub at the corner.

"He loves to hunt rabbits. We'd go out in the back forty and he'd follow their scent and—"

To stop Gramps's voice in my head I called for Wookie and the dog followed me inside. After I got myself a Coke, I popped open my laptop and went to work researching the case of Ava Johansson. Before I decided whether or not to get involved I wanted to get up to speed. I read everything I could find on her case and that was a ton. A pretty young woman presumably held for ransom then murdered by an ex-boyfriend was big news.

Ron Low dated Ava Johansson for a year. By all accounts they'd called it quits amicably enough. She'd told her mother they were still friends. He'd told his buddies there was no one else but he wanted to be free to see other people. Everyone interviewed said there was no big blowup that caused the break and they'd continued to hang with the same group of friends on occasion even after they were no longer together. Even remained friends on social media. From all outward appearances there'd been no drama involved until weeks later when Ava went missing.

It wasn't unusual for Ava to go out with friends and not come home so Ebba didn't report her missing for a few days. Then she became frantic when it appeared her daughter had just vanished into thin air. When Ron also couldn't be found, police felt there was a good possibility the two were just hanging out together. Ron's roommate, Joon Kim, had left the country and when police contacted him in Korea where he was visiting a sick relative, he said Ron had planned a hiking trip.

By the time Joon Kim got back in town, everything had changed. Ebba had received a ransom letter in the mail and, as instructed, she didn't contact police. Instead, she scrambled together a hundred grand and then, following the instructions in the letter, she'd set out to a state park. She dropped off the cash on a path off of an isolated campground and waited for the return of her daughter. When Ava didn't appear, Ebba went back to the path only to find the money gone and a lot of blood in the area so she called the police. It wasn't long before investigators found that there was enough blood in the woods to declare a crime scene and state that Ava would not be coming home.

Ronald Low was also missing and his roommate insisted Ron would never hurt Ava and that he was probably just hiking and would show up any day. Joon explained to all who'd listen that Ron, an avid hiker and outdoorsman, often went off the grid when he hiked. But when police discovered the ransom note had been typed on Ronald Low's laptop he, of course, became the prime suspect.

Despite Joon Kim's insistence, good ol' Ron never did return from his hike.

"If the motive was money," I wondered aloud, "why did he have to kill her once he got what he wanted?"

Wookie rested his hefty noggin on my thigh. I continued to read articles and click pictures and videos posted on news sources and personal pages. I sat at the laptop so long the sun had set and my mouth was dry but I couldn't take my eyes off the latest picture I'd opened of Ronald Low. In every previous picture and video he'd had a scruffy beard but in this picture taken a couple years ago he was clean shaven and looked vaguely familiar. Maybe Ron was a local. Maybe he'd even been a regular when I worked at the gas station.

Getting up from the table I went about the business of refilling Wookie's bowl and then decided on a snack of a bowl of cereal for myself only to realize I had no milk. The biggest problem of being an adult on your own was that keeping cupboards stocked was all on you.

Staring into the abyss that were my cupboards I found a package of ramen noodles. I made the ramen and brought the bowl back to the table to resume my research. The first slurp of noodles took me back to simpler times. Not that my grandmother would ever buy them. Her refusal to buy the stuff had nothing to do with her care for my health and everything to do with making me unhappy. If she even suspected I wanted something, she'd go out of her way to make sure it never happened.

"How do you feel when you think about your grandmother?" Dr. Chen asked time and time again.

"I don't think about her."

I blew into the steamy bowl of noodles. Katie, my best and only friend for many years, would buy us each a cup of the noodles at our high school cafeteria. It had been a real treat for me. I rolled that recollection around in my head as the too-hot salty broth scalded my tongue.

"Ron Low," I murmured the guy's name while staring at his face on my screen.

Rock'n Ron.

The nickname sprang into my head. Startled, I nearly sloshed hot soup on my lap. I put my bowl down on the coffee table and brought my face closer to the laptop screen. I hadn't thought of Rock'n Ron in many years. He'd been a year younger than me in high school and was one of the cool kids who'd hold court in the cafeteria at lunch with the other jocks and the beauty queens.

"No wa-a-y. It couldn't be!" I squinted at the picture where he had short hair and no beard. I tried to imagine the guy on the screen younger and with shoulder-length hair instead of the brush cut.

"Jesus. It's him!"

I punched a few questions into Google and discovered that yes, indeed, we'd attended the same high school. I tried not to think about my school years. Not because school was awful. Quite the opposite. It had been the one place where I'd felt safe. I'd been quiet, on the plain side of pretty and got a tiny bit of second-hand popularity that bounced off my flamboyant friend Katie. *Popularity* might be too strong a word. It was more like the bullies recognized me as awkward but, thanks to Katie, left me alone.

I remembered a time when Katie wasn't around and the jocks were harassing me about something. Ron had walked over and told them to leave me alone and get a life. Besides Katie, he was the only one to ever stick up for me.

I easily found Rock'n Ron on social media sites but it was obvious he'd made no appearance on those pages since Ava went missing. All his pictures were selfies taken in forested areas and rocky beaches. This connection between me and Ava's supposed killer had me very curious and changed my entire perspective on the case. I'd liked Rock'n Ron in school. Had a secret crush on him even.

I delved deeper into some of the interviews and articles, paying special attention to things people had to say about Ron. His parents, of course, cried foul because their little boy would never harm a fly. They even offered a reward for clues leading to his whereabouts. His boss at a sporting goods store and coworkers and friends all said he was a stand-up guy who liked women and hiking and not necessarily in that order. By all accounts Ron was the same guy from my high school. A good guy who wouldn't kidnap and murder his ex-girlfriend.

And yet he apparently had.

And it certainly wouldn't be the first time a "good guy" got into a heated exchange with a girl and killed her. The ransom thing stumped me though. By all accounts, Ron had a simple life. Shared a house with a friend and owned his own car. He worked at a job that gave him the freedom to take off time when he wanted to hike. Why the sudden need for a hundred thousand dollars from Ebba Johansson? Even though evidence proved Ron wrote the ransom letter from his own laptop that was found inside his own room in his own house, my gut said it wasn't that cut-and-dried. Maybe the roommate…

My fingers tapped some more as I researched the roommate, Joon Kim. He'd left the country around the time Ava went missing. Police talked to him while he was in Korea visiting his sick grandmother and he gave police permission to go through the house and do whatever they needed to do to find Ava and Ron. Once he was back and all hell had broken loose, he was interviewed frequently in the media and he seemed just as baffled as everyone else. Mostly, he only said Ron was a cool guy who got along with everyone. When pushed, the most negative thing he could come up with was that Ron was a bit of a womanizer and liked to talk about his conquests and was also a bit of a slob. Joon said he'd met Ava a number of times while she dated Ron and he'd remained friendly with her even after the split. The ransom drop and snatch of the money all occurred when he was still in Korea, leaving him off the suspect list.

Sure the roommate had only positive things to say to the press about Ron and Ava, but I wondered what else Joon Kim would say if he was talking to one of Ron's former classmates instead of the police or the media. He wasn't hard to track down. Joon managed an electronics store in Bellingham Mall just a few miles from where I used to live, and his contact information was on the store's website. I typed up a simple email asking if he'd mind chatting about the Ava Johansson case and included my phone number. Then I shut down my laptop and went to the fridge for a Coke. My phone rang in my hand before I could even fill my glass.

"I know you," Joon Kim said by way of a greeting. "You're the girl who grew up around here. The one everyone talks about who finds bodies using magic."

I cringed. "I'm Julie Hall."

I was going to correct him. Maybe even launch into

an entire spiel about how dowsing rods weren't magic but I was never given the chance because Joon Kim liked to talk and he was already filling my ear with a long dissertation on Ron so I just listened. He confirmed all the things I already knew; that he'd been in Korea during the time Ava was supposed to be murdered in the woods, and that Ron had been an all-round good guy with no hint of craziness and no secret stash of hunting knives dripping with blood.

"But I guess he must've done it, right? I mean, if you're innocent you don't just stay away forever, right? Also, he never came back from his hike at Oak Lake even though he'd promised to bring me to the Bat Caves when he got back. He promised and he wouldn't've just said that if he didn't mean it, right?"

"He promised to take you where?"

"You know…the Bellingham Bat Caves near the Oyster Dome. It was the last thing we talked about. He said he'd take me there because I had a new camera and wanted to take some pictures but I'm not much of a hiker, right? He's been there a lot and it isn't a hard hike but great for pictures. He was going to show me the way. He promised."

The last two words came out on a whine and then Joon was off again talking about photography but I was only half listening because I was remembering high school. There'd been lots of girls to go hiking with Rock'n Ron in their senior years. They'd go to see the Bat Caves and come back with grass stains on their backs. I'd never gone myself, of course, but I had to admit my little crush on Ron did involve a fantasy around seeing those caves and coming home with leaves in my hair.

Joon had paused to take a breath.

"I've taken up hiking myself," I told him. "So did you ever go to the caves and take pictures like you wanted?"

"No. They blocked off most of the trail and closed the parking lot after a small mudslide right after I left for Korea. I just read that it's been reopened this week. Maybe I'll go now."

His tone was wistful and I had a feeling that Joon would never go anywhere without someone like Ron to lead the way. He said he had to go so I thanked him for his time and ended the call. I continued looking through articles online about the case. There were lots of pictures of search parties and one in particular caught my eye. I enlarged it and there, in the back of a crowd of maybe fifty people, stood Ron's mother and father. To my surprise, next to them was Wes, Abel's grandson, with his arm around another young man with a shaved head who I didn't recognize. I imagine a lot of people in the community went out searching but Wes didn't strike me as that kind of guy. Guess I was wrong.

A little more online research brought me to a website Ron's parents had launched to find their son. There was a large grainy picture showing Ron on the day he went missing. The picture was from a convenience store just up the road from his house where he'd stopped before disappearing off the face of the earth. He'd been wearing a fluorescent yellow Seattle Marathon T-shirt and a casual smile that did not imply a mind filled with the kidnapping and bloody murder of Ava Johansson.

After I closed my laptop I settled in front of the TV with my cola and Wookie. A sitcom played canned laughter but my head was elsewhere. I was thinking of the caves. My psychiatrist told me that hiking was good for me. She encouraged me to find peace in nature because, up until recently, nature and I had an adversarial relationship. People died in nature and one of those people had almost been me.

Although the great outdoors and I weren't always on the friendliest terms I did agree to try the new hobby as a way to keep sober, clear my head and heal my broken mind. I have to say that now that I'd done a few moderate trails I actually enjoyed myself. It was a way to be in tune with nature that didn't involve skeletal remains. There was a lot to be said for that.

The next morning was a lot cooler than the previous days and perfect weather for hiking. After feeding Wookie I took him for a run down our street as far as the next driveway, which was a quarter mile away, and then back home. He sniffed every tall weed and shrub and left his mark on all to claim them as his own. When we got back, I showered and ate a handful of dry cereal as I tossed some water bottles and granola bars into my backpack. As I climbed into my Jeep I set a reminder on my phone to stop later and buy coffee, milk, bread and a few other staples. Before long I was driving North on I-5. The closer I got to my old hometown, the more anxious I became but I pushed on.

After all, I was going to be a good thirty or so miles from the farm and, even if I was closer, the land had been sold, and the house and sheds torn down. Nothing there but farmed fields and dust.

I turned off my audio self-help book in favor of music so loud it rattled the windows. Didn't help though. The very air in the vicinity of my old home was toxic and the closer I got the harder I had to work to ignore the memories. Even the exercises Dr. Chen taught me weren't helping but hopefully a hike would help clear my head.

Finally I veered off I-5 away from the direction that would've taken me home. I'd done my research on a hike to the caves so I knew what to expect. Mount Blanchard was part of the Chuckanut range and you got great views from a cliff area known as the Oyster Dome. Hiking to the caves could be arduous but you could cheat and cut the hike in half by driving up Mount Blanchard and parking at the lookout where the hang gliders launch. From this location it would be three miles round-trip. Easy peasy.

I pulled into the lot and turned off the Jeep. Then pulled out my phone and texted Garrett.

Going for a 3 mile hike on Mount Blanchard. I'll message when I'm back at the car.

I turned my phone off before I was inundated with his concerned motherly questions about whether or not I had enough water, proper shoes, a hat, sunscreen... Damn. I forgot my sunscreen. I snagged my backpack from the passenger seat and put on my Mariners ball cap. I also took out the canister of bear spray Garrett had given me, attaching the neoprene holster to the belt loops of my shorts to keep it handy.

It was beautiful here. The sky was the liquid cerulean blue of oceans or a bottle of Bombay Sapphire gin. I breathed in the clean air as I adjusted the pack on my back. The Oyster Dome trailhead was to the west of the parking lot. After about half a mile downhill I came to a junction in the trail with signs that pointed the way to the Oyster Dome, Talus Trail and a nearby lake. There was no mention of the Bat Caves but I knew from what I'd read that I just had to stay to the right for a mile and then I'd find a sign for the caves.

The trail was rocky and, in some places, quite steep. You could see mounds of earth and debris that had been part of the slide that caused the trail closure. I paused a couple times to catch my breath and suck on a water bottle. Just when I was beginning to think I'd missed the marker, an aluminum sign screwed into a massive cedar announced Talus Trail and Bat Caves. To be cute someone had taken a Sharpie and drawn a Batman symbol and someone else had drawn a frown face and scribbled *no bats* under Bat Caves. It wasn't a shock to me since I'd already read that the bats hadn't been in these caves for years.

Finally I reached a field of massive rocks banked by thick brush and skyscraper cedars. Google had shown me that the caves weren't really holes in the mountain like you'd expect. Instead, they were humongous boulders that had piled up and stacked in such a way as to make crevices and caverns. Many of the giant slabs were worn smooth. Walking on them and near them would be dangerous so I chose to sit my tired butt down on a smaller rock under a tall tree off to the side. I still had a clear view of some of the caverns. I had no desire to climb inside any of the caves because I had a feeling all I'd get was a hair full of spiders and a sore back from crouching over.

No spider wigs for me, thank you very much.

I breathed deep and enjoyed the sound of birds around me and a chattering squirrel.

While I drank water and munched a granola bar I thought about bats and nature and my actual existence on the planet and whether or not I was happy yet. That was the thing about being alone in nature. It had a way of forcing you to navel gaze so much you got belly lint in your eyes.

I tossed the bar wrapper and empty water bottle into my bag and, as I did so, I felt a distinct movement from the satchel containing my dowsing rods.

"No-o-o," I moaned.

Saying the word didn't change anything though. Reluctantly, I pulled the rods from the satchel to see if I'd mistaken the movement for anything else like a hand tremor or a localized earthquake. No such luck. The second I was on my feet with the rods in my hands, they swung right.

"Double damn."

Hoisting my pack onto my back, I walked to the right away from the caves, following where the rods indicated. It was a lesser traveled trail but not so tight in the brush that I wouldn't find my way back. However, maybe twenty yards from where I'd been sitting even that thin trail was swallowed by woods and I entered a dark and dank forested area. It smelled of earth and moss and, thankfully, not at all like a dead guy.

But the rods insisted a body would be found, and who was I to argue with a pair of copper wires that had never lied?

Maybe some poor spelunker got hit by the landslide a couple months ago. I pushed branches aside, and the massive tree trunks provided me leverage to lean against as I wound my way downhill. In a small clearing the rods led me across a chunky and uneven rock bed and, just as I stepped from a large boulder back onto the ground, the rods crossed. I took a deep breath and slowly turned to face another of the cave-like crevices. There was a large void made between the boulder and the scrabble of hard earth, a four-foot-high space as black as Satan's heart. Even though I couldn't see inside the blackness I knew someone was dead inside.

Cursing under my breath, I searched my pack and found a small but powerful flashlight that was a gift from Garrett.

Casting light under the rock illuminated scratch marks from various critters at the entrance. Swinging the beam from the flashlight revealed the tattered remnants of a bright yellow Seattle Marathon T-shirt on the badly decomposed remains of Rock'n Ron.

THREE

THIS WASN'T MY first rodeo when it came to body discovery. I knew what would come next. The hordes of law enforcement and the countless questions that would leave me explaining how I'd managed to discover the body of a guy who'd probably been on the Most Wanted list for weeks.

So I didn't immediately make the call. Instead, I took a moment to center myself. If I chose to share with Dr. Chen at our next appointment, she would be so proud. I did the mindfulness exercises that were supposed to stop me from wanting to chugalug a gallon of wine in one sitting.

It didn't work. I still wanted wine.

I took deep, calming breaths and reminded myself of the feel of the hard earth beneath my feet and the scent of cedars and tall grasses. Thankfully, I was far enough away that there was no scent of Rock'n Ron. Then a fat fly buzzed my right ear causing me to smack myself upside the head. It slapped the inner peace right out of me but it also made me laugh.

After a few more minutes I released a long, slow sigh and I got out my cell phone and dialed Garrett's phone number.

"You okay?" he asked by way of a greeting.

"Of course. Why wouldn't I be okay?"

"You usually text me after a hike but you're calling me instead so I thought something might be wrong."

Even though he'd been working on a case that kept him busy night and day the past few months, he always took my calls and returned my texts.

"I'm okay but..."

"But what?" His voice held that serious FBI all-business tone.

"I found Rock'n Ron."

"Who?"

"Ron Low. The guy who killed Ava Johansson. I found his body in the Bat Caves in sort of an out-of-the-way area that probably was blocked by that land-slide a couple months ago."

"Jesus Christ," he muttered. I could visualize him rubbing the back of his neck as he often did when he was simultaneously worried about me, exasperated by my line of work and also trying to balance his own work obligations. "But you're okay?"

"Yes." I explained how and where I found Ron.

"I thought you weren't going to take the Ava case?"

"I said I'd think about it but I didn't find him because I was looking for him. Well, not really." I explained about talking to Joon Kim and how it gave me the idea of hiking here. "So Ron and I went to school together."

"Really? That's a coincidence, isn't it?"

"I guess." I chewed my lower lip and a pause stretched out between us.

"You're thinking about looking for Ava's body, aren't you?"

"Well, we've got the guy who killed her, right? He

probably couldn't live with the fact that he killed Ava so he hiked down here and killed himself. So looking for where he dumped Ava would be a nice way to wrap this up for her mother."

Garrett didn't reply.

"I just feel connected to the case now that I've found Ron." I felt the need to explain.

"Her body could be anywhere."

"True," I admitted. "Obviously, I'm not going to make this my life's work. I'll do a few outings and see if I can't find her."

He sighed.

I gave Garrett the directions to the parking lot where investigators should start their hike and then I asked, "Should I hike back up to my car or do you want me to hang out here with Ron?"

"If nobody's found him before now I'm sure it would be safe to leave the scene alone, but I can't take that chance. I didn't work the Johansson case so I've got to make some calls. Either way it's going to take me and whoever a couple hours to get there with a crew so I'll notify the local law to meet you there in the meantime. Once there's an officer on scene, why don't you leave and I'll call you later for more details. You probably haven't eaten so go have a bite."

I'd shed some weight after dealing with stress in the past year, and it always felt like Garrett was on a mission to fatten me up. I was going to argue but then my stomach growled loudly in protest. Apparently a granola bar didn't cut it after a hike. Garrett advised me that he'd give the officer my number and get him to call me once he was hiking down the trail.

I sat my ass back down on a nearby rock and my hand went reassuringly to the bear spray that was attached to my hip. I cracked open another bottle of water while I stared into the dark abyss that housed Rock'n Ron. A swarm of gnats danced in a shaft of light that pierced the tall trees and bounced off the boulders that hid the body. I pulled my T-shirt away from my chest and blew air into my cleavage as I thought about my former classmate.

"What happened, Ron?"

Various scenarios ran through my head as I considered how the high school Romeo ended up dead in a local cave. He was an experienced hiker and the trail would be considered mild for amateurs. Even if he'd been injured, he would've hauled ass to the main trail and been discovered. So he'd died here. It seemed more than likely he'd hiked here to a familiar place to take his own life after killing Ava.

My cell phone rang and it was the officer who'd been assigned to babysit Ron until a forensic team could arrive. I tried to describe exactly where I was but this guy was obviously unfamiliar with the trail. I instructed him how to begin his trek from the parking lot and said I'd meet him at the metal sign. It wasn't long before the huffing, puffing and sweaty cop met me there.

He introduced himself as Officer Berry. It was hard to resist the urge to point out that his round, red face made him look like a ripe cherry.

"Of all the days to be taking up hiking," he moaned. "Doing it in hundred degree weather would not be my choice."

"It's only high seventies," I corrected. "A lot cooler

than the last few days so we should be grateful about that."

Officer Berry tilted his head and squinted at me in a look that was probably supposed to be annoyance but given the panting and perspiring that was going on, it just made him look constipated. "Right. You're a hiker though so you'd think of it that way."

I guess I was a hiker now. How about that? The thought both surprised and pleased me.

"Doing short hikes might help your mind make a more friendly connection to nature," Dr. Chen said.

When she said that I'd actually snorted. Seriously? People die in the woods. Bad things happen to people out in the woods. People like me.

But maybe not anymore.

"So show me where this guy is."

Okay, well except for the finding dead guy things. Those things still happened to me in the woods apparently.

"It's not much farther." I nodded over my shoulder and started to lead the way. "It can be a bit of a challenge to maneuver around the rocks but just follow me and you'll be fine."

Although it was tempting, I did not turn around every time Officer Berry cursed and grumped as we left the main trail. I went slowly so he'd have no issue keeping up, and I held branches for him and didn't give in to the urge to let them thwack him in the face, just for fun.

"Don't make me give you something to cry about."

A long, deep scar down my back itched at the memory. I hadn't dared to shed a tear.

When we finally reached the cave area that hid Ron, the officer needed to take a moment. He sat down on the boulder across from the cave where I'd rested before. With his elbows on his knees he drew in deep breaths and swatted angrily at flies that wanted to taste the beads of sweat on his neck. I took out my last water bottle and handed it to him, then watched in annoyance as he drank part of it and then wasted the rest when he dumped the remaining water on his head.

Once he'd recovered from the hike as much as possible, Officer Berry got to his feet, took out his flashlight and shined it inside the cave area where I indicated.

"Sweet mother Mary, he's dead as a doornail, ain't he?"

I considered the stretched skin and tufts of hair that remained on Ron's skull and turned away.

"You called it in as Ronald Low, right? I guess it could be him but we don't know for certain."

"That's the shirt Ron was wearing when he went missing."

"I know that," the officer snapped.

I had the feeling he really didn't know what Ron had been wearing and I wasn't trying to be a know-it-all. Not every officer in Washington State had been involved in this case and the feds had worked directly with it too. Still, I didn't like this cop being hostile with me just because he'd drawn the short end of the stick and had to sit here with the body.

He got a little closer to the cave.

"Looks like there's a hole in the skull. Maybe he fell and cracked his head on a rock."

"There was no way he fell and then rolled *up* a rock

bed inside a cave," I pointed out, not caring if I did sound like I knew more than him now.

"I guess an autopsy will tell."

I hooked my thumb over my shoulder. "I'm going to head back now. Garrett—" I stopped myself and corrected that familiarity. "Agent Pierce said that once you were here I could go and—"

"You don't remember me, do you?" Officer Berry asked.

I'd turned away from him but now I looked back. "Should I?"

"When you were working at the gas station I used to come in 'bout once a week. I live about a minute away from there."

"Oh ri-i-ight." I nodded as if it was all coming back to me but—hello—people came and went all day long when I worked at the gas station and I hardly paid them any notice at all.

"So you don't live around there anymore, right?"

So now we're going to make small talk while Rock'n Ron's body is only a few feet away?

"I moved."

"Yeah, after that—" He stopped himself and his cherry face turned more crimson than it had while he was huffing and puffing. It was all coming back to him. The horrible truth of my life that had become the big news that rocked that small town to its core.

"I'm going to head up now," I told him.

"So you found the body using your witching rod things?" he asked my back but I just kept on walking. I owed him no explanation. I was tired of Officer Berry.

The walk back up the trail to my car was arduous

because the sun was really heating things up now. I thought about Ron and what happened to have him wind up dead in a place he used to bring girls for make-out sessions. It unnerved me. Dr. Chen would have told me to spend a moment in quiet reflection or use the tools from my well-being toolbox but sometimes that just felt stupid.

"Screw that," I muttered as I pressed the fob on my keychain.

My throat was parched and my head filled with questions about Ava and Ron. What had happened? I'd started out not wanting to get involved in this messy case but suddenly it felt important to find Ava and untangle this big mess. With the vents of the Jeep pointed full onto my face, I drove back in the direction of I-5 and found a fast-food place close to the highway exit.

Inside, I went to the washroom and splashed cold water on my face. Then I ordered some food and took it to a corner booth out of the sun. I nibbled at the burger and fries but the grease wasn't sitting well with the heat. As I sipped the Coke, a gnawing need in my stomach made me wish it was a nice pinot grigio or even a cheap chardonnay.

Scrolling through my phone I leisurely checked my emails. Every week my website www.DivineReunions. com garnered a number of legitimate requests to find the remains of loved ones. It also attracted quite a few nutjobs who wanted me to repent my pact with the devil.

"You keep messing with the occult so I'm just gonna beat that devil out of you!" Grandma snarled.

I'd almost died as she tried.

God, I wanted a drink. Just one. Bottle.

Continuing through the emails it was easy to delete the crazies. Every week though I found myself turning legitimate people away and it hurt me to do it. Many of them were grieving parents or spouses just wanting to bury their loved ones. Unfortunately, most were just too far away. My fee plus airfare and accommodations was a small price for many seeking that elusive closure. A few months ago I'd happily traipsed away from my Washington home to Florida, Maine and North Dakota. It had been a nice way to run away from my troubles by flying across the country for a day or two of dowsing. It was an adventure in the beginning but then the hotels got lonely and the minibars were too tempting.

Unfortunately, no matter how far away I roamed, the skeletons in my own closet were waiting to greet me when I got back.

As if conjuring my damaged soul made it so, an email reminder of an upcoming appointment with Dr. Chen appeared in my inbox. Therapy was good. It kept me from drowning myself in the hooch my body craved. But that didn't mean I enjoyed it any more than a monthly root canal.

Just before I closed my emails another message popped up. A woman looking for the body of her teenage son who'd thrown himself into Snoqualmie Falls in a fit of despair a couple months ago. Witnesses saw him go over but searchers had been unable to locate his remains.

"Why do they always have to be in the water?" I grumbled.

Suddenly I was aware I'd spoken out loud in the

crowded burger joint, and I sheepishly looked up only to lock eyes with someone across the room.

Katie.

Goose bumps covered my arms as I looked at her. We were the best of friends from the time my mom dropped me at my grandparents' farm when I was six until last year when our entire world burned to ash.

We were both frozen in stunned surprise. She was not the Katie I remembered. Gone was the fancy blond updo and sexy clothing. All that had been replaced by a fast-food worker's gray uniform with orange trim and blond locks in a tight ponytail with four-inch dark roots. The usual look on her face of impish mischief coupled with a fiery playfulness was replaced by this woman who looked afraid to even say hello.

"Hey!" Katie suddenly called out and waved to someone working the counter. "I'm on break, okay?"

I was wrong about her being afraid to talk because she was walking toward me, and I was the one feeling like a cornered animal wanting to bolt from my hard plastic seat before she got to me.

"Hi. I'm Katie Cole." She picked my limp hand up from the table and gave it a firm shake before sitting down across from me. "I don't think we've met but I can tell already we'd like each other."

I just stared at her, mouth agape, trying to find words for the bizarre greeting but none came.

"I just figured since we haven't seen each other for so long and since you never returned my texts or calls months ago that we should just start new, you know?" She picked up my Coke and took a long drink until she was noisily sucking air from the bottom of the cup.

"I don't have the same phone number as I used to."

It was a lame excuse. Katie's number hadn't changed and she'd also emailed me through my website. I'd ignored all contact.

I shook my head then, knowing I owed her more.

"I'm sorry." I blew out a breath. "I guess I just needed to, you know, close some doors after everything."

She leaned back in the booth trying to look cool in her burger uniform. Remarkably she somehow pulled it off.

"Look at me." She waved a hand over her body that was a little rounder and softer than when I last saw her because she'd picked up the pounds that I'd shed. "Have you ever seen me so glamorous? Isn't this just a kick in the head?"

Abruptly, she threw back her head and guffawed, then snorted with the unladylike laughter that I'd always found so contagious. No matter how hard I tried, I couldn't help but join in. I stifled a giggle with my hand but the harder I tried not to laugh, the more chuckles bubbled up until it was a full-on belly laugh that attracted sidelong glances from the other burger eaters.

"It's a little surreal seeing you flipping burgers," I admitted after the laughter subsided.

"Oh I'm nothing as glamorous as a burger flipper. I have the joyous job of being the lobby cleaner and bathroom wiper. I take out the trash. I *aspire* to be the burger flipper."

I smiled at her and barely contained another giggle. It had been forever since I'd laughed like that. I was surprised my body remembered how.

"Hang on a sec." Katie got up and walked behind the counter. She returned with a large container of French fries dumped on a tray next to a lake of ketchup. "Never thought I'd see you walk in here," she admitted around a mouthful of fries.

I thought briefly of confiding in her about finding Rock'n Ron and then I pushed that aside.

"How have you been?" I asked, both wanting to know and dreading the answer.

"I'm going to give you the CliffsNotes answer to that question."

We shared another quick giggle because, in school, CliffsNotes had taken on a comical meaning because Katie had occasionally banged a guy in class named Cliff.

"So the short version 'cause I've only got a fifteen-minute break." She dipped three fries in the ketchup and stuffed them in her mouth. "Horrible. That's how I've been. My life has been a shit storm of epic proportions."

"That's too bad, Katie, I'm sorry—"

"After everything happened…you know…" She waved a hand at me and I nodded because, yeah, I lived it too. "I went about doing regular stuff, right? Figured best way to get over things was to live my life like all that horror movie stuff never happened. I played and partied like all was good."

I nodded.

"But then the universe had to kick me in the vaj while I was down, you know?" She snorted derisively and ate a couple more fries. "Mom died. Had a heart attack right in the middle of giving someone a color."

The news hit me like a punch in my sternum.

"Jesus, Katie, I'm so-o-o sorry." I closed my eyes and thought about Katie's mom. I could almost smell her Opium perfume. She'd run the salon in our small town and, growing up, she'd offered me a glimpse at the closest thing to a normal family life.

"Yeah, it sucks big-time." Katie picked up my Coke to drink, remembered it was empty and put it down again before adding, "Then I found out the salon and our house were both buried in debt up the poop chute. I'd seen the foreclosure notices on the kitchen table, you know? But Mom never said anything and, besides, she'd been in bad spots before and always managed to pull off a save at the last minute. Not this time. Couple days after her funeral I was out on the streets."

I wanted to tell her I would've helped her out if I'd known but we both knew that wasn't true. I'd been in the hospital trying to hang on to the threads of my own sanity.

"I'm sorry," I repeated because I couldn't think of anything else. "I liked your mom."

"Yeah, well, I couch surfed a while until everyone got sick and tired of me. There's only so long people will let a grown woman cry about being an orphan." She smiled the kind of grin that could turn into tears but then shoved more fries into her mouth. "So now I work part-time at a clothing place in the mall and then I snagged this job a couple months ago. Between the two jobs I'm hanging in there. Got a roommate at a place out this way. Of course working these jobs is just temporary. Denny's going to try and get me a job at the casino as a waitress. Good tips and all…"

Her voice trailed off wistfully.

"That would be good," I said.

I found myself wondering if she and Denny were a couple now and then I was angry because why should I care?

For a couple more minutes I just watched her eat her fries and then my phone chirped with a text from Garrett wanting to meet and discuss Rock'n Ron. I replied telling him I'd call him in five minutes.

"Sorry," I told Katie, hating myself for apologizing yet again. "But I've gotta get going."

"Oh sure." She finished off her fries and licked the salt off her fingers. "You still with that guy? The FBI agent?"

I nodded.

"I worked at Big Al's Diner for a bit. Saw your guy blow in and out of town a couple months ago."

I tilted my head and frowned at her.

"Yeah, he stopped at Big Al's for a coffee during the couple weeks I worked there. I got fired the next day because I slept in. This is one of the things I learned the hard way after Mom was gone and I had to fend for myself. Apparently when people hire you they expect you to actually show up at a specific time."

She chuckled and then paused and looked at me. I realized she was expecting me to laugh along with her but I was still focused on Garrett being in my old stomping grounds and not mentioning it. Mind you, he was an FBI agent so most of what he did wasn't stuff he shared with me.

"Too bad you got fired." I gave Katie an encouraging smile. "I remember how much you loved the French toast at Big Al's whenever you were hungover."

"I know, right? It was the best." She sighed and for a second we shared a look that said this was like old times. "Yeah, your guy was sitting in a booth with a guy and I heard the name Arsenault. Made me think of you."

"Arsenault?" I sucked air into my lungs in surprise as my old surname slapped me hard in the face. "Who was he with?"

"Jesus. I dunno. Some suit." She tucked a strand of hair back into her ponytail and then slid out of the booth.

"So, did you say hi to Garrett when you saw him?" I asked, getting to my feet.

"Nah, I made sure he didn't see me. All those memories, right?" She made a big display of shuddering in disgust. "Still trying to keep them away."

I knew all about that.

"You call me and we'll do coffee, okay?" She abruptly leaned in and gave me an awkward one-armed hug.

"Sure." I stared at her back as she walked away leaving me with a ton of questions and only one place to go for answers.

Once I was back in my Jeep I called Garrett.

"Where are you?" he asked.

"I'm at a burger place just off I-5," I answered. "Near exit 242."

My head was swimming with questions about Katie and someone named Arsenault but I didn't want to ask him over the phone.

"I can be there in ten minutes," he said.

I could hear the slam of his car door followed by a moment when the tone echoed as the call went from his ear to Bluetooth.

"I'm finished eating and I don't want to hang around here. I'm leaving now." I started up my own car.

"Wait there a few minutes longer. It shouldn't take long to discuss Ron Low and—"

"Look, I don't want to stay. Why don't you meet me back at my place? I need to walk Wookie and—"

"Why are you in such a hurry?" He sounded annoyed.

"Who were you talking to at Al's Diner a couple months back? Who do you know with the last name Arsenault?"

Dead air filled my ear for ten beats of my heart.

"I can't talk to you about an ongoing case."

"Is it to do with me?" I asked. "Because I don't know of anyone else with the surname Arsenault. I'm sure it's possibly a coincidence but I stopped believing in coincidences a long time ago. So if it isn't about me…"

Maybe it was about my mom.

"I really can't talk to you about this—"

"Tell me!" I screamed, the panic of my verbal assault spraying spittle on my phone.

Dead air again and, this time, I thought he'd disconnected. My heart was pounding so loud in my ears that it was making me dizzy.

"I didn't meet with anyone with the last name Arsenault but, yes, I met with a guy at the diner to discuss someone with that name."

He blew out a breath and I could hear the frustration in his voice. He was talking low and slow, using that placating tone that he used when he felt I was on the edge. I hated it.

"That someone you were discussing was related to me?" It was just above a whisper.

"Hey, I'm on my way. Pick a place nearby where we can sit down and talk."

"Who?" I asked, my voice barely above a whisper. "Who is the person named Arsenault that you'd drive to Blaine to talk about? Tell me."

Again, the pause. As I listened to my heartbeat and the sound of his breathing I could imagine him getting that look in his eyes like he did when he was weighing the outcome of sharing information about a case.

"I was looking for information on your mother, okay?" he blurted. "The name came up in a case and so I was following up and—"

"Why would my mother's name come up in a case you're working when she's been dead for at least three years?"

"Julie, she may not be dead," Garrett replied quietly.

The phone slipped from my hand and onto the floor of the car as I covered my face with my hands and let out a guttural anguished cry.

FOUR

I DON'T REMEMBER the drive home. I do remember
counting all the liquor stores I passed along the way.
There were a lot. If I'd had a bottle of anything hidden somewhere in my house I would've guzzled the
entire thing without breathing. Instead, I snapped a
leash onto Wookie's collar and took him for a hard run.
We ran on the hardscrabble weeds alongside the road
so as not to burn Wookie's paws on the pavement. As
we ran the air sizzled and languid heat came off the
pavement in liquid waves.

My mother, Molly Arsenault, could be alive.

Alive and breathing.

My feet pounded the ground as I tried to conjure
up memories of the woman who birthed me and then
placed me into the abusive care of my grandparents
when I was six. Fifteen months ago, while my life was
circling the drain, I'd managed to track down Molly
Arsenault's last known place of residence with a low-
life named Ted in the town of Marysville. He'd filled
in some painful blanks. I found out my parents had
been married and that's why I'd had the last name Arsenault. My dad died in the Gulf War just after I was
born. Ted also told me that my mom was an addict
who'd left me with my crazy-assed grandparents in
order to go to rehab. Apparently, she'd returned for me

but was told I'd been given up for adoption. My grandmother despised me and there were only two reasons she'd have lied to my mom about me being adopted. She wanted to hurt my mother. And she wanted to continue to hurt me.

"She tossed you out of her car like a hamburger wrapper," Grandma hissed.

"It's okay to be angry with those who've hurt you." Dr. Chen's voice echoed in my head.

I picked up the pace of my run.

Ted had wrapped up my visit by telling me that my mother was a lifelong drunk who also played with hard drugs. She'd gone out for smokes a couple years before I came looking for her and never returned. They found her car on the side of the road near a fast-moving river and she was presumed dead. Now Garrett was telling me she might be alive, and my heart was breaking all over again.

Abruptly Wookie put on the brakes, nearly sending me ass over teakettle into the ditch. It was too hot and he was done with running. When a hundred-thirty-pound dog doesn't want to do something, you aren't going to make him.

"You're right." I put my hands on my knees, bent at the waist and gasped for air. "Enough is enough. Sorry, boy."

We walked back leisurely. I was drenched in sweat and Wookie's tongue lolled out the side of his mouth as he panted for air.

When we made it back to my driveway I wasn't the least surprised to see Garrett's sedan parked there while he sat on my steps. He had a haggard, worried expression on his face.

He got to his feet and started talking but I held up a hand to get him to stop. I turned on the hose at the side of the house and drank from it and then let Wookie lap up some of the fast-flowing water too. Once we were inside I refilled Wookie's water bowl and grabbed a Coke. Wookie collapsed onto the cool tile and went to sleep while Garrett and I took a seat at the kitchen table. I drank half my can before I spoke.

"Talk."

"This is still an active case and I'm not supposed to discuss—"

"Jesus, Garrett, who exactly am I going to tell about your goddamn case? The dead people I find?" I ran my fingers through my damp hair. "You're the only frick'n friend I have in this world." My voice wavered a little. "I can go weeks without talking to a single soul besides you and my shrink."

"So that's what we are? Friends?"

That was an argument for another day.

"You know what I mean." I nudged his foot with mine. "You're all I've got. You're my everything."

"That's really not healthy," he pointed out.

I rolled my eyes so far back in my head that I could read my own thoughts and they weren't kind. "Please. Just tell me."

"I guess I can tell you this much," he began, leaning in to either soften his tone for my sake or to make sure Wookie didn't hear and reveal all his secrets to the media. "Remember that big drug trafficking investigation I was involved with a few months ago?"

"The one that hit the news?" I leaned in too in spite of myself. "The one where you and your guys raided a bunch of places at the same time and seized, like, thirty pounds of meth and twenty pounds of coke and lots of guns?"

He nodded. He was always working on a case, of course, and I heard about the big bust at the same time it became big news in the media.

"We swooped in and hit a dozen houses and arrested a lot of people but not everyone living at those addresses was home at the time of the raids. We got most of them, but some are in the wind. One of the names that came up as a resident in a house was Molly Arsenault."

It hit me hard. I inhaled deeply while I let that sink in. I tried to form a question but all I could feel was the weight of the air around me, heavy and swirling with apprehension. Garrett just waited patiently.

"Where?"

"The house was in Auburn."

An hour away from where I lived now. I closed my eyes and breathed deep. After a while I leaned back and threw up my hands. "I really don't even know what to do with that information."

"That's why I didn't tell you," he confessed. "I haven't even laid eyes on her myself."

"That's not why you didn't tell me." I scowled. "You didn't tell me because you thought it would send me into some kind of psychotic break. That I'd end up back in the loony bin, or, worse, that I'd end up slurping my way through the chardonnay section of the grocery store."

"No." He placed a hand on mine and squeezed. "I just wanted to be absolutely certain before I told you."

"Well, are you sure? Is my mother alive?"

He hesitated and then blew out a long breath. "Until I actually see her for myself, I don't want to say, Julie. We've got her name. Some blurry security footage." He shrugged. "For all I know, someone has just assumed her identity, okay? That happens a lot. If I knew for sure, of course I'd tell you."

I wanted to push him hard for more but I could tell that he'd given me all there was. Or all he could. Either way, I needed to wrap my head around the little that he did manage to confirm. "So you'll keep me in the loop?"

"As much as I can."

Which is really all I could hope for.

He got up and took our Coke cans to the recycle bin outside, then went to the fridge and peered in. "You need to stock your fridge with more than cola and iced tea."

"If you're hungry, I think there's a frozen pizza in the freezer." I came up behind him and wrapped my arms around his waist and stood on tiptoe to nibble the back of his neck. "I'm kind of hungry myself."

He turned around, hugged me tight and murmured "I love you" as I lifted my face to be kissed. His lips on mine were tender and loving until my hands went to the buckle of his belt.

"Bed?" he breathed against my mouth.

I shook my head as I fumbled with his zipper. I wanted him here and now and I didn't want soft, gentle lovemaking in my warm bed. He answered my need with his own and after we both lay spent on the cool tile.

"God, we're good," I breathed.

"You're amazing," he said as he sat up and collected his clothing.

"You're not bad yourself. For an old man."

"Hey!" He played like he was offended and I laughed.

Garrett had over twenty years on me and I loved it when he left mister serious FBI guy behind and became my boyfriend instead of my protector.

Do you think being with an older man is a replacement for a father?" Dr. Chen asked.

The idea was absurd since the way I felt when I looked at Garrett had nothing to do with family.

"We need to do more of that," I told him as I slipped into my shorts and T-shirt.

"If you still lived with me we could do that every night."

My lips went to spit a scathing retort but he quickly apologized.

"Sorry. Not trying to guilt you." He pulled me close. "I love any time we spend together."

I sighed against him. I knew what he wanted. Garrett wanted what he'd had with his late wife and son. That kind of domesticity of everyday family. I didn't know if I could give him that but I did love him with my whole heart. I hoped that was enough.

My phone chimed and I broke our embrace to reach for it. There was an email with lots of exclamation marks from Ebba Johansson. She'd heard about Rock'n Ron.

"Ava's mom knows about Ron Low." I looked at Garrett. "She has questions."

That brought us to the other, more official, reason for Garrett's visit. Since I was the person who found the body, he needed an official statement from me. I filled him in, adding more details to what I'd briefly told him earlier about my having gone to school with Ron and my conversation with his roommate, Joon Kim, that led me to think of hiking to the Bat Caves.

"So you had no reason to suspect you'd find Ron's body there?"

"None." I shook my head. "He was an outdoorsy guy. That hike would've been a cakewalk for him because he knew it well. I don't think he took a bad fall and crawled into the cave to die."

"You're right. That's not what happened. Someone shot him in the head inside that cave. There was a bullet hole in the back of his head and no gun was found nearby so it was not a suicide. Of course, we need to wait for the coroner's report but the big ol' hole in the back of his head is bound to be cause of death."

"Well, a bullet to the temple could mean he crawled in that hole to kill himself over concern he was going down for Ava's murder and an argument could even be made a raccoon or other critter made off with the gun. But a bullet to the back of the head means it was an execution." I dragged my fingers through my hair and thought about it. "I'm guessing you're back to square one on looking for Ava's killer."

"Not necessarily. He could've killed Ava and someone killed him in retaliation."

"What's your gut say?"

"My gut isn't involved here and I'm hoping yours won't be either. I've got enough on my plate with another big investigation and you have other bodies you could be finding. Sure you found Ron but let's leave it at that. This is a hot investigation with at least two deaths now. Let the guys running the show handle it until they find the killer."

"I want to help find Ava," I said. "Finding Ron was an accident but now I feel like I should help to finish this." I pursed my lips. "Unless you think she's not even dead? No body, right?"

"Enough blood left at the scene that it's certain she didn't survive."

"Okay. I know you're not involved in this case but, obviously, you know about it. If you had to guess, would you say it was Ron who killed her and then he just got taken out, like you said?"

"You know we look at those closest first. Ransom note was written on Ron's computer so he was involved somehow. His roommate was out of the country at the time Ava died but I guess he could've hired someone to do it and set up Ron." He shrugged. "There are a lot of possibilities. Ebba had an insurance policy out on her daughter but it was taken out years ago to benefit the business and she's now lost a hundred thousand against her business by paying out the ransom, so she sure doesn't look like she killed her daughter."

"Was Ava dating anyone else after Ron?"

"Investigators looked into a couple other guys she was dating but I don't think anything came of that. Right now, I'm guessing they're starting from scratch with the discovery of Ron Low's body." He pinched the bridge of his nose, squeezed his eyes shut and sighed. "The autopsy will be done and until we have proof about how and when Ron died, the supposition that he was murdered is not to leave this room. Don't go sharing that with Ebba Johansson."

I made a motion to turn a key at my lips and nodded.

He was on his feet then and making his way to the door. "See you tomorrow, right?"

When I looked at him blankly he reminded me I had an appointment in town. He'd marked it on his calendar.

I followed and, before he left, he kissed me long and slow and in a way that almost made me ache for the normal life he craved. I watched his dark sedan back out of my long gravel driveway and waited until it disappeared down the road.

Rather than email Ebba, I decided to give her a call. Since it was late afternoon I tried her first at the business line listed on her card but the receptionist told me she only came in a couple times a week to that location and today was not one of those days. Next, I dialed her cell number and she answered on the first ring.

"Thank you so-o-o much, Julie! It means so much to me that you found that horrible Ron. I guess you've taken my case and we didn't even discuss your fee yet," Ebba announced, sounding immensely pleased. "I can't believe you've already found Ron! What a coward to take his own life instead of facing up to the consequences. Do you think that Ava's body could be nearby? Did you search?"

I asked why she thought Ron took his own life and she said that when the officer called her she asked how he died and they said they found a bullet hole in his head. So much for keeping everything on the down low until after the autopsy report. I patiently explained that finding Ron's body was purely accidental but she wasn't buying it. I also told her that I hadn't searched for Ava at the Bat Caves because if she'd been killed at the state park where the crime scene was, there was no way even a hiker like Ron would've hauled her body down that trail.

"The fact that I found Ron had nothing to do with your request to look for Ava."

"Right. You don't want law enforcement knowing that you're working for me. I get that. You have no idea how much it means to me that you're willing to help bring my girl home."

"I…um…"

Part of me wanted to turn her down flat and make Garrett very happy but a bigger part of me wanted to know how my old high school crush ended up dead in a cave and a suspect in the murder of his ex-girlfriend.

"I will do a little searching but if it looks like there are no leads of areas to look, I'm going to drop the case. Agreed?"

I told her how to send me an initial deposit of a thousand dollars by electronic bank transfer and she agreed to send me the money immediately.

"I don't have a lot to go on," I admitted. "But I'll start searching the area where…you know…" My voice trailed off because there was no easy way to say it.

"Where they found all that blood and where the asshole killed her."

"Right."

"And when will you go there?"

"Tomorrow. First thing."

"I'd like to be there when you go."

"That's not necessary. The area has already been widely searched. I'm only going there for my own peace of mind and, obviously, I'd call you if I found anything at all related to Ava."

The news reports all talked about the location being in the Mount Baker-Snoqualmie Forest along the Nooksack River but I was going to need more of a starting point than that so Ebba promised to email me the exact location.

I realized she must be somewhat relieved that the body of Ron was found but she wouldn't be so reassured if she knew that Ron had been murdered himself and maybe wasn't the person who killed Ava.

Later that evening I was having popcorn and cola for dinner while watching a sitcom when my phone chimed with a reminder of an appointment tomorrow with my psychiatrist. I cringed. My appointments were down to once a month now but that still meant a drive all the way to downtown Seattle. The monthly appointments usually meant Wookie and I would spend the night at Garrett's. He would get our favorite pizza—sweet fennel sausage, roasted peppers and provolone from Serious Pie—we'd cuddle on the couch to watch a movie afterward and sometimes make love right there in the living room. Honestly, it was the one ritual that made therapy worth it.

I debated only a few seconds before picking up my phone and emailing my psychiatrist that I needed to cancel. Almost immediately my phone rang in my hand. It was her and I knew that if I didn't answer she would keep trying until I finally did.

"Hi, Doc."

"Why are you cancelling?"

She'd plucked me from the brink of crazy last year with many hours of therapy and strong medication. If she had her way I'd still be seeing her weekly instead of monthly. I'd like to know how a wound was ever supposed to scar over if you kept peeling away the scab.

"It's job related. I have to drive two and a half hours north of here tomorrow for a job. You're an hour south from home. It puts a cramp in my day."

"The next day then?"

I pursed my lips and tried to think of a good excuse besides *I don't wanna*.

"Fine."

"How are you at this moment?"

It was a loaded question. Did I tell her about finding a body today, running into Katie, or kick off a verbal interrogation by saying I'd discovered my mother could be alive. "Fine. I'm fine. Really."

Might as well make her earn her two hundred dollars an hour at our next session.

We set up the time and I texted Garrett to let him know about the change. He was a scheduler. The second he got my message he'd be on his phone calendar rearranging things. He replied immediately saying he loved our time together today and was really hoping for tomorrow to spend the night together. Then he added he was happy to see me the next night and ended his text with a heart emoji. I knew he was somewhat disappointed in the delay and he'd probably already been fluffing Wookie's doggie bed in his apartment. The thought made me smile and then wince because sometimes I didn't know why I ever moved out.

"Moving out and buying your own place must have made you feel empowered?" Dr. Chen asked.

"Was it empowering or just another way to run away?" I mumbled, answering the voice in my head.

Abruptly I pushed those thoughts aside and sat down to make a plan to find Ava's remains. As promised, Ebba had emailed the location of the camp and I used a map and satellite images online to check the area where all that blood had been found. It was as good a place as any to start but, let's face it, even though that was probably where she died, if her body was nearby the cops or the numerous frequent search parties would have found it. I was guessing that Ron, or whoever the killer was, just stuffed her body into the trunk of his car and drove her somewhere else to be dumped. Ava could be anywhere in the seventy thousand square miles that made up Washington State, or even the whole country.

I was tired. It had been a long, emotionally charged day. I climbed into bed, set the alarm on my phone for the ridiculous time of six a.m., then pinched my eyes shut and hoped for a dreamless sleep.

"What do you dream about?" Dr. Chen asked.

Bodies.

Gramps.

Grandma.

Drowning myself with bottle after bottle of wine.

"Nothing. I don't dream."

My body relaxed into the cool sheets and I positioned myself perfectly so that the light blanket exposed my feet but covered the rest of me, and the table

fan on my dresser blew, as I liked it, across my body
but not in my face. Then my phone chimed.

"Shit."

I'd neglected to turn off my phone notifications.
Normally I turned off sounds for everything except
texts from Garrett when I went to sleep so that email
messages from people searching for bones wouldn't
wake me up. I couldn't resist checking the message.
It was a rambling email from Abel saying how he
couldn't sleep and was stuck on one of the Candy
Crush levels and so he'd been thinking about me and
his grandson, Wes, and did I know that Wes actually
grew up in my old home town and that he was single.

I know you two didn't hit it off right away, but I didn't
get on with his grandmother at first either.

He ended the email asking me to call him to talk
about it if I had the time or inclination. I didn't have
either so I turned off the sounds on my phone.

When the alarm on my phone went off hours later
it felt like I'd just closed my eyes. Wookie had crawled
into bed next to me in the night and managed to take
over the entire bed. I found myself clinging so close to
the edge of the mattress that I nearly tumbled onto the
floor trying to reach my phone to shut off the alarm.

"You have your own bed." I gave the dog's solid
body a shove. "When we lived in our trailer you
wouldn't have dreamed of sleeping in my bed. All this
fancy living is making you soft."

He stretched then jumped off the bed as I got to my
feet, and came over and licked my bare feet in apology.

"You are not forgiven." He licked me some more. "Thanks for the bath but I'm still going to need a shower."

I filled his bowls with water and kibble and let him out to pee while I scrolled through my phone. That's when I realized that it was almost nine and not six.

"Damn. Damn!"

I'd screwed up in setting the time and now I was hours behind in my day. Once Wookie was back inside I hustled into the shower. While I stood under the spray and washed the sleep from my eyes and Wookie's slobber from my ankles I debated bringing the dog with me. He enjoyed car rides and would love the chance to romp in the forest once we got to the state park.

I'd just started toweling off when Wookie went insane in the front room. It was his someone-is-at-the-door bark followed by his just-say-the-word-and-I-will-chew-their-face-off snarl.

Tightening my bathrobe around my waist, I made my way to the living room. Someone was knocking at my front door. In the year I'd been here, I don't recall ever using that door. The side door into the kitchen was the one I used. I peered out the picture window and saw a young woman with shoulder-length lime-green hair and wearing cutoff denim shorts and a zebra-striped tank top. She had a couple grocery bags in one hand and more at her feet, and every time Wookie barked she nearly jumped out of her skin.

"Can I help you?" I shouted through the door.

"Um. Grocery delivery!" she shouted back.

"I didn't order any groceries."

"Some guy called Frank's Foods in town and asked

us to make a delivery. He put it on his card and everything."

Wookie was growling so much that his spittle was spraying the door as he threatened to gnaw his way through it.

"Hush!" I put a hand on Wookie's head and, like a belligerent toddler, he still woofed except now it was quiet like he was muttering under his breath.

"Look," the girl called, "I don't need you to sign or anything so how about I just leave them here."

I watched through the window as she put the bags down on the front stoop and began walking back to a small Hyundai that was the same bright green as her hair.

"Well, crap."

After a split second debate I took off after her, pinching the top of my robe and wincing as my bare feet landed on every sharp pebble in the driveway. I reached her just as she was opening her car door.

"Sorry," I said breathlessly. "I didn't mean to be rude. It's just that I really didn't order any groceries."

"Yeah, like I said—" she started.

"Some guy ordered them," I finished.

"Yeah his name was Barry or Gary or—" She scrunched up her face.

"Garrett?"

"Yeah. Garrett."

I blew out an exasperated breath and she smiled.

"That your dad? Is he making sure you eat right or somethin'?" She tucked her hair behind her ears, exposing the oddest double rings over the first and second joint on a number of her fingers.

"Definitely not my dad but sometimes he acts like it." I smiled and then shifted my weight awkwardly from one foot to the next. "So how does this work? Do I give you a tip or something?"

"I'm not sure on account of we don't do delivery, like ever." She shrugged. "Guess your Garrett guy talked Frank into it and next thing I know I'm driving out here."

"He can be convincing."

"I guess."

We stared at each other a second.

"Well, I think I'm supposed to give you something for your trouble," I said. "Come inside and I'll grab my purse."

She looked at the house, where Wookie had resumed his overprotective attack mode of machine gun barking.

"Don't worry. He's all bark."

"I'm good."

"You don't like dogs."

"Not even a bit," she admitted.

"Wait here then."

I jogged back to the house, carried in the bagged groceries and then spent a couple minutes tracking down my purse. I was Googling the proper tip amount for grocery delivery while I walked back to her car but I couldn't figure it out so I just handed her a ten.

"Wow. That's too much." But her multi-ringed fingers snagged the bill and it disappeared into the front pocket of her cutoff shorts.

"I appreciate you going out of your way especially since you don't usually do deliveries," I said.

She nodded, climbed behind the wheel of her car and started it up, or at least tried to start the vehicle. The car wouldn't turn over. She popped the hood and we both stared at the motor.

"Goddammothertruckershitwaffle car."

"Yeah," I agreed. "Maybe you just need a boost. I've got cables around here somewhere."

We attempted to give the car a jump with my Jeep but that wouldn't take either. I wanted to get on the road but I couldn't exactly leave her stranded in my driveway. She tried calling her boss to come get her but his number went straight to voice mail.

"With me out here there's nobody working the front till," she said, running ringed fingers through green hair. "So he won't be answering the phone 'cuz it's in the back."

"Well, I was just going to get dressed and head out the door myself. How about I drive you back to the store and you can send someone to tow your car?"

"That would be great." She glanced up at Wookie barking through the window. "I'll wait right here."

It didn't take me long to dress and put the groceries away. My fridge wouldn't know what to do with all the fresh produce, milk and cheese—and my cupboards had never held so many kinds of soup with varieties I'd never heard of and labels that boasted organic this and healthy that. It was a really nice thing for him to do but it annoyed me too.

Soon I was out the door and hauling my green-haired passenger into town.

"I'm Tracey Cook," she announced after riding a couple minutes in silence.

"Nice to meet you, Tracey Cook." I smiled at her briefly before returning my eyes to the road. "I'm Julie Hall."

"Oh I know who you are."

"You do?"

"Everyone does."

"Everyone as in...?"

"As in everyone in town. Which isn't a lot, of course, but I think we topped four thousand last year."

"You're saying everybody in town knows me? How?"

"Oh, sure. You probably hadn't even moved in when everyone in town knew your business. You're the girl from up in Blaine that used her inheritance to buy a house here after things went to Hades in a hailstorm and—" She looked at me. "Sorry 'bout that." Then she continued, "Also, you find dead people so there aren't too many people like that around."

"Am I the local freak?"

She just blinked at me.

"You know, the local attraction. Come one, come all to see witchy girl with her dowsing rods."

"I wouldn't go that far."

"Maybe I need to up my game. Throw a neon sign on the front yard and learn to read palms." I giggled at the idea.

"You can't blame people because they're going to talk 'bout stuff like someone new. Plus, you finding ol' Corny Dooley made someone money too so—"

"Wait. What? Finding that old man made someone money?" I gave her my what-the-living-hell look.

"Sure." She shrugged. "People were betting how

long it would be before you used your sticks to find a body while living 'round these parts. Of course ol' Abel couldn't bet on account of he hired you to find the graves at the church."

"People have been betting. On me." I shook my head slowly. I guess just because I'd been avoiding spending time in town and getting to know my neighbors didn't mean that they didn't already know about me. Life in a small town made me want to pack up again and move back in with Garrett in his high-rise condo in downtown Seattle where people only nodded hello to each other if they had to ride up the same elevator.

"Don't get twisted about it," Tracey said. "It is what it is."

I hated that saying.

We pulled up to the only grocery store in town and I waited for her to get out.

"You know, you should tell that Gary guy that the Fred Meyer one town over delivers and they have a bigger selection and better prices."

"I don't think he'll be doing this on a regular basis."

"Okay. Whatever." She climbed out of the Jeep and then dug out a pen and paper from her purse and scribbled something on it. "We have a stitch and bitch meeting every Thursday night at seven o'clock." She handed me a piece of paper with her name and number on it. "We take turns hosting. It's my turn next. Send me a text for the address if you wanna come."

"What's a stitch and bitch?"

"We knit, gossip and just drink a lot of herbal tea."

"I don't knit."

She shrugged. "Some do and some don't and some drink wine instead of tea."

With that she closed the car door and walked into the small grocery store. As I pulled away from the curb my head was swimming.

Once I'd had a moment to digest all that I'd heard from Ms. Tracey Cook the green-haired grocery clerk, I used the voice-activated Bluetooth feature in my Jeep to dial Garrett's phone number. When it went to voice mail I left a message.

"Did you know that the people in this town know a-a-l-l-l about me and were actually placing bets on when I'd find a body? And now, thanks to you, I have an invitation to something called a stitch and bitch? Oh and thanks for the groceries." I waited a beat. "Don't do that again."

I disconnected the call and began to play one of my audio self-help books through the speakers. The narrator's voice was surprisingly upbeat as she informed me about the physical benefits of relieving PTSD through yoga and meditation.

I hit the highway and turned up the volume of the book as the narrator talked about forgiveness. Dr. Chen loved to give me tidbits about that.

"You don't have to forgive the people who hurt you in order to make peace with your past."

"Sure."

I didn't want to make peace with my past. I wanted to incinerate it.

After heading north an hour, I took exit 236 to get onto Route 9. I stopped at a gas station to fill up the tank, use the washroom and grab a Coke and a candy bar. I still had almost ninety minutes of driving to go. Back in my Jeep I took a moment to scroll through my phone. Ebba Johansson had emailed to ask when I was going to the site, but hadn't yet sent my deposit. If she didn't send it by end of day, I'd have to send her a reminder.

For the remainder of the drive I switched audible books to one that was motivational. I'd probably listened to dozens of these books over the years. They all had that cheerleader *Rah-rah-rah go-o-o team!* feel to them but they were like my crack.

It should've been peaceful taking the forest-lined Mount Baker Highway into the North Cascades National Park, but I had a love-hate relationship with the woods. People died in the forest and those who wanted to kill you could easily dump you there. Taking up hiking to find the beauty in nature helped but it didn't steal away that unease in my gut. I figured I was only a few miles away from the campground now so I plugged the address into the navigation system so I wouldn't miss my turn.

As it was, even with the annoying lady's voice telling me to turn right I nearly blew right by the faded wood sign that indicated the turnoff toward the campground. The trees were so tightly knit they caused the smaller drive to be camouflaged in shades of evergreen.

The road was loose, rutted gravel that split into a fork after a mile but the navigation system gave no indication of left or right. I stopped the Jeep and stared down each of the roads as far as I could and was rewarded by a small directional arrow pointing right for the camping area. A quarter mile down, the road sharply cornered right and I had to two-foot the brake or I would've slammed into the back of a news van.

"What the hell?"

I steered around the vehicle into a small parking area for the campground, which was chockablock with cars and vans emblazoned with television and newspaper logos. I pulled up alongside Ebba Johansson's red BMW and was immediately surrounded by reporters shouting at me. Ebba was holding court in front of a picnic table. She made eye contact with me and I waved her over. She sauntered over and I yelled at her to get in and unlocked the doors.

She climbed into the passenger seat. "I was wondering if you were still coming because you said you'd be here early and—"

"What is going on?" I snapped. "Why are all these reporters here?"

"Well, I invited them."

"Why on earth would you do that? I'm trying real hard not to freak out at you so start talking."

Our picture was constantly being taken so I resisted the urge to strangle Ebba or even give her my death glare.

"There hasn't been as much coverage lately. I need to keep my Ava in the news so people won't forget her." Her voice broke at the end of the sentence.

"You should've warned me."

"I'm sorry. You'll still help?" She reached over and put a hand on my arm and I could hear the *click click click* of cameras snapping this emotional shot. Grieving mother pleading with weirdo witch girl who finds bodies.

"I'm not walking into the woods with my dowsing rods and being followed by a bunch of nosy reporters."

"Okay. I'll make a statement and tell them to leave."

"They won't go," I told her, my voice cutting. "Why would they? They're hoping I'll find a body and each one of them wants to be here if that happens. They didn't drive all the way out here just to watch us have a touching moment in a car." I sighed. "Tell me about that day."

"Well, I'd received the ransom note a few days before saying that he'd release Ava for one hundred thousand dollars. The letter came in the mail to my house and said to get the money ready and told me where to meet them in four days with the cash. I was told no police or they'd kill her."

She spoke so quietly that I had to lean in to hear her over the sound of reporters outside.

"In the meantime the police were launching their investigation?" I urged her to continue.

"Yes, but they only knew she was a missing person. I didn't tell them about the ransom note. They came over and searched her room. Called her friends, that kind of thing, but they weren't taking it very serious. Until I got that letter I was worried but I still thought she'd show up on a friend's couch somewhere. She often didn't come home for days at a time if she was out having a good time." She gave me a look that said *kids, right? Whatcha gonna do?*

"So you got the money ready?"

"Well, that wasn't as easy as it sounds because even

though I've got all these spas and the house my money was tied up. It's not like I had a hundred thousand in my savings account. I had to go to the bank and they were a big help in helping me leverage everything to the hilt."

"So you got the cash and then you came out here at the day and time it said?"

"So I packed up the money in a small backpack and came here. The instructions said to drop off the bag on a black rock that was down the trail, and Ava would come out. I dropped the backpack on that rock, which was out of sight from the parking lot. Then I went back to my car and waited for Ava. After an hour of waiting I got worried." She took a deep breath. "So I walked back down the trail. The pack with the money was gone and there was a lot of blood on the ground and no sign of Ava. I called the police and they got here right away. Brought dogs and everything but…nothing. The dogs lost the scent of them only a few feet from the drop-off spot."

"Were there other campers here that day? Any other cars?"

"Nobody else was here. This campground was closed for the season and reopened a couple weeks later."

"So the two would've hiked here together and then he hurt her here…but then what? He couldn't've carried her far. You called the police and—"

"And they came." She looked down at her hands folded in her lap as if trying to keep back the tears. "I can't tell you how long it took the police to come. I was a wreck. Running around the woods screaming Ava's name over and over."

The click of the cameras and the reporters pressing into the car made me feel like a fish trapped in an aquarium. I wanted to flip them my middle finger but resisted.

"I should start looking. You know that this is kind of a formality," I told her. "I'm sure the police, park rangers and the FBI combed every inch of these woods looking for Ava."

"They did." Ebba nodded, swatting a fly away. "But they didn't find her. You could find her and I'd like to come with you."

She was dressed inappropriately for any kind of a hike. She had a large white purse hooked over her shoulder and wore white Capri pants, a pink blouse and rose-colored sparkly wedge sandals.

"You're dressed for the mall and I doubt you're going to find anything to buy on that trail unless you want to haggle with a squirrel for his nuts. If you want to wait for me in the parking lot, it'll make this a lot easier."

"Easier for who? You?" She laughed. "If I'm paying you, I have a right to watch, right?"

"Technically you haven't paid me yet. You still need to send me the deposit."

"Oh. Right. I forgot." She pinched the bridge of her nose and squeezed her eyes shut. "I'm just so overwhelmed right now."

"I know you have a lot on your mind," I said gently. "I'm going to head down the trail. I'd prefer to go alone. Maybe you could keep the wolves from nipping at my heels." I hooked a thumb to indicate the reporters.

"Okay. I'll try."

After I snagged my bag from the back seat we hopped out of the vehicle.

"Hey, Witch Girl, did spirits tell you Ava's body was here?" shouted a reporter, while a cameraman stuck a lens in my face.

"Can we get a picture of you with your dowsing rods?" asked another.

My feet ate the ground toward the far side of the lot where a trail was visible and Ebba followed. It wasn't hard to spot since a tree on that side of the camping area had become a makeshift memorial with dried flowers and ribbons tied to its trunk.

"Could we get a picture of the two of you in front of the tree?"

I kept on walking.

"Ebba, what made you hire Julie Hall and her magic wands?"

Ebba stopped at that question and I just kept walking.

"I want my daughter found. I need to bring her home."

Her voice broke into a sob and I felt horrible for her. She was a mom who'd lost her daughter. All the reporters paused and focused on Ebba, sensing an emotionally charged clip as she struggled to regain composure.

"I can't bear to know that she's out there. Alone. With the animals in the forest." She nodded toward me. "Please let Julie do her work and, if anything comes of it, I'm sure you'll all know soon enough."

They asked Ebba more questions. She was openly crying now and they were in a feeding frenzy. I wanted to take advantage of the reporters being distracted so I sprinted far enough away that I was out of sight.

Ebba's email to me stated there were a few trails that led away from the campground and I was to take the path that was directly behind the picnic table. I walked to the table and placed my backpack on top to take out my rods. Carved into the wood were dozens of names inside hearts and uninventive curse words but right across the center of the table, carved deep and with care, was engraved: *Ava we will miss you forever.*

It made me pause and give thought to the pretty twenty-five-year-old blonde who'd had friends who cared and once loved Rock'n Ron and who had her entire life ahead of her. Did Ron bring her here to this spot, take the cash and kill Ava anyway? If he did, who killed him and why?

A massive hemlock tree that had to be two hundred feet tall guarded the start of the trail. A makeshift memorial of dried flowers and weatherworn teddy bears surrounded the base of the tree. Ava's friends had found out the location where she'd died and taken hours out of their day to make the drive to this secluded campground just to pay their respects and chose this tree and picnic table. If it were me there wouldn't be a single person besides Garrett who would bother.

After I attached my bear spray to my belt loop I started out. With my rods in hand I stepped into the trail and breathed deep the smell of earth and old growth forest. My sneakers crunched on the hard-packed dirt and branches as I followed the trail that wound through the thick woods. There were wolves in this forest. And bears. Neither of which appreciated being surprised so I hummed a little as I walked and sighed a wish that Wookie was with me. Had Tracey Cook not been so freaked by the dog, I would've brought him along.

It wasn't far at all. The place Ebba left the cash and where Ava was murdered was only a few dozen yards down the path. I reached the large flat rock that was the scene where she'd been killed. Even though we'd had rain since, the bottom of the rock was still spattered red. I paused a moment and took in the area. Although I wasn't far from my Jeep and the campground, I was completely obscured by dense shrubs. If Ebba had left the pack with the money here and returned to her vehicle to wait for Ava, she would not have been able to see her daughter being killed. I tilted my head and listened to the forest. Birds, bugs, a breeze rustling the tops of the trees, and I could also hear the muffled voices of the journalists. If Ava had screamed, her mother would've heard her.

"Why didn't you scream, Ava?" I whispered to the forest but a squirrel's chatter was the only reply I got.

It was entirely too Mother Nature for my liking.

FIVE

I'D BEEN EXPECTING some kind of marking by police around this rock location but there was none. Whatever crime scene tape and staked out markings had long since been taken down which, of course, made perfect sense. Probably dozens of campers had hiked down this trail and walked right over the soil where Ava's blood had drained and become part of the ecosystem.

With my hands extended holding the dowsing rods out I walked quite a ways before realizing I'd gone too far. There is no way someone, anyone, would've carried deadweight this far. Turning around, I followed the trail back. The rods never flinched and, honestly, I hadn't expected them to. Investigators had scoured this area and volunteers had fanned out far and wide to search as well. If she was nearby, she would've been found. As I approached the large, flat rock, I noticed another less traveled trail off to the side. Others had broken twigs and pushed through the shrubs here too, but there was no harm in seeing where it went.

I walked steadily on the tight trail while I hummed "Stay away bears" and "Screw-off wolves" in a fun little singsong that wasn't going to be a chart topper. The rods never moved, except briefly when I tripped over a log. The trail curved and I stopped short when it brought me to a walking bridge over a ravine.

"Damn."

I felt fear trickle with sweat down my spine as I contemplated my next move. I could turn around and go back to the other trail. I didn't have to go over the bridge but it was only a half dozen yards long and wasn't very high up.

"Still a bridge," I told myself.

I heard Dr. Chen's voice in my head.

"When you feel strong enough you can face your fears and you'll find it very empowering."

"Won't feel much empowered if I fall to my death over the side or pee my pants out of fear trying to cross it," I grumbled under my breath.

I could see the headlines now: Water Witch Plunges from Bridge and Pees Pants. I took in deep, cleansing breaths and practiced some mindfulness meditation.

Then I told myself to pretend there were a couple ice-cold bottles of Riesling waiting on the other side. That did it.

The bridge was sturdy and didn't shift under my weight. Had it wobbled, even a little, I would've screamed and possibly found my death over the side and onto the rocky ravine below. My eyes focused straight ahead and my feet propelled me forward. I would not look left or right because the edge of the bridge was a siren's call that would tempt me to climb the railing and jump over.

When I reached the other side, I dropped my pack and rods on the ground, put my hands on my knees and wiped away the tears that had drenched my face.

"You are such a frigg'n baby."

I wiped my damp face with my palms and took a

few minutes to find my breath. I took out a water bottle and emptied it into my parched throat. Then I gathered my stuff and continued on the trail nonchalantly as if I hadn't just seen the face of my own death.

It was only a couple minutes later that the trail came to a stop, opening up onto a gravel road. Following the sounds up ahead, I realized that the trail had opened onto the second fork in the road. Although it would've taken some effort to drag a body this far, someone as fit as Ron, the avid outdoorsman, could've heaved Ava through this trail and then tossed her into his car. If the car had been parked down this fork in the road, it wouldn't have even been visible to Ebba when she turned into the campground.

When I walked back into the campground clearing, the reporters were waiting. They swarmed me and pummeled me with questions. I walked stoically toward my car without cursing them out like I wanted. Somebody should give me a medal for that.

Ebba had been sitting at the picnic table and, when she saw me, got to her feet and ran over to my vehicle.

I rolled down the passenger window and whispered that I hadn't found anything but had a few more questions. I told her I'd call her in a few minutes. She nodded not looking at all surprised that I'd returned without the exact location of Ava's body. She knew her daughter wasn't here because she would've been found already.

At least she got the publicity she wanted. Ava's face would be headlining the news again tonight. So would mine. Although I should be used to the witchy name-calling, it still stung. When I started up my website

I'd given a few interviews to benefit www.Divine-Reunions.com but journalists weren't interested in the lengthy, legitimate history of dowsing. They didn't want to hear that grave divination didn't make me a sideshow freak. They wanted to ask about the vortex of doom that was my old home. Questions were about fifteen months ago when I met and worked with Garrett to help find a serial killer.

I drove out of the campground, relieved that the reporters didn't follow me. A few minutes later I called Ebba on her cell phone.

"I'm sorry," I said. "I know you understood it was unlikely that I'd find Ava today but I'm sure you were still hoping. Unfortunately, these things rarely go as planned."

"If anyone can bring my daughter home, it's you," Ebba said emphatically.

I appreciated her vote of confidence but it wasn't that easy.

"There's a really good chance I won't find her," I said gently. "I'm going to try, of course, because you hired me." I looked around the vastness of the forest around the road. "But she could be literally anywhere in the state or the country."

Ebba didn't respond for a long while and I was beginning to think the call was dropped.

"Hello?"

"I'm still here," she replied so I waited.

The sun was now high in the sky and it burned my skin through the window. I turned up the a/c and accelerated. I wanted to get the long drive over and get back to Wookie.

"When her dad died I didn't know what to do. We'd never had much money. He was a laborer who brought in enough to keep a roof over our heads and food in the pantry and, honestly, I never wanted more than that."

I thought about the Ebba I knew who was always dressed to the nines, and had a hard time imagining her living a lower class lifestyle.

"When he got sick I took a retail job to help pay the medical bills but the bills kept coming long after his heart gave out." She sighed long and wistfully. "I didn't have an education. I'd always just stayed at home to be a mom. Ava was just entering school at that time so it was a good time to get some training. When she went to school, so did I. I took classes to become a massage therapist and then worked retail at night. I barely made enough to pay the rent and her babysitters but it was worth it. I opened one spa location at a single casino and soon many spa locations at many Washington casinos. Ebba's Bliss is a name recognized for the epitome of perfection when it comes to massage."

"Ava must've been very proud of you for all you accomplished."

"You'd think that but, no, Ava really didn't care." Ebba gave a derisive snort. "As long as there was money for the things she wanted, she didn't care how I got it. I worked long hours myself and then I hired others. It took years to get my name out there but my reputation grew so I became known as the best of the best. That's why the local casinos and hotels were happy to have us." I could hear the pride in her voice. "My massage studios are now inside of nearly every major casino hotel in the state and I wanted Ava to be a part of it because I'd done it for her. She was un-grateful."

Ebba had pulled herself up from poverty as a single mom and a widow. Although she said she did it for Ava, I doubt her daughter saw it that way.

"Still, she was my daughter and I wanted us to be close so I kept on trying," Ebba said. "And now it's too late."

"I'm so sorry."

Those weak words were all I had to offer. She was grieving. The pain of losing a loved one carries on far beyond the time the sympathy cards and phone calls stop and way beyond the time of casseroles being dropped at the house.

"What did Ava do for work?" It was something I didn't remember reading about in the news articles.

"When she did deem me worthy of her presence she answered the phones for the spa at the same casino where Denny works." Her tone was so bitter it surprised me.

"You sound angry about that."

Ebba chuckled. "My daughter was a spoiled brat." She quickly added, "That was my fault, of course. I'd given her everything. Life was one big party for her. She'd come to work when it pleased her. It was a glorified allowance I paid her hoping that she'd actually get an interest in the business one day. That's why she thought she could date a fool like Ron Low."

"I went to school with Rock'n—" I stopped myself short. "With Ron Low." I cleared my throat. "He was extremely popular with the girls."

"He broke her goddamn heart." Ebba blew out an

angry breath. "My daughter wasn't good enough for him. She caught him screwing someone else and broke it off but she would've taken him back. Ava begged him to take her back. Why she would want to be with him is beyond me."

A pause stretched out between us and I told her I'd talk to her another day.

"But what's next?" she demanded.

"I'm going to think about that," I told her. "I'll let you know."

She persisted to pepper me with questions until finally I'd had enough. "There is no science to this. I'll have to figure out where to go looking next."

"But you did other things before. Dowsing not just with rods but with a string. I heard about that somewhere."

My hands tightened on the steering wheel.

"Who told you that?" Then I shook my head. "Never mind. I don't want to know." It was probably Denny. I ran fingers through my hair that was still damp with sweat. "It doesn't work that way. Yes, I used pendulum dowsing successfully a time or two but it hasn't worked since—" I stopped myself. "It doesn't work for me. Let's leave it at that. I need to stick with my dowsing rods, which means I need to give a thought to the best place to go next." I was anxious now to end this call. "If you think of any suggestions of anywhere else you think she might be, let the cops know and then let me know. I've gotta go."

I hurriedly punched End Call on the navigation screen to disconnect. Ebba Johansson had brought up the idea of pendulum dowsing and now I couldn't stop thinking about it. I drove fast and rolled down my windows so that the wind whipped my hair around my face.

Yes, I'd done pendulum dowsing before.

It was how I saved Katie.

It wasn't difficult. You swung an object from a string and asked questions to narrow down answers. Easy peasy if that was your thing. I'd tried it after the end of my old life but never got it to kick in. That part of dowsing was obviously dead to me now. Why had I agreed to take on this case? Just because my old high school crush was connected and it made me curious was a dumb reason. I was beginning to wish Ebba Johansson had never stepped foot on my driveway.

I'd finally relaxed, and was listening to a motivational book on audio when my cell phone rang. The display on my dash announced the incoming call was from Joon Kim. I reached to hit End on the dash and ignore the call but hit the Accept button instead. Damn.

"Hello! Hello!" shouted Joon Kim.

"Hi," I replied, trying to keep the disappointment from my voice.

"I heard about Ron. You found him, right? Good for you! And you found him in the Bat Caves, which is really kinda weird after I told you about the caves!"

Did everything he said have to sound so excited? Couldn't I just be left to drive in broody silence?

"So what now?" he asked me but then I heard him busy talking to a customer in his store so I guess he really didn't want an answer.

"I'm kind of busy." There was more chatter in the background so he obviously wasn't paying attention to me. I reached over to disconnect the call while grumbling about him wasting my time.

I started thinking about Ava Johansson and how her mother had called her a spoiled brat. Ebba had given her everything but Ava hadn't cared. It was polar opposite to how I was raised in poverty and abuse and maybe that was what had set me on edge. Abandoned by my own mother—who might very well be alive—and having to deal with someone else's mom who was going to extraordinary lengths to try to find her dead girl. Maybe all this drama hit too close to my own aches.

Then again, maybe I'd just been in therapy far too long and should stop overanalyzing things.

I let up on the accelerator before I got a ticket and rubbed the back of my neck. Ebba's admission about her daughter's behavior made me realize I knew next to nothing about the girl beyond what was painted in the media. Of course all the papers and TV had colored her as this beautiful young woman who'd been kidnapped and killed by her ex-boyfriend. There was more empathy and money to be made glorifying the qualities of the victim than there would be in stating she acted like a lazy princess. Maybe the answer to finding Ava was to get to know the real person. I called Joon Kim back.

"Hello-o-o!" he cried. "If you have bad cell service come into my store and I'll fix you up."

"I don't have bad cell service; I hung up on you because you were busy."

"Oh."

"How well did you know Ava Johansson?"

"How well do we ever know anyone, right?"

Great, now he was going to get all philosophical on me.

"You must've seen her a lot? She'd come over to visit Ron, and since you lived there…"

"Well, sure, she'd come to see Ron but not me, right? I was, like, the fifth wheel except the third wheel. If you know what I mean."

"I'm just trying to get an idea of what kind of person she was."

The talkative Joon fell silent for once.

"What time do you take your break?" I asked.

"Anytime I want because I'm the manager," he boasted.

"I can be at your store in half an hour," I told him. "I'll buy you lunch."

Joon agreed and at the next exit I turned around so I was now headed north.

I was at Bellis Fair Mall trying to squeeze my car into one of the last available spots when I got a text from Joon that he'd meet me at the Chipotle in the food court and that he was wearing a straw fedora. I thought he might be joking about the hat until I spotted him standing in the line to get his food. I walked up and introduced myself.

"You're skinnier and paler than in the pictures I've seen of you." He tilted his head and looked me up and down.

"What pictures?" I frowned and then realized he'd seen me in the media. "You saw me on the news and stuff."

He nodded and smiled as if my trauma of a year ago was a photo op.

"Nice hat," I remarked. "Makes you look like a cross between Justin Bieber and Frank Sinatra."

"That's what I was going for." He gave me a fist bump.

We waited while the food line inched forward and he complained about the mall being overrun by Canadians and that was why the lines were so long.

Once we were seated and he was digging into his burrito I started my questions.

"Did Ron and Ava fight a lot?"

"Not really."

"But sometimes they did?" I pushed.

"Ron was an easygoing guy, right? He wasn't the type to fight with anyone. Ava would get wound up… usually about her mom…and Ron would just let her rant so if they had a fight, it was more her than him."

I nodded. "Did Ava complain about her mom a lot?"

"A ton." He shook his head. "Too much."

"Tell me about Ava."

He chose to ignore that question. "So you found Ron down in the Bat Caves after I told you about the caves so, in a way, I'm the one who found him, right?" He puffed out his chest and grinned proudly with a dollop of salsa clinging to the corner of his mouth.

"Sure. You're a regular Sherlock Holmes except you didn't know that's where Ron would be, only that he liked to hike there."

"It's all about clues, right? I gave you the clue and you ran with it."

"More like I hiked with it."

"Touché." He grinned and winked at me. "You just had a feeling in your gut that he was there after I said it, or what?"

"I wish it was like that but it wasn't. Lately I've been trying different hikes, and when you mentioned the caves it made me think of…" Of all the times in high school I wished Ron would take me down to the caves for a make-out session. "It made me realize that would be a nice easy hike that was about my speed. Not too hard."

He looked at me like he didn't believe it, then picked up his burrito and took another huge bite.

"But you don't act surprised that he was found dead," I pointed out. "Some people probably thought he was still on the run from killing Ava."

"I guess I'm not really surprised."

Or grieving. "Why?"

"Anybody who'd kidnap their ex-girlfriend, send a ransom note to the mom for a hundred grand and then kill her in a park after getting the money…" He gave me a twisted smile. "I figured if he could do all that, there's no way he could stand to get caught, right? Besides, Ron's the type of guy who'd die in jail, you know? Me? Give me my game systems and I'd never leave my room if I didn't have to eat, poop or work."

"Ron needed more than games, food and pooping?"

"Yeah. He had to be outside and hated being stuck inside. He liked to smoke a little weed, do a lot of hiking and just be in nature, right? Being in a prison cage like that…it would've killed him. He's better off like this."

"Better off dead?"

He might have been right on some level but that sounded pretty cold to me, and I was starting to dislike Joon Kim.

"What's your opinion on why he'd do all that? She caught him cheating and broke it off. Why kidnap her for ransom if all he wanted was to live a simple life? And why kill her?"

Joon took off his hat, placed it on the table next to his food and rubbed his receding hairline as he thought about that. "He was always talking about traveling the world and hiking all over. He hated working at the sporting goods store. Ava always told him she'd get part of her mom's massage business eventually and, when she did, they could sell it off and travel together. Of course that was when they were still getting along and she thought she was his only piece of tail."

"Things got angry after that?"

"Not on Ron's side." Joon slurped from his drink. "Ava went ballistic but Ron acted like he didn't care that she ended it. Obviously he cared big-time though, right? Maybe he realized he made a big mistake cheating on Ava. Could be that he still wanted to hike Machu Picchu instead of Mount Baker, ya know? Maybe he saw that hundred grand as a way out of this stupid town."

He sure made it sound plausible.

"Is that what the cops thought?" I asked. "That Ron wanted the cash so he could get out of this map dot?"

"Sure. That's what the cops even told his mom and dad. I'd just gotten back from Korea and went to visit his folks, yanno, to pay my respects and say how lousy all this was, and the cops were there talking to them about Ron's possible motives."

"What do you think went wrong that he didn't just take the money and see the world?"

"Chickened out, I guess."

Except Ron didn't kill himself. Someone shot him in the back of the head and took the gun with them so someone else was involved in this mess. I looked at Joon with new eyes.

"And you were in Korea when Ava was murdered, right?"

"Yeah, my grandma was sick."

"But she'd already been missing when you left. Just that no one thought anything of it yet. Just figured she was partying with friends."

He slurped his drink.

"So when did you get back?"

"A couple weeks after they say she was killed, why?" He shoved the remainder of the messy burrito in his mouth and then talked with his mouth full. "Oh you think I had something to do with it or something?"

I cringed at the gooey food in his mouth. "You're not exactly bawling your eyes out here. Did you have something to do with any of this?"

"Hey, I cried about it, okay? I might not be crying now but I had my moments. Of course I didn't have anything to do with this. If I did, I'd have all that money, right? Do I look like a guy with a ton of cash in my pocket?" He waved at himself. "I've got it going on, but not a hundred grand worth."

"Yeah you're a rock star." I handed him a napkin. "Except for the sour cream beard."

"Not a designer label here, yanno." He wiped his face. "I'm a walking ad for knockoffs."

"Let's get back to Ava. She breaks up with Ron and I understand she tried to get back with him. Did he take her back? Were they a couple when you left for Korea?" I realized Ebba didn't think so but a mom was seldom the first person to know about their kids' romantic relationships.

"When I left they were still broken up. Not for lack of trying on Ava's part though. She was willing to get back together if he'd swear off other girls. He just told her he wanted to relax without a relationship for a while. He was chill like that but not her, right? Ava was freaking out. Kept coming by the house but Ron was never home. He worked and hiked. That was it. She could be a handful, though, and wouldn't take no for an answer. Maybe he just flipped out, right? Guess he did."

We were quiet a minute. He scrolled through his phone while I scooped up guacamole on chips and ate a few.

"What was Ava really like?"

"What do you want to know?" He took a couple of my tortilla chips and double-dipped the guac, stuffing the chips into his mouth.

I tried not to look revolted as I pushed the bowl toward him. He could have them. "I mean besides how Ava was like with Ron. What was she like as a person? Did you like her?"

He chewed and chomped my chips and noisily slurped his fountain pop while he considered his answer and I waited patiently.

"Fun but also kind of mean." Joon licked a green dollop of guac that clung to the corner of his mouth. "Not an outright bitch but the kind who'd give you an unsult."

"An insult?"

"No, an insult tucked inside a compliment. Unsult. She'd make snide remarks and backhanded compliments so you'd think she was being nice and later you'd think and go…huh?"

"Oh." I thought about that and then asked, "She was like that to everyone or just Ron?"

"Everyone. Like if she saw me wearing this hat today she'd say," he carried on in a singsong voice mimicking Ava, "'Oh, Joo-o-o-on, look at yo-o-o-ou! I've never seen anyone be able to pull off that kind of hat!'"

"Gotcha."

"Yeah, so sometimes you think she's giving you a compliment but if you really think about it, she's not." He slurped the remainder of his pop then reached for mine. "But considering where she came from, it's no wonder she turned out like that. I mean, have you met her mother?" He made a big display of visibly shuddering. "That woman is a class A beotch."

I blinked in surprise. Ebba was stuck-up, maybe, but a bitch? "Did she come to your apartment often?"

"Ava or Ebba?"

"Either."

"Ava was there every single day when she was dating Ron. Sometimes she'd even come over when he wasn't around to get away from her mom and we'd just hang. A couple times Ebba showed up to scream at her about getting her ass to work but Ava would just blow her off." He smiled, apparently proud of Ava's defiance. "If I had the day off and Ron was at work, Ava and I'd watch Netflix all day and game and stuff. She was cool like that."

"So you were close with Ava?"

He gave me an abrupt nod and his face screwed up and for a second I thought he was going to cry.

"Don't be telling the cops that, or nothing. I don't need that headache. Besides, Ava only came over on account of Ron. When Ron was around she only had eyes for him. She'd come over hoping to catch him when he came home from work but mostly he went out after so it was just me and her. We chatted a lot. Sometimes she'd come to my store when she was shopping in the mall and then we'd come right here to Chipotle." He sighed and said wistfully, "She liked the salad with chorizo."

"Did you two ever get together…you know…as a couple?"

"Oh no-o-o." He shook his head emphatically. "Ron was her goal. Not that I wouldn't have given her the ol' Joon torpedo if I'd had the chance but she wanted Ron so I had to respect that. I mean she could be a mean girl but she didn't sleep around so…"

Maybe Joon wasn't as casual about his lack of torpedoing Ava as he claimed. Could be he arranged for the kidnapping before he went to Korea and somehow Ron found out so Joon killed him too. I looked at Joon sitting across from me casually scrolling through his phone and it seemed unlikely the guy cared that much about anyone or anything.

Suddenly he held his phone out to me to show me

a selfie taken with Ava sitting almost exactly where I was right now. They were making goofy duck faces and doing peace signs with their hands.

"What's that around her neck?" I leaned into the picture and then enlarged it. "Some kind of key?"

He flipped the phone around and looked at it. "Yeah she always wore that."

"A key to your place? One that Ron gave her?" I asked.

"Nope. She was wearing it the first time she came over. I don't think she ever took it off."

"Do you have any other pictures of her?"

"Sure. Ava was picture happy. Always wanting me to snap her pic and send it to her so she could load it on Instagram and Facebook." He tapped his phone and then handed it to me. "Just scroll through that album."

There were a couple dozen pics of Ava and Ron together and apart and also pics of each of them with Joon. Most of them were in the house, which was a complete pigsty. In a lot of the pictures there was pot and booze littering the coffee table. Marijuana was legal in Washington and it didn't strike me as a surprise that Ron might partake in a little weed but the house looked like a party place and that took me back a bit.

"How much did Ava like to party?"

"Quite a bit." He took back his phone and slipped it into the pocket of his shirt. "We all did. Except she liked to go out to the clubs, the casinos, bars… I'm more of a party-at-home kinda guy."

"Could you send me any pictures you have of her?"

"Sure." He shrugged. "But why?"

"Just trying to get a feel for who she was as a person and you know what they say about pictures being worth a thousand words."

He tapped repeatedly on his phone and soon my own cell phone was chiming with incoming messages.

"What about hiking?" I asked. "We all know how much Ron loved it. Sounds like that's what he lived for. Was that something Ava was into?"

"Oh, she tried." Joon rolled his eyes. "She bought all the most expensive gear and was always asking Ron to bring her along but, of course, she couldn't handle the bigger trails. Ron took her along a couple times but he liked a challenging outing and didn't want to babysit a newb." He glanced at his phone. "I gotta get back to work."

We got to our feet.

"By the way, how's your sick aunt?"

"My aunt?" He tilted his head. "You mean my grandmother? The one I visited in Korea when all this exploded with Ava and Ron?"

"Oh yeah, your grandmother."

"She died."

"I'm sorry to hear that."

He shrugged. "She was really old." He slipped his hat back on his head and we gathered up our food containers and wrappers and brought them to the disposal area.

"Are you still living in the same house that you were in with Ron?"

He nodded. "I've got a new roommate. He's not as much fun as Ron but he isn't as much of a pig either."

"I never would've guessed Ron to be a slob," I admitted. "But then I didn't really know him at all."

"Since you're here, maybe you should talk to the people he worked with at the sporting goods place." He glanced at his phone and rolled his eyes. "Gotta go. Call me if you have any more questions and…" he leaned in and whispered in my ear, "good luck with finding Ava."

I decided to take Joon's advice and head down to the other end of the mall to talk to the employees that worked with Ron at the sporting goods store. I came around the corner of one leg of the mall and nearly slammed into Abel's grandson, Wes.

"Oh. Hey." I nodded to him. "Thanks for getting those graves uncovered for your grandfather."

"Sure. Whatever." He looked over his shoulder, uneasy. "Took me five minutes, so no big deal."

"It was a big deal for your grandfather," I pointed out. "By the way, do you know where that big sporting goods store is?"

"The one where Ron used to work?" He pointed down a leg of the mall to our right. "It's down that way. At the end."

"You knew Ron?"

"Went to school with him. And you." He gave me an awkward grin.

"Sorry." I scratched my head. "I don't remember too many people from then." I cleared my throat. "But that reminds me, I was looking at some pictures online about that Ava Johansson case and I saw you in one shot taken of the search parties."

"Yeah, I tried to help out a couple times." He shifted from one foot to the other.

"That's really nice of you. You had your arm around

a guy with a shaved head and he looked really familiar to me. Do you remember who that was?"

"Jay Low. Ron's older brother."

"Oh." That took me by surprise. "I didn't even know he had a brother."

We stared awkwardly at each other for a couple seconds.

"Well, I've gotta go."

I said goodbye and watched as he hurried off in the opposite direction.

I headed in the direction of the sporting goods store. I had to pass a buffet restaurant where I'd taken Gramps for his birthday. I thought about him unbuckling his pants because he'd overeaten, and a smile slipped onto my face before I could stop it.

Get outta my head, Gramps.

I was itching to leave this mall now and all that this town represented to me. At the sporting goods store I found two people who'd worked with Ron and remembered him. Unfortunately, there wasn't much they could tell me except that he was a nice guy and everybody liked him. One of them mentioned that Ron liked to use his employee discount to stock up on the best hiking stuff and that even with the discount it still cost him a lot. The clerk showed me a pair of hiking boots Ron had purchased just prior to the whole Ron and Ava fiasco. They were nearly five hundred bucks. The ransom money would buy a heckuva lot of gear. Still, some fine Gore-Tex boots and an exotic location to wear them didn't seem like good enough motivation to hold Ava for ransom to the tune of a hundred thousand.

Although I nearly died at the price of the boots, I didn't leave the store before trying them on for myself. My feet felt amazing. If I ever got beyond the less skilled hikes, I would have to come back and buy a pair.

I picked up a coffee for the road and made my way back to my Jeep only to find that one of my rear tires was completely flat.

"Ugh." I crouched down and examined the rubber. There was a gash in the sidewall that meant I wasn't going anywhere with a simple refill of air. "What the hell?"

After making a call to a local tire place I ended up spending more than those hiking boots for a new tire.

"How did it happen?" I asked the guy as I was handing him my credit card.

"Either you swerved this bad boy and kissed the curb pretty damn hard with your tire, or someone sliced it for you." He handed back my card and a paid invoice. "Looks like a slice to me. Plus look at the back of your trunk. Someone pried that open. While I'm here, I can fix that for you too."

I went to the back and felt along the back where tool marks showed the back had been popped open and even now wasn't fully closed.

"You got any enemies?"

The question chilled my blood.

SIX

BESIDES THE FACT that I found dead people, my life was pretty simple. I had no friends and no enemies that I knew of but the mechanic's question still rolled around in my head. Did someone slice my tire and break into my car, if they did, what would be the reason? That kind of behavior felt juvenile and vengeful. The tire guy managed to rig the latch in the back so the trunk could stay closed and then I was on my way.

By the time I was close to home, I'd decided that one of two things had happened. Either I'd sliced the tire on a rock bouncing along the rutted roads in the park earlier in the day, or I'd been the recipient of parking lot rage by maybe parking too close to someone at the mall.

My thoughts on that changed when I pulled into my driveway and was greeted by Wookie bounding down the road to greet me.

"What in the world?"

I slammed the Jeep into Park and jumped out. Immediately, Wookie nearly toppled me over when his massive body slammed into mine. He licked me non-stop and was bouncing around as if to proudly announce that he'd been outside for hours. I looked at him and then at the house. I went through the process of my leaving that morning. Even though I'd been distracted by little Ms. Green Hair, Tracey, there was no way on this planet I'd left the doors wide open, and it was highly unlikely Wookie had spontaneously grown opposable thumbs.

I texted Garrett 9-1-1, which was our code for this-is-important-so-call-me-now. And he didn't disappoint. My phone rang immediately.

"Are you okay?" he asked.

The emotion and fear behind the question made me feel like the luckiest girl in the world for having an FBI officer who loved me even if he did send me groceries like I was too stupid to feed myself.

"I'm fine but I've been out all day, just got back and Wookie greeted me in the driveway."

That sank in for a beat.

"I take it you didn't leave him outside?"

"No."

"Is the door open? Windows broken?"

"Not that I can see. I haven't gone inside. I'm still in the driveway."

"Good. Don't go in the house. Get inside your vehicle and lock the door until I get there. I'm leaving Seattle now."

I agreed because that sounded like a good idea to me. The last thing I wanted was to walk inside and confront whoever had sprung a furious hundred-thirty-pound Rottweiler without becoming a meal themselves. I eyed Wookie skeptically to see if there were any signs that he'd recently chomped a chunk of ass. He just stared at me panting with his tongue lolling out the side of his mouth. I kept a spare water dish for Wookie in the trunk for when we went out together. Who knows how long he'd been outside in the heat?

"Thirsty, boy?"

I rubbed his head as I dumped the contents of a water bottle into the bowl and put it in on the floor of the back seat for him. Then we both hopped into the Jeep and I turned up the a/c while I stared at the house. The only sounds were the hum of the vehicle and Wookie noisily lapping up his water in the back.

It was going to take Garrett at least an hour to get here. Was I just supposed to sit here until then? I half expected to see a couple guys come running out my house wearing balaclavas, holding revolvers and carrying sacks of loot over their shoulders. Except I was kind of lootless. No sack of gold and jewels or a safe. They'd be really disappointed. Wookie climbed from the back seat onto the front passenger seat and placed his fat head in front of one of the air-conditioning vents.

"What happened, boy?" I asked.

I'd been sitting and frowning out the window of my car for probably ten minutes when a bright green Hyundai pulled up behind me.

"Now what?"

Tracey jumped out of the car carrying a square pink box and approached my Jeep.

I rolled down the window and forced a smile. "Hey."

"Hi there." She grinned back. "Looks like I arrived just in time 'cuz you're just getting home."

"Um." I didn't know what to say so I just looked at the pink box and then up at her face. "Did you forget something?"

"I did!" Her smile grew wider until Wookie growled

over my shoulder. She took a step back. "How about I just give you this through the window and be on my way?"

"What is it?"

"Cake," she announced proudly.

"Cake?" I blinked at her, trying to understand.

"Yeah, when your guy called in your grocery order he asked us to bring you a cake but we didn't have any proper birthday cakes done up yet on account of our baker was late getting in so I figured I might as well drop it off on my way home when I'm off shift."

"A birthday cake?" I parroted. I was tempted to roll my eyes and make a loud raspberry sound of annoyance but she looked so damn proud of herself I just said, "Thanks. You didn't have to do that."

"Well, it was your guy who ordered it and obviously you can't have a birthday without cake now, can you?"

Apparently that wasn't true because I'd actually never had a cake for my birthday before. Ever. We didn't do birthdays growing up and I didn't do them now either. I'd asked Garrett not to make any kind of a big deal about the day. He'd followed my request for no gifts but apparently cake was exempt.

"Do you feel like you missed out on part of your childhood because you didn't have the usual gifts and celebrations? Christmas? Birthdays?"

"Everybody in the world is born. It's stupid to celebrate something we can't even control."

"You okay? Your face got all weird." Then Tracey's jaw dropped and her eyes grew big. "Holy shitake mushroom, did I just ruin some kind of surprise?"

"No, you didn't." I shook my head. "I didn't know

Garrett asked for a cake. I'm surprised because I honestly don't usually make a big deal out of birthdays."

"That's silly." She made a face. "Why not whoop it up and holler just because you're alive?"

When I didn't reply and Wookie kept growling she took a hesitant step forward and handed me the cake through the window.

"Enjoy your cake."

"Hang on."

Instead of grabbing the cake I rolled up the window and climbed out, leaving the car running so Wookie could have the cool air.

"That sure is nice of you coming all the way out here with cake," I said. "I... I um..." I looked at Tracey and then after blowing out a long breath told her the truth. "I came home to find Wookie out of the house. Somebody let him out so that means somebody broke in."

"No kidding?" She looked at the house and then looked at me. "And on your birthday of all days!" She looked personally affronted by this. "I had a boyfriend forget my birthday one time. Not even a card so, obviously, I had to kick him to the curb but this—" she waved at the house "—is a much worse birthday kick in the ass than that."

It was comical how she seemed perfectly outraged and aghast that such a thing had happened on my birthday. I almost giggled at her reaction but managed to hold it in.

"Yeah, it sucks."

"It sucks big-time." She nodded.

"It sucks harder than an anteater at a picnic."

"That's lame." She laughed. "So you're just waiting

in your car until you get the nerve to go inside? Should we call the cops or something?"

"I'm just waiting for Garrett to come and check the place out and make sure everything is okay before going inside, but he's coming from Seattle so it'll be a bit."

"I'll just call the cops instead. That'll be quicker." She thrust the pink box in my hands and dug out her phone.

"No!" I nearly shouted and she eyed me curiously. "Because Garrett is kind of, well, he's law enforcement, so…" I smiled awkwardly. "I'd just rather it be him because maybe it's nothing, you know?"

She nodded slowly but I could tell she didn't get it at all. "Well, it's too bad on account of now we'll just have to sit here and eat that cake because we can't just sit here and do nothing else."

I blinked in surprise and then pointed out the obvious that we didn't have any forks or knives or anything and she said something resembling "Pshaw" and went to her car and retrieved about a dozen fast-food napkins from the console and an uncomfortably large kitchen knife from under the seat of her car. Then she marched these things over to a small shade tree a few feet away from the driveway and plopped herself down in my grass, leaving me no choice but to follow with the cake.

She popped the lid of the cake box then handed it to me and said, "Smile." Using her phone she snapped a picture of me staring down at the white birthday cake with the pale blue buttercream frosting flowers that looked like the typical birthday cake others always received. It said *Happy Birthday Julie* in pink icing across the middle. I found myself blinking back tears until Tracey stabbed it with her large knife of questionable cleanliness. She carved out a large slice of cake and handed it to me on a stack of napkins.

"Of course, you get a flower and part of your name because it's your cake. That's the rule."

"I had no idea there were rules about cake."

"Not all cake. Just birthday cake."

Tracey sawed off a hunk for herself and I watched her stuff cake into her own mouth before attempting it myself. It was so sweet it hurt my teeth but I managed to eat the entire large slice, blue flower and all in record time.

"What's your cell phone number?" she asked when she was sawing off another slice of cake for each of us. I hesitated and she rolled her eyes. "I'm gonna send you the picture of you with the cake so you can post it or whatever. Maybe you want it for a memento of the day, you know?"

I rattled off my number and thanked her when seconds later I received the picture of me staring incredulously at the boxed cake.

Eating large quantities of cake on my front lawn with a stranger while my house may have been burgled was a strangely intimate thing. We sat staring at the house with the icing-covered knife between us ready to slice cake or a robber. The sun and sugar relaxed me enough to try and talk to Tracey and not be weird.

"So you got your car fixed. That's good."

"Yeah it was just some thingamabob," she replied. "How old are you?"

"Twenty-seven today."

"Same!" she exclaimed like this gave us a connection on a new level. She tilted her head and looked at me. "You don't act twenty-seven. Or talk it. I woulda guessed you to be, like, thirty or something."

"How does twenty-seven act?"

She thought about that. "Like everything is still possible instead of impossible and like birthdays are still a big deal because it's not like you're sixty or something. What did you do last year?"

I was in the loony bin this time last year. "Not much." *Three hundred thirty-one.* I changed the subject. "I like your rings."

"They're finger splints. I have a connective tissue disorder called Ehlers Danlos. My joints randomly pop out and I'm super bendy." She looked at me stone faced. "Guys seriously love it but it also kind of sucks because it hurts like a bastard."

"Oh. Sorry."

"What's our plan for if some crazed guy comes running out of your house?"

"Well, we could stab him with your cake knife. If he didn't die from the wound, he'd probably get diabetes. It's a slower way to go though."

"You're funny when you're not uptight."

We each ate another piece of cake. When Garrett arrived his black sedan roared up the driveway, slammed into Park and he hopped out like a man on a mission to save his girl from a home invasion and possible death.

He glanced at my vehicle still running with Wookie licking the inside of the windows and then he looked at me sitting with Tracey under a tree with cake crumbs down my front. He looked utterly confused.

I got to my feet and introduced him to Tracey.

"You ordered me groceries and, apparently, also cake." I hooked my thumb at Tracey. "The cake arrived a few minutes ago."

"Oka-a-y." He looked at Tracey and stuck out his hand. "Nice to meet you." Then to me. "Happy birthday." He gave me a quick kiss and then pointed to the house. "Anything new happen?"

"We haven't gone in at all," Tracey piped up. "We've been waiting for you to give the all clear but there have been no bandits or hooded serial killers running out while we've been here on the lawn eating cake."

"Okay, I'll check it out." He nodded seriously and then pulled me into a brief hug and whispered in my ear, "You have icing on your nose." He wiped his index finger across the tip of my nose and licked it off.

He pulled a revolver from his shoulder holster and slowly approached the house. My heart pounded because even though it seemed unrealistic that someone would still be holed up inside, my man was armed and ready to do battle for me.

"So he's like a cop or something?"

"Yeah, something like that," I told Tracey.

"And you like them much older and straitlaced, huh?"

"What?" I startled because I'd been staring so intently at the house after Garrett went inside. "You mean Garrett? Yeah, he's in his mid-forties."

"Daddy figure, right?"

She elbowed me in the ribs and gave a chuckle but it pricked me with annoyance, just like when Dr. Chen suggested the same thing. Why couldn't I just love him because I loved him? Why did he have to be replacing something I never had?

I ignored Tracey's comment and after what felt like forever, Garrett appeared on the front steps, yelled "All clear!" and waved us over.

"I gotta get Wookie out of the car." I nodded to the dog. "So you might want to—"

"Say no more." Tracey held up a hand. "I'm outta here." She walked to her car. "Thanks for sharing your cake!"

"Thanks for delivering it," I replied and I actually meant it.

Once the little green Hyundai was out of the driveway, I turned off my vehicle and Wookie bounded toward the house, more than a little excited to see Garrett.

"So nobody was inside obviously," I said as I climbed the steps carrying the pink box and what was left of the cake. "Sorry to make you come all this way for nothing. I just don't know how Wookie got loose, and it freaked me out but maybe I just didn't close the door all the way and—"

"The back patio door was smashed."

"What?!"

My eyes got huge. I looked past him to see that there were only jagged shards from the frame where the glass door used to be. I put the cake box down on the table and grabbed Wookie by the collar so he wouldn't wander over to the broken glass, even though that was probably how he got out in the first place.

Garrett took charge because he was good at that. He pulled my sofa and a couple chairs to block access to the area so I didn't have to hang on to Wookie. Then he swept up the glass while I checked to see what was missing from the house. Then he called a glass company one town over to make an emergency trip out. There was a large rock the size of my head that had obviously been tossed through the window. Even though Garrett had swept the glass, I pulled out the vacuum to make sure I got it all. I didn't want Wookie getting a sliver in his paw.

At first I didn't notice anything amiss or missing. Then I realized my laptop was gone.

My emotions were all over the map. I felt angry and violated and wanted desperately to punch a hole in the wall and drown my sorrows in wine. Not necessarily in that order.

While waiting for the glass company to come and replace my door, we took a seat at the kitchen table. We nibbled crackers and cheese and drank iced tea while I kept shaking my head and mumbling, "Jesus, why would someone—"

"Not exactly the best way to spend your birthday," Garrett said, then held up his hand to stop me. "I know you don't like to celebrate but still it's a crappy way to end any day and, from what I saw on the news, looking for Ava Johansson wasn't exactly a resounding success either."

I cringed when I thought of all the reporters. "It was just a starting point. I wanted to see where she was killed. Unfortunately, every news truck in a hundred-mile radius loved a chance to catch Ebba in tears with the water witch girl carrying her sticks." I rubbed the back of my neck. "She called them, you know? Said she wanted to make sure Ava's face got back on the news."

He nodded. "I'm not surprised. Families of victims often try to keep their loved ones on the news, hoping it'll solve the case. Sometimes it works and witnesses come forward."

"If Ron was murdered it looks like maybe he didn't act alone to kidnap and kill Ava," I reasoned.

"I'm sure the investigators are looking into a possible partner there."

"And Ebba had no reason to kill her daughter, right?"

"Do you think she killed Ava?" His eyebrows went up in surprise.

"No, I just know you always look at family first."

"They had life insurance policies taken out on each other years ago through Ebba's Bliss, and I guess that could be a motive because Ebba is leveraged to the hilt with her business, but the woman is a workaholic and I don't think she ever took a day off until this happened with Ava. Every second of her days before and after were accounted for. She reported her daughter missing before there was sign of a kidnapping and then took a lot of cash out of her business, so it feels unlikely she's involved. Joon Kim was looked at strongly but it's hard to kidnap and kill someone when you're across the world. Although he could've been working with someone too, right? The whole case is a disaster." He reached for my hand and my fingers entwined with his. "That's why I'd prefer you stay away from it."

"I get that." I nodded. "But I feel like I need to solve this thing because of Ronald Low. We weren't close or anything but we went to the same high school and, well, he stuck up for me a couple times. Even if it turns out he killed Ava, I need to find out."

"That's what investigators are for."

"Yeah, I know." I ran my hand through my hair. "Look, don't lose your mind here, but I should probably tell you I had an issue at the mall today too."

"What kind of issue?" His fingers tightened on mine and I pulled my hand away.

"I met up with Joon Kim to ask about Ava and Ron. While I was chatting in the food court with him, someone may have slashed one of my tires."

"What!"

"And broken into my trunk."

He was on his feet pacing. "You should've called me right away." He pointed at me angrily from across the kitchen. "Why are you just telling me this now?"

"When it happened I figured it was a one-off, you know? Maybe I parked too close to some guy and he took it out on my car." I got up and walked toward him. "Anyway, I had a tire place come out and fix it and it's all good."

"It's not all good." His face was red with anger. "Your car and your house get broken into at the same time so I'd say that's as far from good as it gets."

I went to him, wrapped my arms around his waist and pressed my cheek to his chest. His body was rigid with anger.

"I'm sure it's nothing," I breathed against him. "Someone hurt my stuff but they didn't hurt me. They could have done these things while I was around but they didn't, so they're probably just bad luck in one day."

I felt him soften as he returned the hug.

"I'm going to look into it."

"Of course you are." I smiled and lifted my face to his. Then he kissed me tenderly and hugged me tightly.

"By the way, thanks again for the groceries and also thanks for the cake." I left his embrace and nodded to the pink box. "There's still a lot left. You want some?"

"I thought you'd never ask."

He tussled my hair as he walked over to get plate, knife and fork. And just like that we were okay again. He wasn't the FBI agent needing to save the girl and I wasn't the victim needing constant protection.

While he was carving a slice for himself, he said, "You and grocery girl managed to put a pretty big dent in this cake."

"My teeth still hurt from the all that sugar." I laughed. "I'm no longer a birthday cake virgin."

"That was your first birthday cake?" His eyes darkened with that same sad look he always got when discussing my less-than-stellar upbringing. "Your first cake and you made a new friend all in one day." He tapped the tip of my nose. "Next thing you know you'll be throwing dinner parties filled with the local green-haired girls and taking selfies together."

"Hah! Calling her a friend might be a bit of a stretch."

But I had to admit I wasn't totally averse to the idea of a friend. At one time Katie'd been my best friend but then she'd hurt and betrayed me. I no longer wanted to run her over with my Jeep, but there wasn't going to be any girl time in our future.

"You know I have to ask…" I let my voice trail off and Garrett looked up from his cake and shook his head.

"No sign of your mother."

I sighed and pushed the hurt aside.

A few minutes later some crime scene tech guys showed up to do fingerprinting and I had to snap a leash on Wookie to stop him from making a meal out of them. Garrett greeted them outside and took them around the back of the house to show them what he wanted them to do.

Afterward I told Garrett, "I really believe it was probably just teens wanting a laptop. Throwing a big rock through the glass doors and then snatching it off the table isn't exactly the work of mastermind criminals."

"To us, Wookie is a gentle giant." He put his hands on my shoulders and looked down at me. "But there is no way somebody broke that door and sauntered in here without your dog tearing a hunk of flesh from their bodies."

"Oka-a-ay." I'd anchored Wookie's leash to the leg of the kitchen table and now I looked at him. "Maybe he did though." I shrugged. "There's a good chance some reckless teen is at the ER right now getting a couple dozen stitches in his ass."

"And your tire being slashed?"

"A coincidence."

Garrett took me by the hand and led me to the bathroom off the hall and pointed to a window that was open about four inches. "You always leave that open when you shower."

"Well, yeah, because I don't like it getting steamed up, and the fan isn't strong enough to totally clear it out. I don't want mold growing in here like what happened in my trailer. Besides, I always put the lock on it so it can't open beyond that amount." I pointed to the small lock in the track of the window. "And it's not like anybody could fit through there."

Garrett stepped closer to the window. "There are some sesame seeds in the track and a bit of bread." He nodded toward the floor. "And a greasy smear down the wall."

I saw what he meant and realization dawned.

"They pushed a burger through the window and drugged Wookie so they could break in."

Tears burned my eyes as I turned and slammed my fist onto the bathroom counter. I hurried back to the kitchen where Wookie was sprawled out on the floor next to the table. I dropped to my knees and hugged him hard. He was all I had from my life before and all I wanted.

"I should bring him to the vet right away."

"He's fine. If it was something more lasting he wouldn't have been romping around the yard when you got home."

I buried my face in Wookie's thick neck and choked back the tears because he was the only family I had left.

Unless your mom is alive, a voice whispered in the back of my head but I choked and tamped down that small whisper.

Over the next few hours the guy came to replace the glass door and Garrett made sure he installed some better locks on all the windows. Even though Garrett took out his credit card I insisted on paying the absurd overtime rate. Still, I knew that if someone wanted to get inside my house and drug my dog, there wasn't a lot I could do about it.

Garrett made a bunch of phone calls dealing with

whatever I'd dragged him away from to come and rescue me. He used his hushed FBI businesslike voice that carried over from another room. While he did that, I sat on the sofa and checked my emails on my phone. I was grateful my laptop could be replaced and I wasn't going to lose much on it since I stored things online anyway. Most of my laptop work involved email, invoicing, Googling locations and playing card games. When I opened my email inbox there were a few requests through my Divine Reunions website asking for help finding loved ones. When I was already working one search, I tried not to muddy my thoughts with others. I wanted to find Ava, or at least give it a good effort before thinking about finding someone else.

There would always be others. The dead don't care but those left behind need something to bury and a graveyard to visit in an elusive search for closure.

I read three emails from Ebba Johansson making suggestions about where I should look next for Ava's remains. Her first message was a mere suggestion and her second was a tad bossy. Also, she'd failed to send me the e-transfer of my deposit. I wasn't desperate for the money but I found it very odd. You want me to work for you immediately but you don't want to pay me? Ebba dressed well, drove an expensive car and had a chain of massage studios in various casinos around the state. But Garrett said her business was leveraged to the hilt, and I'm sure taking the hit of losing a hundred grand didn't help. I had a feeling she was holding off paying me anything until I found Ava's remains even though I'd pointed out firmly that there was a chance I would not find her. I considered dropping the case altogether but, admittedly, I was curious now and wanted to see it through.

I sent a reply to that third email saying I was going to take some time to plan out my next thoughts. I informed her I'd get back to her once I had a firm direction in mind and once I'd received her deposit.

It wasn't about the money. I'd done pro bono jobs before. Poverty-stricken families deeply grieving for closure had hired me by scraping together whatever cash they could and, at the end of the day, I'd declined their payments. It felt like a good karma thing to do. I put the phone down on the side table and looked around my house. Mine. When Gramps died I wanted no part of the inheritance but Garrett and my doc encouraged me to sell off the farm, donate some to charity and take the rest and turn it into something good.

"Everyone grieves in their own way. He was your grandfather and he raised you—"

"I don't want his house. His money. His messed-up legacy."

"You could take it and make something good out of it. Turn it into a positive."

This house and trading in my old Jeep for a newer model had been part of the good. At least that was what I told myself every time my dark thoughts told me it was blood money. And today it didn't feel like good. Both the house and the vehicle had been tainted. My inheritance was cursing me.

"Here's a small birthday gift."

Garrett interrupted my thoughts and I stared at him as he held out his phone. I didn't reach for it.

"You got me a cake, which, actually, might be the start of a new tradition."

"Really?" He sat down next to me on the couch and placed the phone screen down on my lap.

"Yeah, not just for birthdays though. I think I'll start eating birthday cake on any day of the week randomly. It occurs to me that I could've been eating cake for breakfast on a daily basis. I'm an adult and there's literally nobody policing this kind of stuff, is there?"

"That's true. You could eat cake morning, noon and night and when your teeth start to fall out from the sugar, you can get dentures and I'll love you anyway."

I choked out a laugh at that but could only stare nervously at his phone on my lap. "Whatever is on your phone…is it going to make me happy? Is it a present?"

"Not really a present. I don't know how you'll feel about it."

I leaned my head against his shoulder and counted to ten. Then I picked up his phone and turned it over. It was a grainy picture of a woman who looked in her mid-forties. She had waist-length dark hair, high cheekbones, a bow mouth and a slim nose that reminded me of my own.

Bringing the phone to my face I stared hard at the picture, memorizing everything from worn Keds on her feet to the crease between her thin eyebrows and the long, bony hands that emerged from a flannel shirt.

"My mother?" My heart pounded so hard in my chest and ears that I was worried I wouldn't hear the answer.

"Yes."

SEVEN

My mom dropped me at my grandparents' farm when I was six years old saying she'd be back in a week but that turned into never. I had no memories of being with her. The earliest recollection was the back of her head driving away down the dirt road as she left me on the farm. I had one worn photo of her taken when she was in her late teens, probably around the time she had me. I'd long ago fixed in my mind every minuscule particle in that four-by-six photo and now looking at this aged version of her I knew I'd recognize that mouth and those eyes anywhere.

"Send me that picture, please." I reluctantly handed him back his phone. "So she's alive? For sure?"

He hesitated and my stomach clenched.

"As far as we know, but…" He put a hand on my thigh and squeezed. "All we know about her is that she's a known associate of those in the local meth trade. I don't know if she's using but, even if she's not, it's a hard life. Often a short one."

I nodded.

He tapped his phone and a second later my own cell chimed with the incoming picture.

"Thank you."

He put an arm around my shoulders and I curled my

feet up on the couch and leaned into the crook of his arm where all felt right with the world.

Even though questions about my mother swam in my head, I wasn't going to give them a voice tonight. I needed to chew on it for a while.

Garrett stayed the night. We started off lovingly but then as I lay in his arms he tried unsuccessfully to convince me to pack up and come stay with him so I could be safe. I angrily refused and we fell asleep with our backs to each other. I slept like the dead and woke up to the sound of distant banging and the occasional whirring of a drill.

I reached over and felt the lump that was Wookie in the place where Garrett had been. The dog stirred and yawned loudly, sending unpleasant dog breath my way.

A fresh round of hammering started outside and I pulled my pillow over my head.

"What is that man doing?" After a yawn and stretch I reached for my phone and saw it was nearing noon and I nearly jumped out of bed. I'd slept eleven hours. The only other times that happened was when I was drugged in the psych ward or because I'd had help from a couple bottles of chardonnay.

I followed the welcoming aroma of coffee into the kitchen and poured myself a mug. Wookie's food and water bowls had already been replenished. The new patio door was open and I carried my coffee out to the concrete patio. Garrett was on a ladder against the house wearing a tool belt and Wookie was looking up at him. I wanted to yell and demand to know what he was doing but I didn't want to startle him and cause him to fall. After some more thumping, whirring and few curse words Garrett glanced over and saw me standing there. He offered me a sheepish smile before climbing down the ladder and walking over.

"Good morning." He leaned in to hug me and I took a step back.

"You are a sweaty mess." I laughed. "How about you hug me from afar?"

He bent and gave me a quick kiss. "Glad you slept late. You obviously needed it."

"And you obviously had some demented need to trade in your FBI badge and become Mr. Fix-it? What exactly is going on?" I stepped closer to the ladder and looked up to see a security camera. "Seriously?" I crossed my arms.

"Did you know that Costco sells these in a 5-pack and once they're installed you can monitor them on your phone? And they were pretty reasonable too." He grabbed me by the elbow and walked me around the house, proudly pointing to the locations of all the cameras that were now going to track my every coming and going. I struggled with being somewhat relieved to have the surveillance while hating that he never bothered to even ask me before installing the cameras.

"I'm glad you're in touch with your inner handyman this morning but did you think to even ask me before running out and spending hundreds of dollars on equipment that makes me look like a paranoid survivalist?"

We were standing in the shade on the side of the house and I was trying my best to look pissed off. He pulled me into a hug and I screamed in mock horror at being against his damp, sweaty body. The harder I squirmed the tighter he held me, and I slopped some of my coffee on both of us during the simulated struggle. I was glad that the anger of the night before hadn't carried over to this morning but I had mixed feelings about these cameras.

"Look, you won't come stay with me and I have to do something to keep you safe. Someone went to serious effort to drug your dog, smash your door and steal your laptop and possibly the same someone attacked your vehicle."

"I know you feel this need to protect me, and the nature of your business makes you think of everything as a big crime." I drank from my coffee cup. "But it's still possible it was a simple break-in to snatch my laptop and a stupid parking lot rage thing that's done now."

I walked back inside the house and he followed me.

"You don't think you were targeted?"

I thought about the chances of my house being broken into and my vehicle vandalized on the same day.

"I guess it's a possibility," I admitted. "But if they targeted me just to take my computer—" I shrugged "—they're going to be really disappointed. I store all my stuff online and I've changed all my passwords already. I don't even store any good porn on it so…"

The last bit got a tight smile from him. "Yeah, but you're working on that Ava Johansson case. All this could have something to do with that. Ava is dead. Ron was killed after that so that means we still have a killer on the loose. Think about that."

I chewed my lower lip and nodded. I took a seat at the kitchen table with my coffee cup, Garrett went and poured a cup for himself and joined me.

"Maybe I should ask Joon Kim to recommend a new laptop. That last one was too heavy anyway."

"Joon Kim? As in Ron Low's roommate Joon Kim?" Garrett wiped the sweat from his forehead with a tissue he pulled from his pocket.

"Did you get any information from him about Ava and Ron when you met at the mall?"

"Not much." I shrugged.

"Don't forget that Ron's old roommate essentially told you where to find his body."

"Yeah, but he only mentioned wanting to hike there. I was the one who decided that sounded like a good idea."

"Maybe you should stay away from Joon Kim."

"He was in Korea at the time this all went down with Ron and Ava and he's not even a suspect so—"

"Everyone's a suspect until the killer is caught," Garrett grumped.

He got up and got himself an ice water and brought it to the table. He drank his water with that pinched look he gets when he's trying to figure something out. Abruptly he slid his chair next to mine, pulled out his phone and showed me how to operate the app that would allow me to spy on my own house.

"So frigg'n stupid," I mumbled.

"Not stupid. Smart."

With reluctance I downloaded the security application onto my phone at his insistence and then checked each of the cameras. "All right, Mr. Paranoid, it's all set up."

"It's not perfect. Your long driveway is obscured by

so many trees I can't get the whole view but at least every entrance to the house is covered."

"Oh yay," I said sarcastically.

He laughed and went off to have a shower. Afterward he proceeded to make us breakfast using the groceries he'd had delivered. If he hadn't been here I would've had cereal and probably eaten it dry because there'd be no milk. Now Garrett made us ham and cheese omelets with hash brown potatoes and orange wedges on the side. I guessed that before his wife and son were killed by a drunk driver, omelets, hash browns and fruit were a regular Sunday morning ritual. Maybe even pancakes with happy faces for his little boy. That made me hurt for him.

All this domesticity was nice but I didn't crave this home life the way he did and never would. Probably because I'd never had it in my life. Breakfast growing up was whatever I could sneak out of the cupboard when Grandma wasn't looking, or whatever extra granola bar Katie brought to school for me.

While Garrett washed the dishes I scrolled through the emails on my phone and discovered that Ebba had sent the deposit for my services. It was a few dollars short but I wasn't going to freak about a few bucks.

"What do you make of Ebba Johansson? What do the agents working the case say about her?"

Garrett put the last plate on the dish rack and dried his hands on the towel. "What do I think of her as a person, you mean?"

"Yeah."

He leaned a hip against the counter and thought about it. "Wasn't my case so I never met her personally. The agents said she appeared overwhelmed and angry someone dared kill her daughter."

"Grief stricken?" I asked. "In the early days when it was determined that Ava was killed and not just kidnapped, did she fall apart?"

"People handle grief differently. I don't remember hearing that she came apart. She stopped working for a while and got quiet and determined. She had an assistant from one of her massage places take over the business and she put the company up for sale. I heard she was going to retire."

I nodded.

"She imploded."

Maybe she still wanted to retire but was waiting to bury her daughter first. My heart ached a little for this strong woman who'd built a career from nothing and now the business was all she had left but she wanted to walk away from it.

"Any suggestions about where I'd find Ava's body?" I asked with a sigh.

"If law enforcement knew where she was, they would've put this case to bed already. I'm guessing wherever you think she could be, it won't be there."

"Then I guess I'm going to be driving all over Washington State with my rods in my lap." I was only half joking.

"I want you to make sure you start setting your house alarm on a regular basis too. I know you said you set it when you come to my house for the night, but you'll need to set it every time you leave from now on."

I agreed.

"And when you do go out and search, please send

me messages about where you are." He got up from his chair. "I've gotta get to work. I'll see you later when you come into town for your appointment." He kissed the top of my head. "Be safe."

"You too."

I stood up and pulled him into the kind of kiss that should've drawn him back to bed. Instead the romantic moment became a comical one when Wookie sauntered over and nudged his large head between us to get in on the group hug.

"You're cutting in on my jam," I told Wookie as we watched Garrett pull out of the driveway.

My phone chimed when Garrett walked outside. The screen showed me a notification that the side door had opened and allowed me to click to see the camera view.

"This is going to be a big pain in the ass."

I showered then talked to the insurance company about the window and replacing my laptop. After that was over I tried to do some business on my phone. Reading and responding to emails wasn't difficult but I couldn't enter Ebba's payment into my accounting software as easily without benefit of a laptop. I sent Joon Kim a text asking for recommendations. I told him the capabilities of my old computer and that I didn't need much more than that but I wanted something more lightweight. His text reply had me scrolling through my phone forever. Way more information than I ever wanted to know. The bottom line was that he told me his store actually had a big sale on this week and I should come and take a look.

I looked at Wookie and worried my bottom lip with my teeth. What if the laptop thieves came back and this time gave him a lethal dose of whatever laced grub they fed him yesterday?

"It's too hot to leave you in a car," I said to Wookie. "And I'd rather not leave you home after what happened."

He tilted his head from one side to the other trying to understand my ramblings. Then I had an idea. I called up the vet's office in town and told them about Wookie being drugged the day before.

"He seems perfectly fine now but I'd really like a complete checkup to be sure."

The receptionist told me I could drop Wookie off and come back for him in a couple hours.

"It's not exactly a spa day," I told Wookie. "But at least you won't be home being tempted by toxic burgers."

I packed up my backpack with the rods, just in case, and a couple water bottles, granola bars and dog treats. Then we made our way into town. Wookie was happy to come along for the ride but the minute he saw we were at the vet's he wasn't quite as impressed. I snapped the leash onto his collar and tugged and cajoled him and bribed him with treats to get him into the waiting room. A friendly young woman greeted us wearing a smock that had colorful cats all over it.

I told her who we were and admonished Wookie for nearly pulling my arm from the socket. "Stop it! Sit!"

The receptionist pulled a treat from her pocket and managed to take Wookie's leash and coax him to the back. When she returned to the counter I told her I had errands and I'd check on him when I was on my way back.

"We have arrangements with the doggie daycare next door so, if you want, we can send him over there once we're done here. They'll keep him right up until eight o'clock this evening. The dogs love going there. It has both an inside and outside play area and even a kiddie pool." She handed me a business card from the counter. "It's a full-day rate if it's longer than four hours."

That might take pressure off to rush back. "Can I call and let you know?"

"Sure." She smiled.

I stuffed the business card into my jeans and walked back to my Jeep. I was about to climb into the vehicle when I heard the distinct musical sound of the Candy Crush game. When I turned I was face-to-face with Abel.

"I didn't return your email," I said by way of a greeting.

"No, you did not." He tapped away at his phone and then cringed. "Dammit!" With a sigh he pocketed the device and smiled up at me. "It's okay. I know you've been busy."

"How'd you know that?" I asked, wondering who'd been talking.

"Everyone knows that." He chuckled and I was reminded again why living a few minutes outside a small town did not make me immune to gossip.

"So-o-o, just going for a walk?" I asked him, anxious to be polite but firm because I wanted to talk to Joon Kim about computers and a few other niggling thoughts.

"Wes had a big job in Arlington so he asked me to

walk his bulldog over to the dog daycare." He nodded to the small shuttered house-like building next to
the vet office. "I'd keep him with me but that mutt's
as dumb as a sack of rocks and eats socks." His smile
broadened. "I'm a poet and don't even know it."

I smiled back. "Well, enjoy your day dog-free then.
I have to head to Bellingham to buy a new—"

"Laptop, right? That's what I heard you got stolen."
He shook his head. "A real shame that we can't leave
our doors unlocked like the old days but then we didn't
have Candy Crush in the old days so it wasn't all fun
times, you know."

"Right." I took a step back. "So I'm going to go
and—"

"I bet you haven't had breakfast."

"Actually I have and—"

"Then coffee. You look like you could use a cup."

I began to protest but it was hard to say no to those
black eyes that were almost hidden behind droopy lids
and deep lines. "Sure. I'd love a cup of coffee."

Minutes later we sat nearly knee to knee in the only
coffee shop in town. Abel talked about the blazing
heat the past couple weeks and moaned about global
warming while I wished I was already on my way to
the mall. The waitress brought us each a mug of coffee
and an apple oatmeal muffin that Abel insisted would
change my life.

"So-o-o...about your grandson, Wes. Although I
appreciate the suggestion that we might...you know...
I actually have a boyfriend already."

"You cut right to the chase." He waggled a finger
in my face. "I like that." He took a bite from his muf-

fin and mmm-mmmed in delight, then washed it down with a slug of coffee. "Wes's wife up and left him last year, taking everything except that damn dog. He used to be a lot happier kind of person but now he's miserable so I'm always trying to find something to lighten his mood. I feel bad she just up and left him like that." He shook his head and frowned. "It don't seem right."

"I'm sure it's hard for him. I've heard divorce is like a death and you need time." I put my hand on his. "You're a good grandfather and I'm sure you know it's hard for him to grieve but you just gotta let him do it."

"Oh it ain't that hard to grieve." Abel pulled his hand away and winked at me. "I've probably lost more loved ones than you've ever even had."

That wasn't exactly difficult considering how short my list of loved ones was: Wookie and Garrett.

"I'm kind of an expert in the arena where the grim reaper visits." He smiled. "I guess you are too given what you do for a living." He took another bite of muffin and another sip of coffee. "I just figured since you lived in the same town growing up and you're about the same age…"

He smiled at me hopefully.

"It takes more than having a couple things in common to make a relationship, Abel." I laughed. "So we grew up in the same area then maybe we saw each other around. I wasn't much of a socialite back then. I'm not now either."

"Maybe you don't have to date him. Just be his friend." Abel thumped the table. "There's no such thing as too many friends."

Oh sweet Jesus he's not going to stop until I agree to date his loser grandson.

I didn't answer, just sipped my coffee.

Abruptly, Abel polished off his coffee and brought the mug down on the table with a thud. "Wes tells me he used to hang out with that Jay and Ronald Low too. Ron's that fella who killed that girl so, you see, you have things in common to talk about."

"He hung out with Ron?" I thought about Wes's picture in the back of a search party crowd.

"You could meet him here. Have a coffee and a muffin. Help him get out of his funk. Introduce him to some of your girlfriends."

"How close was Wes to Ron?" Maybe I would have to have coffee with the guy. I cringed a little.

"They just saw each other sometimes. Did some hiking together. See that's another thing you and Wes both like to do. Hike." He pointed at the muffin in front of me. "Take a bite. You won't regret it."

I broke off a golf-ball-sized piece of muffin and stuffed it in my mouth while I thought of the right thing to say. "Wow. That really is delicious."

And I wasn't just saying that either. Abel waited patiently while I finished the muffin and then signaled the waitress for refill on our coffees. I asked her to bring a couple more muffins to go.

"So you'll do it?"

"Do what exactly?" I asked.

"Call up Wes and invite him for a coffee? Just as a friend, of course."

As much as I dreaded the idea of spending five minutes with Wes, it wouldn't hurt to talk to someone else about Ron.

"You've got my number and email. Why don't you pass those along and ask him to message me."

"That's great." Abel looked immensely pleased.

"Now tell me this, is it true that people in this town were laying bets about when I'd find a body around these parts?"

"Well, sure, people like to keep entertained."

And now I was suddenly the sideshow freak? *Ladies and gentlemen, pay attention to our dowsing girl who will amaze you all with her ability to find the dead and chew a good muffin at the same time.*

"I don't like to think everyone around here is talking about me."

"Missy, people are going to talk about you no matter what. That's just a known fact. Relax about it. Nobody means you any harm."

I didn't know about that considering the break-in of both my car and house but there was obviously no arguing with Abel about it. He insisted on paying for my coffee and numerous muffins. Then he made shooing motions, dismissing me to go and get my new laptop. He said he was going to sit a while in the coffee shop and I left him crushing candies on his phone.

I hadn't even driven out of town when Garrett called my cell. I told him about my conversation with Abel trying to fix me up with his grandson.

"It was awkward."

"Do I have to worry about this guy muscling in on my girl?"

"Not in a million years." I laughed. "Besides, you've

got a much nicer ass than Wes does. But, if you'd like I can give Abel your phone number so he can call you up and tell you what an upstanding and misunderstood guy his grandson is."

"Don't even joke about that. The last thing I need is to be bribed with muffins to try and hook up his grandson with any women I know."

"They are very excellent muffins." I chuckled and then gave the phone a loud kiss before I disconnected and concentrated on driving.

At the shopping center there was no sign of Joon Kim at the electronics store. When I asked about him a pleasant fortyish woman said Joon had called in sick but had told all the staff to take care of me if I showed up. If I'd only wanted to buy a laptop I could've found a place closer to home or even bought one online. I also wanted to pick Joon's brain more about Ava Johansson.

"Okay. Show me what you've got."

Half an hour later I left the store with a computer that was probably far more than what I needed for my small business. I was promised that I got the best deal around and that I'd love it. I stuck the boxed laptop on the floor of my back seat and looked up Joon Kim's address.

Joon lived ten minutes away on a street around the corner from an elementary school and a block from a Fred Meyer grocery store. The house was small and tidy from the street with a fair-sized yard and not where you'd expect a couple of single guys to be living. I parked out front not sure what to do next until I saw Joon Kim sitting with a beer in hand on the front porch watching me. I grabbed the bag of muffins and climbed out of the car. He looked surprised but then got to his feet and waved me over.

"Sorry to stop by uninvited," I began. "But—"

"But you wanted to see where Ron lived, right? Part of your investigation."

"Yeah, but if you're too sick—"

"Needed a personal day with my friend, Bud." He lifted his Bud Light. "Want one? Or wine?"

More than anything in this goddamn world.

"No." I licked my lips. "I'm good. Thanks." I handed him the bag. "I brought you a couple of muffins. They're awesome."

"Thanks. So you want the grand tour then?"

"If it's okay with you?"

He shrugged and headed inside. The house was hot and stuffy, making me wonder why he didn't have every window open to create some kind of a breeze. There wasn't a lot to see in this twelve-hundred-square-foot home. The living room had a leather sectional, a large flat screen TV and a coffee table littered with game controllers. Down the hall were the three bedrooms. His own and that of his roommate were pretty much what you'd expect from young guys. Clothes piled in the corner, unmade beds, the stink of sweat from sheets past their prime. The third room was done up as an office. A large desk and long tables were littered with computer parts, towers and laptops all in various states of repair.

"I dabble in computer repairs," he told me. "As a side. Makes me enough bucks to pay for a trip back to Korea once a year."

He told me the office used to be Ron's bedroom and I stepped inside to take a better look around.

"You never thought of moving out of this place after everything that happened?"

"Nah. What difference would it make? The cops would still come round to ask me questions periodically no matter where I live. Besides, I'm getting a smoking deal for this house because it belongs to my cousin. Took me a while to get a roommate to replace Ron because nobody wanted to sleep where an ex-killer might've screwed the girl he killed, yanno?"

"I could see that being a problem."

"So I turned Ron's room into my office and that took care of that. The new guy is fine with the sleeping arrangements." He'd taken one of the muffins from the bag and took a large bite. "Damn. That's a fine muffin. You bake these?"

I laughed at the question and shook my head. "What happened to all Ron's stuff?"

"He didn't have a helluva lot." Joon took a swig from his beer. "The police took any electronics like his laptop and GoPro. His mom came by yesterday and took his clothes and stuff. She didn't want his bedroom furniture so I donated it to a charity."

"So all his belongings are gone?"

"She left one box of stuff."

Joon walked to the corner of the room and grabbed a banker's box from a shelf. After pushing some computer boards aside he dropped it on the table and popped the lid. I looked inside. Books on hiking trails. A map of Washington. More books. A yearbook from my old high school. A couple of bright blue foil packages with small white print on them. A well-used bong and a lot of bottles of vitamins and minerals with names I hadn't heard of.

"You want that stuff you can have it."

"Thanks." I picked up one of the bottles. "Milk thistle. Did he take all of these?"

"He was always taking something." Joon rolled his eyes. "He had some kind of blood condition and had a nurse come here sometimes but he was all about beating it using healthy alternatives."

"Was he really sick?"

"Nah. Struck me more like this was something he just had to manage and that it was no big deal."

"Did he smoke a lot of weed too?"

"Define a lot."

I couldn't and it really didn't matter. I replaced the lid on the box and noticed a wall calendar tacked up over his desk. The picture for the month was of a woman receiving a back massage surrounded by candles. The ad in the center of the calendar was for the Ebba's Bliss spa.

"You keep in touch with her?" I hooked my thumb in the direction of the calendar.

"Not really." He turned around and headed back toward the living room and I followed. "I heard from her a lot in the beginning when Ava was first missing but she got tired of asking me the same questions and hearing the same answers. She always had a dozen reporters following her too so it was very annoying. I mean, I was out of the country, right? I didn't know anything about where Ava could be or why Ron went nutso."

"Which do you think is more unlike Ron, that he

would kill his old girlfriend or that he'd kidnap her and demand a hundred grand?"

He seemed taken aback by the question. "What difference does it make?"

"None," I admitted, putting the box down at my feet. "Both seem pretty far away from the kind of guy I thought he was in high school but how about now? Did he seem like the kind of guy who'd kill someone in a rage, or do something crazy like kidnap his girlfriend to make a buck?"

"No, of course not," Joon said. "Obviously I never thought the guy was capable of any of that kind of shit or I wouldn't've asked him to be a roommate, right? He was an easygoing guy. Nothing fazed him. He went to work. Hiked. Screwed girls. Then hit Repeat."

"But you definitely think he did it. He kidnapped Ava for a hundred grand and then killed her and took off with the money and then…"

"And then couldn't live with it and killed himself in those Bat Caves," Joon finished firmly. "Absolutely. Hey, the cops found the ransom note sent to Ebba on Ron's laptop, right? And nobody had access to that laptop but him."

"How do you know?" I asked. "I mean, people were coming here all the time, right? His friends and lovers. You and your friends."

"I guess…but I'm sure he had a good password on his computer." He stuffed the last of the muffin in his mouth and dropped the bag containing the other one on the table. "Sure the cops hacked it but the average person wouldn't know where to begin."

"You would though."

That suggestion made his face go dark. "I was in Korea at the time."

"Yeah, I don't mean you personally," I quickly added with a smile. "I just mean that you probably get people who lock themselves out of their computers all the time and so you'd know how to help them with stuff like that, and so would other computer pros."

"Well, yeah. Happens all the time." He finished off his beer and I followed him into the kitchen as he opened the fridge and got another. "Sure I can't interest you in a drink?"

I stared a little harder than necessary at the can as he popped the tab and put it to his lips.

"I should go. Thanks for your help and also thanks for setting me up with the new laptop." I picked up the box of Ron's things and headed for the door.

"Anytime" was what his mouth said but his eyes were cold and I got the impression he wouldn't be sending me an invite anytime soon.

"By the way, do you have the contact information for Ron's family? Maybe I could give them a call."

He dug his phone out of his pocket, tapped a few keys and then my own cell phone chimed. "Done."

"Thanks." I started down the steps and he called out to me.

"You got your new laptop in the car?"

I nodded.

"Don't be doing that in this heat. It'll mess it up. Let it get to room temperature before you start it up for the first time."

I thanked him for the advice and was almost at my

Jeep when an idea occurred to me and I walked back. "What about his car?"

"Whose?"

"Ron's. He supposedly drove all the way to the state park with Ava in order to meet Ebba and get the money. I'm assuming he did that in his vehicle, right? So he kills her there but her body is never found at the scene so he must've stuffed it in his car and taken her somewhere."

"Cops found his car parked in our drive out back. If there was any sign he put Ava in that car all bloody and stuff, the cops didn't share that with me. Not that they would anyway. Maybe he rented a car."

"Maybe. So the police impounded his car as evidence and still have it?"

"Far as I know."

I put the box of Ron's stuff on the passenger seat then walked around and started it up. It was fiery hot inside the car and I hoped I hadn't already damaged the laptop. I rolled down the windows to let out the heat while the air-conditioning started up. While I waited for the vehicle to cool a bit, I thought about where I should go now.

I opened Ron's box again and looked through it. I pulled out the high school yearbook from beneath the stack of hiking books. I hesitated. Those years weren't good to me and I didn't really want to dive into the painful memories of that horrible time. Still, I couldn't resist opening it.

Of course, a lot of people had signed the inside covers of his book. Lots of *Best wishes!* and *Don't forget me Rock'n Ron!* He was a popular guy.

In the upper right of the page someone had taken up a large amount of space with a heart done in red felt pen. Inside the heart was a sappy message in a loopy, flowery script with hearted Is and lots of Xs and Os.

And suddenly I knew exactly who I needed to talk to about Rock'n Ron.

EIGHT

KATIE WASN'T AT the fast-food place when I walked in a few minutes later looking for her. A guy at the counter told me she was on her lunch break and had walked to the coffee shop next door so I headed that way. I found her hunched over her phone in a far corner with a large backpack at her feet.

"Can I get you a refill?" I pointed to her empty cup.

She looked up, startled to see me, and smiled.

"If you're buying then I'm drinking," she replied. "Although that means a whole lot more if we're talking real drinks and not stupid coffee." She glanced at her phone. "I've only got about ten minutes left on my break."

I grabbed us each a coffee and also got her a lemon scone because I remembered how much she liked them.

"So-o-o…" She sipped her coffee. "Rock'n Ron, huh? Is that just a screwed-up situation, or what?"

"Totally," I agreed. "So you heard that…"

"That you found his body when all of Washington has been looking for him for weeks?" She smirked. "Yeah. I heard." She nibbled the scone. "You find that Ava girl yet, though? She's the one everyone's really looking for."

I shook my head.

"But you're looking, right?"

I nodded.

"Then I guess you and your rod thingies will find her, right? That's like your full-time gig these days, huh?"

"Yeah. It is."

I waited for the smirk or for her to tease me for it but all she said was, "You make good money at that?"

"Enough, I guess," I replied, hoping she wasn't going to ask how much I made.

"Guess you don't need much on account of you sold Gramps's farm and bought your own place, right?"

I picked up my coffee and became eager to change the subject. "You and Ron dated in eleventh grade, right?" I sipped tentatively at the hot coffee.

"I doubt anyone could call what we did dating." She took a large bite of the scone and then washed it down with her drink. "Gotta say he had a way to rock a girl's world, you know? I mean a lot of guys know how to sweet-talk their way into a girl's pants but Rock'n Ron knew what to do once he got those pants off." She sighed. "The things that man could do with his tongue."

I shifted a little in my chair.

"What's wrong? Too early in the day to discuss cunnilingus?" She laughed, then tilted her head and regarded me. "You always had a thing for him, didn't you?"

I felt a hot blush creep up my neck. "I think everyone did."

"That's a fact. I remember he stood up for you a couple times when the jocks were giving you a hard time."

I planned on repaying him by finding his killer.

The rest of the scone disappeared into Katie's mouth. "That's why you're here? To talk about Ron."

"Ava's mom hired me to try and find Ava's body. I never met her but I was thinking maybe you had."

"Ava Johansson…" Katie drew the name out long between her lips, which were parted in a strange smile. "Now that girl was a piece of work."

"So you knew her?"

"Sure. I'd see her out clubbing. At the casinos. At the local bars saddling up to whoever looked like they'd buy her a few drinks."

Sounded like she was describing herself. "How do you mean she was a piece of work?"

"How?" Katie sipped her coffee. "In every way, that's how. Always jumping from guy to guy depending on what she could get out of them." She held up her hand. "Not that I'm shaming here, right? I've been known to have my share of boyfriends myself."

"That's the truth." It slipped out before I could stop it but Katie only giggled at my honesty. "There was a time I could hardly keep track."

"And I kept trying to toss some your way but you were never interested."

"In your snaggle-toothed or limp-dicked castoffs?" I chuckled. "No, thanks. Getting back to Ava, I got the impression Ron was the one cheating. Maybe they both were. Guess they were cut from the same cloth, right?"

"Nope. Totally different. Ava didn't seem the type that could really get attached. She was always in it for Ava and looking for something better. Ron, he loved women. Sure he slept around but when you were with him, he only had eyes for you and he really cared, you know? He made a girl feel special but he never made promises and then broke them. He wasn't cruel."

"The fact that he kidnapped and killed Ava kind of makes that inaccurate," I pointed out.

"Huh. Yeah, that's true, isn't it?" Katie drummed her fingers on the table. "The whole situation is messed up."

"Since you guys were together a bit I was wondering if you knew any more of Ron's secret spots."

"Secret spots?" She wiggled her eyebrows.

"You know what I mean." I laughed. "His make-out locations. Other than the Bat Caves because, obviously, that one's been covered."

She leaned forward on her elbows. "You think he killed Ava and dumped her body at one of those spots?"

"I have no-o-o idea. I'm grasping at straws here," I told her honestly. "Just need something to go on."

She sat back and thought a minute. "So you need my help, huh? Tell you what. I'll think about it and send you all the places that come to mind if you'll buy me dinner next week. Somewhere decent." She tucked a wayward strand of hair back into her ponytail. "If I have to eat another burger I'm going to start mooing."

"Sure. I could do that. When will you send me the list?"

"When I get around to it."

With Katie everything had a price and she liked things on her own terms. It was amazing how being away from someone for a while allowed you to see them more clearly. Still, for all her faults, perhaps part of me had missed her and maybe it would be good to do dinner and put the tragedy of the past behind us.

We walked out into the hot parking lot and I pressed the key fob to unlock my Jeep.

"So that's the only reason why you came to find me? To ask about Ron?" Katie fell into step beside me. "I figured you were back to ask me about that FBI guy talking about your mom. Is he trying to find her?"

"He's working on it," I told her, opening my car door. "Looks like she's alive but involved in drugs so…" I shrugged to make it seem like I was okay with however it played out.

"Yeah, the guy he was lunching with that time looked a little sketchy."

"What did he look like?"

"Old. Like maybe fifties. Skinny as all heck. Bald and had a long goatee that was braided."

My head started spinning because Katie had just described Ted. Mom's ex-boyfriend and the last place I'd gone looking for her myself.

"Nice ride," Katie commented as she looked beyond me into my Jeep. "A lot better than the old one you had when we hung out. Did I mention I had to sell my Mustang after Mom died? I'm rocking that old piece of crap these days. When it runs. Other days I take the bus."

She pointed to an old brown four-door sedan with rust holes in the fenders.

Katie loved her metallic blue 1972 Mustang. I couldn't imagine her taking a bus.

She sighed as she walked away and then called over her shoulder, "Good to see you got something good when everything went sideways."

I didn't reply. I didn't like to think of the Jeep as the

profits from that horrid end to my old life. If I thought about it like that, I couldn't drive it.

I started up the vehicle and spent a minute checking my phone. I received a notification from the security app that there was movement on one of the cameras at my house. My heart pounded as I opened the app and clicked on the camera. A wild brown rabbit was nibbling grass in my backyard. I exhaled on a loud laugh.

"Bring on attack of the bunnies!" I was so relieved I almost cried. Almost immediately I received a text from Garrett saying not to worry, it was only a rabbit. Obviously he was keeping tabs on the security system too.

His next text was: Where are you?

He also seemed to be keeping tabs on *me*. No big surprise. I wanted to ask him about Ted and why he'd met him at the diner and not told me who he'd talked to about my mother. I knew he struggled with keeping things confidential, and if Ted was part of his current investigation that would be the reason he hadn't mentioned his name. Still, it annoyed me so my reply to him was a selfie with me sticking my tongue out.

See you in a few hours, he texted.

My psychiatrist appointment was later this afternoon. I needed to gather Wookie, pack an overnight bag and make my way to Seattle.

After I returned to the vet's office and paid the bill they gave me a coupon for the doggie daycare next door.

"If you're a new client at the doggie daycare you also get a coupon for buy-one-get-one massage," the receptionist said, thrusting a pale blue slip of paper into my hands.

"I don't need one."

I wasn't big on the idea of someone rubbing my body unless that someone was Garrett. A massage would mean having to explain the keloid scarring on my back from years of abuse at the hands of my grandmother.

I tried handing the coupon back to her and she laughed.

"It's not for you." She pointed to Wookie, who was tugging so hard on the leash my shoulder was about to dislocate. "The doggie daycare does them. So many dogs really love it and it's good for them too."

I thanked her and folded the blue paper and tucked it in my back pocket as we headed out the door.

Wookie was thrilled to get home and he did a breakneck run around the rooms in a fit of energy that made me laugh, particularly when he came skidding along the tile in the kitchen.

"We gotta get going." I rubbed the dog's head. "Can't be late for the shrink 'cuz she'll charge me for the time even if I'm not there."

My phone chirped a text from Garrett just as I was locking up the door behind us.

You better get going. You're going to be late.

I looked up at the security camera and lifted my shirt to give him an impromptu peep show.

Ni-i-ice, was his reply followed by some heart emojis.

Sure, I was making it all seem like fun and games

but I was getting a little ticked off about the whole thing.

"We're going to have to talk about you spying on me," I grumbled under my breath as I loaded my bag and Wookie back into the Jeep.

After I fought through the slugfest that was Seattle traffic I gave Wookie a quick run around the block and then took him up to Garrett's condo. He had his own dog bed, toys and dishes already there and he immediately made himself comfortable. Before heading to my appointment I left him a note: *Can't wait to see you, Mr. Sexy! Xoxo.*

My therapist's office was only a couple blocks away and by the time I was done my session, Garrett would be home with a pizza.

Dr. Abbey Chen specialized in Post-Traumatic Stress and Trauma. After a lengthy hospital stay where I was more medicated than treated, it was recommended that I see Dr. Chen. Her website boasted that she treated clients in a professional and confidential setting that felt safe, comfortable and nonjudgmental. I might feel safe there but after all these months the air of judgment was thick even if it was all of my own making.

She asked about events since my last session. When I'd first started therapy I'd just sit there and not talk at all but it pained me to pay her fee and not get anything out of it. Even though I knew I wasn't nearly as open with her as I should be, I'd come a long way over the course of the past year. I started today's meeting by giving her the abbreviated version of my life over the few weeks since I'd last seen her. When I mentioned running into Katie, her eyebrows went up in surprise.

Then I added the news about my mother, and Dr. Chen sat forward in her chair and looked as shocked as I'd felt. Then we did the question-answer tango.

"How did you feel when Garrett told you that your mom might be alive?"

"Confused."

"Did seeing Katie bring back memories of happier childhood times?"

"No."

"Do you feel the skills you've learned here helped you to walk over that forest bridge when at Ava Johansson's crime scene?"

"Sure."

"Do you still hear your grandmother's voice saying negative things?"

"Sometimes."

"Do you think you'll pursue a friendship with this new girl, Tracey?"

"Not sure."

"How long has it been since you thought about taking a drink?"

"Five minutes. No…two."

"Are we ever going to get beyond your short monosyllable answers?"

"Probably not."

Dr. Chen was patient, encouraging and full of helpful tricks and exercises to deal with triggers that caused my mind to get sucked into quicksand thoughts and made me spiral into hell. Triggers were when something innocent like going on a hike and having to walk over a bridge made me want to curl into the fetal position and suckle on a chardonnay nipple. I guess things like mindfulness exercises and deep breathing helped at those times but, honestly, part of me wondered if all this navel-gazing in therapy was really helping or if I was just too scared to stop going.

"Do you feel like coming here is a waste of your time?" the doctor asked, reading my mind.

"Maybe," I admitted. "I'm coming 'cause I'm scared not to."

"What do you think would happen if you stopped coming?"

I shrugged but I did know that without someone holding me accountable the temptation to drink might get stronger. The monster in my belly that screamed "Feed me wine!" was a whole lot louder if I went a long time without seeing her, and the medications I'd been on in the beginning felt a bit too good to have lurking in my medicine cabinet.

"Do you want to start coming less?"

"No." I didn't want to start drinking again. Or worse. Maybe get pulled into dark thoughts and not be able to claw my way out.

"Julie? What do you think would happen if you didn't see me?" she repeated.

"Can we make our next appointment a little later in the evening?" I asked, avoiding her question.

We booked another time and day a few weeks later and then, as she walked me out, Doc suggested I contact Tracey to go for a coffee as a way of getting beyond my comfort zone and making the community feel more like home. She also commended me for continuing to go on small hikes as a way to clear my head and find peace but said they didn't count toward that if those hikes turned into body-finding missions.

Apparently there was no such thing as a twofer here.

While I was walking back to Garrett's apartment I tried to enjoy the moment. The sun was warm on my body. The city was bustling around me and everyone seemed Friday-afternoon happy. Except for me. I felt uneasy in my own skin as I thought about having a mother out there somewhere and she might actually care that I wasn't given up for adoption like she'd been told.

She might care and I might matter.

Or not.

Immediately following that thought came a temptation, not for the first time or the tenth, to relieve the ball of tension in my gut with a drink. Just one glass… even one sip.

Up ahead a woman flipped her waist-length hair and leaned in to hug the man walking beside her. I picked up my pace until I closed the gap between us with my heart pounding until she glanced over her shoulder and I realized she wasn't my mother. Besides the long hair, there wasn't even a glimmer of resemblance but, for some reason, my hopes had soared. The regret and aching hit me in the chest like a blow that took my breath away.

By the time I was opening the door to Garrett's apartment I was miserable. Then Wookie bounded over and climbed my torso to lick my chin, and Garrett pulled me into a welcoming hug.

"My two guys." I smiled as I kissed one and petted the other. "And pizza." I kicked off my shoes and headed to the living room. "What more could a girl want?"

And I meant it. Even in the darkest places inside my head, I knew I was damn lucky.

While we ate pizza and drank cola Garrett regaled me with humorous stories about the drama in the lives of the goofy unnamed people he worked with, which he spun in a purposeful way to tweak a laugh out of me in spite of myself. I knew what he was doing. Every time I had a therapy session and returned brooding and angry with the world and my sucky past, Garrett put in a huge effort to turn my mood around. He was one of the good ones. Despite his own personal demons of losing a wife and son, he'd been able to get his act together and still be a good person. I wanted that for myself.

We finished the pizza and turned the television on to watch an action flick. I cozied up to him and nestled my head into the crook of his arm. About an hour into it, my mind grew restless. Try as I might, thoughts of my mother giving me up kept slinking back to the front of my mind. Garrett was intent on watching the movie but I didn't care. I reached for his hand and he lifted my face so that he could kiss me. I lost my horrid thoughts of past trauma in pleasure of our kisses.

Near dawn, as we lay spooned in his bed, I dreamed of the back of my mother's head going down the road after she'd said goodbye to me on my grandparents' farm. In my dream, my mother turned around but then her face had become my grandmother's and the sweet goodbye moment turned violent. I woke up shaking and in a cold sweat.

Garrett placed a comforting hand on my thigh and

then fell back to sleep. There'd be no sleeping for me now so I dressed in sweatpants and a T-shirt and took Wookie for a brisk morning walk around the block. The city was already alive with throngs of people hurrying to their destinations. I kept Wookie on a short leash so he wouldn't get trampled or snarl at other dogs. It was not the relaxing run in my backyard either of us enjoyed.

When we got back, I made coffee. While I listened to the gurgle and spit of the coffee maker coming to life I went to the dining table where we never ate and shuffled through Garrett's paperwork looking for anything to do with my mother or her ex-boyfriend. Nothing jumped out at me. The only files around were about another case that was meaningless. I hated myself for going through his stuff and hated more the burning to know about my mom that made me itch with need.

Garrett woke and showered an hour later and he found me still sitting at the table, all files pushed aside and my hands wrapped around my third coffee.

"At the table, are we?" he joked.

"Yes, we're high-class now. You'll have to drink your coffee with your pinky out."

As he bent to kiss me I noticed him scan the table and see the obvious way I'd pushed the papers and stacked them.

"Looking for stuff about your mom?" He walked over to pour himself some coffee.

"Ted," I replied. "Tell me about you meeting Ted at Big Al's in Blaine. Katie was working there. She saw you. She described Ted so I know it was him." The words came out biting and the tone was accusing even though I hadn't meant it to be so I softened it a bit, adding, "Please."

He pulled a chair up next to mine and reached for my hand. "When did you see Katie?"

"I ran into her at a burger joint where she works."

"Can't imagine her flipping burgers."

"Yeah, well, apparently she wants to flip burgers but only gets to take out the trash." I reached over and tugged on his baby finger. "Remember we're fancy now so you have to drink with your pinky out."

He laughed and elaborately brought his mug to his lips in a pseudo-posh way that made us both chuckle.

"To answer your question, I'm not hiding anything from you that would keep you from finding your mother. I'm not the bad guy here." He put his coffee mug down. "Yes, I met with Ted. It was to do with this case but, yes, since I knew he once was together with your mother I did ask about her. He chose to meet at that diner. Said he was meeting a friend up that way. How was it seeing Katie?"

I filled him in on seeing her the first time after finding Ron Low and about seeking her out a second time at the burger place to get more information about Ron.

"It must be hard seeing her," he said softly.

I thought about that.

"Sad." I sighed. "It just makes me feel sad. For both of us."

He nodded in understanding and we both sat there quietly until our phones chimed in unison. We looked at each other and snatched up our phones, realizing the notification was the alarm system at the house.

A spider had built an elaborate web across the camera lens at the back patio door and was scurrying back and forth across the camera. We burst out laughing.

"First an attack rabbit and now I'm under spider siege."

We had a good giggle about it. It would be a perfect moment to bring up how much I hated him keeping such close tabs on me but laughing was a great way to end my overnight stay and so I just left it. I figured that once I was done with this Ava case, things would settle down and I'd look at having him either take down the cameras or remove the app from his phone. Garrett headed off to work to do federal agent things and Wookie and I climbed into my Jeep to go and do my kind of finding the dead things.

Traffic was bad because it was always bad on I-5. Wookie bounded back and forth in the rear seat, antsy to be done with the ride, and I felt the same way. I tuned the radio to a news report that stated there'd been an accident but it had been cleared so traffic should begin to lighten. That meant it would lighten up by tomorrow long after I was done with this stretch of road. Next up was an update on the case of a teenage boy who'd taken his boat out fishing at Blackmans Lake. The boat had been discovered capsized yesterday but there was no sign of the boy. The sheriff's office had been out since daylight and was using six divers but the lack of visibility in the murky water was a huge obstacle. They could only see less than two feet beneath its inky depths at most.

I did not make a specific plan to drive to Blackmans Lake. That part of the state was nearly an hour past my place so not exactly on the way. However, before I knew it I was on my way there.

I pulled up next to the sheriff's vehicle on the stretch of the parking lot next to the boat ramp. I unloaded the bag that contained my rods and snapped a leash on Wookie.

"Sorry ma'am," an officer said as I approached the boat launch. "We're not allowing anyone near the lake today because—"

"I know why." I handed him a creased business card that I'd dug out of my bag. "Can you give this to whoever's heading up the search? Chances are they know me."

He looked at the gray business card with www. DivineReunions.com in raised purple lettering and frowned. "Wait here."

Wookie pulled me off to the edge of the bushes that banked the lot. He was anxious to repeatedly leave his mark on this new-to-him forested area. He was just peeing on his second or third bush when one of the divers approached and called me by name.

"Julie!" He waved and slowly walked over, his shoulders slumped with fatigue. "I didn't know you'd been asked to help."

"I haven't been asked but I was kind of in the neighborhood."

"Well, that's great. Need all the help we can get." He nodded toward the lake behind him. "Boat was found with all the life jackets still in or around it so, you know, this is definitely a recovery job and we could use you. You want to try by boat or walk around?"

The water looked calm so I suggested he take me

out by boat and asked if someone was available to keep an eye on Wookie.

We climbed in the boat and pushed away from the launch area and I prepared my dowsing rods. As soon as I pulled them from the bag I was fully aware of the eyes of law enforcement watching me from the bank as well as hard stares of the red-eyed and weary clutch of people nearby who were no doubt family. The boat skimmed ever so slowly across the water and I only half listened to the voices of the two other divers on board as they showed me the areas they already checked and complained about the murky waters of the lake. I was focused only on the rods in my hands.

The hot sun baked my head but a cool pine breeze breathed release on my neck. It was a beautiful, peaceful spot but all water was murderous if given a chance and a fool without a life jacket. It took less than ten minutes for my dowsing rods to cross over and make a distinct X at a reedy bend in the lake.

"Here!" I shouted.

The others in the boat donned their gear. Minutes later the divers dragged the lifeless body of a teenage boy from the gray water of the lake, and the anguished, heartrending cries from a woman on the shore shattered the morning quiet.

NINE

I DIDN'T WANT to stick around as officials dealt with the distressed family and the body. My job was done and as soon as we returned to the boat launch I climbed out and headed over to the officer who had Wookie.

"Thanks." I took the leash from his hand and he walked with me toward my Jeep.

"Are you kidding? Thank *you*. We could've been looking for that boy forever in that lake."

"Well, until he floated to the surface anyway," I pointed out. "I just sped things up a bit."

The woman's loud, racking sobs echoed across the lake and hurt my heart.

I loaded up Wookie then climbed into the driver seat but the officer was still talking so I rolled down the window.

"How do you do that thing you do with those metal sticks?"

"If you have the knack they'll help you find water."

Gramps said that the first time he gave me rods to use. He'd taken me out of the house to keep me away from Grandma, who was on a particularly vicious rage that morning, and my body already bore the welts of her wrath.

"I don't know how they work," I told the officer, which was the absolute truth. I reached for a water bottle in my cup holder and took a long drink. It was warm but it was wet and my dry throat was grateful.

"So you think you're going to find that Ava Johansson?"

I lowered the bottle from my lips and frowned. "How do you know I'm looking for Ava's body?"

He shrugged. "People talk. You found the boyfriend so, yeah, people are saying you're on the case." He shrugged with palms up. "But if you're not looking for that girl, it makes no difference to me. I'm sure she'll turn up eventually."

"Her mom asked me to see if I can find her," I admitted.

"Not surprised. Must be hard on her not knowing where her girl is. Unfortunately, Washington is a big place, you know? Finding that girl is like a needle in a haystack and her mom, well, she wanted all officers searching for her girl."

"Makes sense, right?" I said. "I mean, if it was your kid, you'd be frantic and you'd be pitching a fit until she was found."

"Sure." He nodded. "No insult to the woman intended but giving somebody a massage isn't the same thing as finding a body. Best to leave it to people like us who know what we're doing, right?"

In my experience most people could be a little frantic about finding the remains of their loved ones. Hysterical even.

"You're probably wanted over there." I nodded to the clutch of officers gathered around the body and a second group around the family.

"Yeah, I'd better get to it."

When he started to walk away I called out to him. "If you were searching for Ava, where would you look?"

"Me personally?" He walked back to my window with chest a little puffed up with pride.

"Yeah, you personally."

He looked pleased to offer his opinion as his face scrunched up in concentration. "It's gotta be near where he killed her, right?"

"In the state park?"

"Yeah, I know we searched that entire community high and low but I still think she's gotta be in the park somewhere."

"You don't think he drove her body somewhere and dumped her?"

"Oh yeah that's entirely possible. She could be any-where." He spread his arms wide. "Needle in a hay-stack. Like I said."

Thanks for being the least helpful person on the entire planet.

I tried to give him one last chance to redeem him-self. "I know the evidence is stacked against Ron Low. The ransom note came off his laptop, he went missing at the same time she did, and now he turned up dead himself but, if it wasn't Ron…or if he was working with a partner and it could be anyone else…who would be your next guess?"

"Maybe that roommate."

"Really?" I blinked in surprise. "But he was in Korea when it happened. Kind of hard to be across the world and commit a kidnapping and murder, right?"

"I don't know." He took out a tissue and dabbed at

the sweat that was beaded on his forehead. "But there's something about that boy that's just…off."

I thought about Joon Kim on the drive back home. When I used the hose on the side of the house to water my wilted flowers, my phone chimed to announce there was someone activating the camera on that side of the house.

"No shit, Sherlock. It's me." I blew out an annoyed breath as I clicked on the app and then pocketed the phone.

The next sound announced a text from Garrett: Traffic must've been awful. Welcome home.

I just sent him a kissy emoji. I didn't want to explain I'd been sidetracked by finding a body in a lake. He'd find out soon anyway, once it hit all the news stations.

I let Wookie run in the yard for a few minutes and then we went inside and I filled his water and food dishes for him. While he slurped his water and chomped his kibble I started up my new laptop. The entire process of getting everything up and running took entirely too long. By the time things were ready to go, my stomach was grumbling and demanding food so I made myself a grilled cheese sandwich. I brought the sandwich and the laptop to the sofa and turned on the TV as background noise while I went through my emails.

One email in particular stood out. James Low. Ron's father. It was simple and to the point: Thank you for finding our son.

While I nibbled my sandwich and sipped a can of Coke I debated how to reply. There was a lot I still wanted to know about Ron and, although parents seldom knew everything, I felt like it would be a good place to start. I remembered the website Ron's parents had put up for tips to find their boy. Both the media and the public had dragged them across the coals for putting up such a public request when he was the perpetrator and not the victim. When I clicked open the page now I noticed the section to submit tips had been taken down and the only thing on the website home page was a statement saying Ron had been found and the family was asking for peace and privacy at this difficult time.

I was about to invade that solitude and disturb that peace as I picked up my phone and looked at the message from Joon Kim forwarding the Lows' home phone number.

James Low answered the phone and I introduced myself.

There was a poignant pause followed by, "Thank you for finding our boy."

"I'm truly sorry for your loss, Mr. Low, and I know this is a horrific time for you and your wife but I was hoping I could come over to talk about Ron."

"Why?"

The simple question stumped me.

"Well because I, um, I was hoping to get more information about him and—"

"You're working for Ebba, right? That's what we were told. That's why you found Ron when and where you did."

"I'm working for Ava's mom. Yes."

"And you're hoping we can tell you where our son dumped her body. Well, that's not going to happen,

Julie, on account of we don't think our Ronnie killed that girl so if you don't mind—"

"I don't think so either," I blurted trying to stop him from hanging up on me. The air stretched between us on a fat pause.

"Is that so, or is that just what you're saying?"

"Look, I knew Ron from high school and, well, he was nice to me. He stuck up for me when others didn't. He sure didn't seem like the kind of guy who could hurt a flea."

This was all true. Although he could've snapped and killed Ava, even if he did Ron had still taken a bullet in the back of his head so he was also a victim here. I was doubtful the coroners had shared that with the Low family yet and it sure couldn't come from me.

"But you *are* working for Ebba."

"I am."

"Then I got nothing more to say to you."

"But she hired me to find her daughter's body, not to find evidence against Ron," I said hurriedly. "And if I *do* find her body, it could prove who killed Ava, and that could clear Ron's name."

There was another lengthy pause and if it wasn't for background television noise coming from his end of the line, I would've thought he'd ended the call.

"I don't want my wife to know we met. She doesn't need the heartache. She's getting her hair done in town tomorrow morning at ten o'clock," he said quietly into the phone. "You can come to the house then and I'll give you a few minutes of my time." He rattled off the address and added, "Don't be late." And then the call went dead.

"Looks like it's a work day tomorrow." Wookie was on the sofa next to me and I rubbed his head. "Maybe you can give that doggie daycare a try rather than staying home alone. You know, in case someone tries to slide you a burger laced with sleeping pills again."

He yawned and rolled over for a belly rub.

The next morning my alarm went off and I padded to the kitchen in only a long tank top with an open back. I let Wookie outside to do his business first and listened to my phone chime as the app for the video camera announced movement. I texted Garrett to tell him this was getting beyond annoying. He replied with a thumbs-up emoji. Big help.

After Wookie was back inside I filled his water and kibble and then started on coffee for myself. My phone chimed again at the same time that Wookie began going crazy at the front door. The hair stood on the back of my neck as I checked my phone and then I rolled my eyes because walking toward the house was the green-haired girl, Tracey, holding two cups of coffee. I frowned at the app watching her get closer. Wookie sounded like he wanted to go through the door and take a pound of flesh.

"Just a sec!" I shouted through the door and then I instructed Wookie to go to his bed, which he did in a sulky manner.

I ran to the bedroom and slid on a pair of sweatpants. When I opened the door I did it quickly and carefully so Wookie wouldn't be tempted to escape.

"Hey," she said holding up the coffees. "You looked like a Starbucks latte kind of girl." She thrust a paper cup into my hand.

"Um. Did Garrett ask you to bring me coffee now? Because really that's just messed up and a little stalkery."

She laughed and sat down on the concrete steps at my door. "No. It's my day off and when I don't have to work I always drive the ten minutes to Monroe and get a Starbucks and I was thinking to myself, I bet that Julie girl doesn't even know there's a Starbucks that close and I bet she'd really like a latte."

"Oh. In that case, thanks a lot." I sat down next to her, not sure what to make of this girl and her bizarre assumption about my coffee habits, which, for the record, was entirely off base. I was not a fancy coffee kind of girl.

"Cheers." She tapped her cup against mine and then we sat there sipping our drinks. "So I heard you found that kid at Blackmans Lake."

"Yeah."

"That's your gig then? You drive around and find wayward bodies and stuff? It's like you're some kind of superhero and finding dead people is your superpower."

I cringed and slid a sidelong glance at her to see if she was joking. "I guess all I need is a cape or something and maybe a tiara."

Tracey smiled but her face was otherwise impassive as she wrapped her hands around her coffee cup and I noticed the double rings that were braces around her knuckles.

"Those braces ring things…" I pointed to her fingers, wanting to change the subject. "You said it's some kind of condition."

"Ehlers Danlos." She took a drink. "It's a genetic condition that means that all my connective tissue is confused. Held together with more spit than glue so all my joints do weird things. Including my fingers."

"Oh."

"I've had more surgeries than I'd like to count just to keep everything connected but I'm not a complainer. We all got our own stuff going on."

We sat there on the steps sipping our coffee and listening to sparrows chirp in the bushes nearby. Neither of us said a word and it was kind of nice so I found myself regretting that I was going to have to break the moment.

"I have an appointment in Blaine and I need to drop Wookie off at doggie daycare before so-o-o…" I got to my feet.

"I could come with you on your appointment." She got up and smiled excitedly. "All superheroes need a sidekick, right?"

"I'm not a superhero." My words came out snippy and I quickly added, "I'm meeting with a family member who lost someone so I really need to just do it alone."

"Sure. Of course. I understand." Her words were serious now and the previously animated look on her face was shut down.

I'd hurt her feelings. Christ. "But, hey, maybe you can come with me another time, you know? Four eyes are better than two, right?"

"You mean that?" Her eyes brightened. "That would be so cool and I absolutely would not get in your way at all."

"Thanks so much for the coffee." I raised the cup, and as I turned away I immediately realized my back was visible and I felt exposed.

"Wow." She said it quietly and her cool fingers lightly touched my back and traced the deep, grooved scars caused from a grandmother with a whip made particularly to inflict as much pain as possible.

I flinched away. "Don't."

"Sorry," she said quickly. "I got a ton of scars too so I wasn't judging or anything."

She turned and lifted up the back of her shirt exposing a thick keloid snake that ran up the length of her spine. Her scar was obviously surgical and not brought on by someone repeatedly trying to beat the devil out of you when you were a child. Still, she was trying to connect with me on that level so I just gave her a friendly smile.

"Oww," I said in empathy.

"Spinal surgery when I was a kid."

"I guess we've got scars in common," I said, anxious to go now. "So I'll see you around then."

"I got your number so I'll text you next time to see if you're free instead of just popping by, okay?"

"Sure." I waved goodbye and walked back inside the house. I started to get ready to leave and it wasn't even five minutes later when Tracey fired me off a text.

See you soon! with happy faces and a superhero emoji.

I sent her a thumbs-up in reply.

I really liked her so I hoped she wasn't going to turn into a pain in the ass.

Seconds afterward Garrett also sent a message saying that he liked my new coffee buddy but next time I should invite her in. I could've replied explaining Tracey didn't like dogs. I could've also raged at him to mind his own business and that he was crossing the line. Instead, I just ignored the message and prepared for my day.

Ron Low's parents lived only a couple miles from the property I once shared with Gramps, him in his house and me in my trailer, just over a year or a lifetime ago. It was hard to be in that area. I played an audiobook so loudly my windows shook as I turned down their gravel road and spied the single wide trailer claiming a weed concrete pad in the center of a few acres of farmland. My breath caught in my throat and my stomach clenched with fear. It could've been my place. My cramped trailer surrounded by wannabe fields that lay fallow.

I probably would have barfed if I didn't practice every one of Dr. Chen's deep breathing and mindfulness exercises right there in my Jeep. I sat in my vehicle a long while, until the white curtains in the dingy kitchen window parted and I felt eyes watching and questioning what I was doing having a meltdown in my car.

"This isn't my home," I told myself, climbing out of the Jeep.

Swallowing my fear, I strode strong and purposefully to the door and it was thrown open before I even raised my hand to knock.

"Wondered if you were coming in or writing a book out there," Mr. Low barked. "Come in already."

I stepped inside, relieved to see the interior of the trailer was not at all like my old place. It smelled of pine cleaner, and the décor was very feminine with any available space covered in crocheted doilies and lace.

"Sit," Mr. Low instructed, pointing to a seat across from him at the small dining nook.

Just getting up from the table was a bald man a few years older than me. I recognized him as the one standing at the back of the search party with Wes's arm around him.

"You must be Ron's brother, Jay," I said.

I held out my hand and he wordlessly shook it.

"You want me to hang around?" he asked his father.

"We're good," Mr. Low announced.

Jay headed down the short hall and disappeared into one of the bedrooms. I took a seat at the nook table and Mr. Low sat across. He picked up a mug of coffee and drank without offering me one. This wasn't a social visit and he was making that clear.

"My wife will be back from the salon not long from now. She can't… She won't… I don't want her to see you here."

"I understand."

"You couldn't possibly."

He didn't have the market cornered on loss or grief and I could fill a book on my own but I wouldn't deny him his. Grief was its own demon that made a home nestled deep in your gut. It could be fed and stirred by a simple token and today I was that reminder to poke and prod. He was angry but he'd earned it.

"You found our boy and that's the only reason I invited you over."

"I appreciate that and so I'm going to get right to the point. You don't think Ron killed Ava."

"I sure as hell don't." His hands went to fists on the top of the table before he relaxed them and wrapped them around his coffee mug.

"And you don't think he kidnapped Ava and demanded a hundred Gs from Ebba Johansson?"

"Nope, and that just ain't me standing up for my boy and defending what's mine. Ron just wasn't that kind of guy. He didn't give a rat's ass about money. He worked just enough to pay for what he needed. He could've had more…worked harder…gone to school…made something more of his life…but he turned all that down."

"You're saying he could've gone to college but chose not to?"

I tried not to sound judgey but he obviously heard it that way.

"We had money set aside for it." He leaned forward and stuck a finger in my face. "We'd put away a little bit every month since the day the boys were born. When it came time, well, he just said 'nah, you two enjoy it.'" He choked on those last words and cleared his throat. "Those were his exact words." I waited while he drank some coffee and then he continued. "All that boy wanted was to work enough to pay for a roof over his head, food in his mouth, and all that gear he needed to hike here and there. He loved the great outdoors. That was his calling."

"Did Ron ever talk about traveling so he could hike at more exotic places?"

"Sure. Hiking was all he ever talked about. That boy would've traveled to Timbuktu if it had a good trail and he had the money."

A hundred thousand would've gone a long way toward feeding that hiking obsession.

"If Ron didn't do it, then who?"

I watched him drink the rest of his coffee and then put the mug back down while he slowly shook his head.

"I got no idea who would've kidnapped and killed that girl. If I could've picked anyone, it would've been that Joon Kim boy that lived with Ronnie. That boy always rubbed me the wrong way but they say he was in Korea and, as far as I know, they haven't yet invented a way for someone to be in two places at one time."

"Mr. Low, what did you think of Ava?"

He shrugged. "I didn't think much of her at all, actually. Me and my wife only ever met her one time and we weren't all that impressed. Jay met her a couple times at Ron's house and he said the same thing."

"Why weren't you impressed?"

"She was just too full of herself. Oh she was friendly enough but acted like she was all that and a bag of chips. I could tell she thought the world owed her a living. Spoiled. That's what she was. Spoiled. She was the type that thought her shit didn't stink."

If talking smack about the dead could cause them to smite you, Mr. Low was about to be struck dead.

"If she was so bad, what do you think Ron saw in her?"

"He probably just saw her as a piece of tail. Ron liked the ladies and they liked him back. He was far away from anything near getting serious with anybody and definitely not Ava Johansson."

"How do you know? I mean, you said you'd only

met her once so how do you know they weren't serious? Did he say that?"

The questioned seemed to confuse him as he blinked at me. "Well, we only met her the one time but then we only ever met a handful of girls he dated. My wife was always after him to get more serious. She was ready for grandbabies and told him so on every occasion. Ron always told his mother he just hadn't met 'the one' yet and she'd always tell him you gotta be with them longer than five minutes to find out if they're right for you." He smiled a little when he added, "My boy just wasn't done sowing his wild oats, if you know what I mean."

And speaking of all that oat sowing… "Where were some of Ron's favorite places to go?"

"You mean hikes and such?"

"Hikes, or day spots or even places he liked to go overnight?"

"Just in the parks and stuff, you know."

I did not know and this was getting me nowhere. "Yes, I know he liked to hike but I was wondering if there were any special locations he liked to go."

"Well, sometimes he liked to head across the border and drive up to Whistler, but he hadn't done that for a while because he'd been sick."

"Sick?" I tilted my head a little. "Like he had the flu or something?"

"No, he has an inherited condition where he has too much iron in his body. Not a big deal really because he took care of himself and saw a nurse regularly."

He told me the name of the condition but I'd never heard of it. I remembered Joon Kim mentioning it too.

"Ron was good about taking care of himself. Sure

he had pain because of the iron thing and it stopped him from going on longer drives for a while, but otherwise he was good and strong."

We sat there then staring at each other. I'd run out of questions and I could tell Mr. Low had run out of patience as he got to his feet to see me to the door.

I dug a business card out of my pocket and held it out to him. "If you think of anything I should know, please give me a call."

He didn't take the card.

"If you find that girl they'll be able to prove it wasn't Ron so just go and do your job."

I thanked him and left.

Jay Low was staring furiously at me from a bedroom window. The message was clear. I was not welcome back.

After I started up the car, I took my dowsing rods out of my pack and lay them across my lap. If they were going to twitch at all to indicate I was driving by a body, I wanted to be prepared. Not that I thought Ron would've hauled Ava out to his parents' place to dump her in the fallow fields, but who was I to say for sure.

The rods never shook or moved at all when I drove away.

I steered back onto I-5 and I didn't even realize I'd taken the exit toward my old home until I was on the parallel road and the old driveway was in front of me. I violently steered the Jeep onto the shoulder and slammed on the brakes. My heart pounded so hard it felt like my ribs would crack.

My mind was filled with dark quicksand thoughts. From where I sat I could make out the exact location

where Gramps's house had been before the new owners had demolished it. I felt a cold sweat dampen my
body as I stared into the distance and there, just down
the road, my old trailer was a silhouette on the horizon. I flung my car door open, leaned out and vomited
repeatedly until there was nothing coming up but bile.

Three hundred thirty-three.

I broke every speed limit on my way home and
didn't breathe easy until I pulled up to the doggie daycare to get Wookie. One look at his goofy face and his
butt wagging happily made my heart swell. Wookie's
power licks did not disappoint. I wondered if I was the
first client whose eyes brimmed with tears at the sight
of their dog after only a few hours apart. I knelt on the
tile floor at the payment desk and hugged him tight.

The cheerful young man running the daycare was
telling me about how they'd become so popular in the
small community that they'd developed a waiting list and
that I'd been lucky to get Wookie in for a day on such
short notice. I was only half listening as he described
the services they offered in addition to dog-sitting that
included grooming and the massage services previously
mentioned by the vet's office. It wasn't until the Ebba's
Bliss name came up that my ears perked up. I broke
Wookie's embrace to get to my feet.

"Did you say Ebba Johansson? I mean Ebba's Bliss?"

"Yes, I did." He beamed proudly. "Most people don't
know that Ms. Johansson trained in veterinarian massage and then offered special training to our groomers."

"I wonder why she would do that when she has a
chain of massage studios in the casinos?" I wondered
then realized I'd spoken out loud.

"I'm guessing she loves animals and believes in the therapeutic benefits of massage," he replied.

"Of course. That's it."

I was beginning to realize there was a lot I didn't know about Ebba Johansson. It was time I did a little research about this woman who hired me to find her dead daughter.

TEN

Before I left the doggie daycare, I questioned the worker about their massages but he didn't seem to have any answers beyond their rates and the supposed therapeutic benefits. He couldn't explain anything about the training including when it had happened and where.

"You need to talk to Kim." He reached behind the counter and handed me a business card. "She's the head groomer and she oversees the pet masseuse part of the business."

I took both the business card and Wookie home.

After a dinner of popcorn and iced tea I put my feet up on my coffee table and dialed the number on the business card. Kim answered on the first ring. She was totally cool with me asking a lot of questions.

"A lot of people are wary about massage for dogs. They think it's some kind of scam but I've seen wonderful results with many of our clientele."

"The dogs you mean."

"Yes. Some of them have old injuries or they're senior dogs with arthritis, and the deep tissue techniques we use help to increase circulation and promote healing, and many see increased range of motion after just a few treatments. If you had a backache you probably wouldn't think twice about going for a massage."

Actually, I'd think more than twice. I'd probably

think a hundred times and still come up with "There is no way in hell you're rubbing my body." But I was willing to bet others found massage relaxing.

"Tell me about the training involved."

Kim told me that they were trained at the daycare facility by a person certified in Canine Sports Massage Therapy.

"And that person was Ebba Johansson, I understand? I was surprised to hear that because I know she runs massage centers at some of the casinos. For people I mean."

"Yeah, well, she said she became interested in canine massage when her own dog enjoyed massage at home. She got her training specific to animal massage and then wanted to spread that love. Isn't that wonderful?"

Wonderfully lucrative I bet.

"It must've been pretty expensive for you to take the course and have Ebba come out and train you."

"There were two of us from the daycare and it cost us each a thousand dollars for the training. That probably sounds like a lot but we can do canine massage off the premises too. We're not limited to only offering our services at the facility. We both do home treatments as well. If you're ever interested, I'll give you a discount for your first treatment."

Based on the information I already had, a canine massage treatment was fifty dollars. After twenty sessions the doggie masseurs would recoup their money. I'm guessing it was a nice little side business.

I thanked Kim for answering my questions and promised to bring Wookie in soon for one of their treatments. Wookie's ears picked up at mention of his name. After I hung up I gave his head a rub.

"Don't get your hopes up. If you want a massage you're going to have to do a lot more around here than just scratch yourself and lick your balls."

As if on cue, Wookie raised his head and began to growl deep down in his throat. My phone chimed and my hands shook as I clicked open the motion detector app just as Wookie bounded off the couch and ran to the side door of the house and began snarling and barking like a maniac. The app showed a raccoon had knocked over Wookie's outside water bowl and was hightailing his bandit face out of there as Wookie snapped angrily at the door.

I walked over, patted him on the head and sighed with relief. "Thanks for keeping me safe from that cute black-eyed thief." I reached into the cupboard where I kept his treats and hand him a chew bone.

My phone beeped an incoming message from Garrett: Just a raccoon.

I sent him an eye-rolling emoji because no kidding!

"Do you think part of what appeals to you about Garrett is the fact that he's a protective father figure since you never knew your own dad?" Doc asked.

"Trust me, the things I like to do with Garrett are not fatherly."

Now I resisted the urge to fire off another text to Garrett telling him to stop acting like a worried dad. Part of me hated it when he fussed over me but I knew a bigger part liked that he worried about me so much and wanted me safe. I'd never had someone care so deeply about my welfare before.

"Boyfriends are supposed to take care of you," I grumped as I refilled my iced tea and returned, with Wookie and my laptop, to my place on the sofa.

I turned on the television to a silly sitcom and opened up my computer to do a little research on Ebba Johansson. I started with what I already knew. Ebba owned a franchise of boutique spas located inside casinos. It all appeared to start with the casino closest to the one where I used to live. The one where my ex-boyfriend, Denny, still worked. Denny had been the one who'd told Ebba to look me up.

I got up from the sofa and went to the kitchen and found Denny's drawing exactly where I'd left it. The sketch of his profile with the word bubble that read "Hey! She's a stuffy old lady but she could use your help." The drawing where a more beautiful, ethereal vision of myself in a sundress was flipping him the bird as I walked away.

I stared at the drawing, letting it pull me in to a simpler time when Denny and I were lovers and my cramped trailer was home, the gas station was work and Gramps was just Gramps.

"It's okay to miss your grandfather. It's okay to grieve the loss of that life," Dr. Chen said.

"It wasn't a life. It was a lie."

I did something then that I never thought I'd do in a million years. I texted Denny. His phone number was one of only a handful I knew by heart and I sent the message before I could change my mind.

Got time for coffee? It's about Ebba.

I put my phone down then because Denny was casual about cell phones and it wasn't unusual for him to let the battery run down or leave it at home. He lived the humble kind of life that didn't involve having his hand Velcroed to a digital device like most of us.

When I woke up in the morning it was because my phone was chiming. Two notifications from the security camera that detected motion. When I checked, there was only the industrious work of a spider that had managed to swathe a swarm of flies in the white thread of his web.

A text from Garrett said I should use my broom to brush off the web. I was about to send a snarky reply when I noticed another text had come in. From Denny.

Coffee is good. Today? Big Al's? 11?

I chewed my lower lip as my finger hovered over the letters awaiting my reply. After a deep breath I quick typed See you then before I could change my mind.

I sat on the edge of the bed and put the phone back on my nightstand and drilled my fingers nervously through my hair.

"This is a bad idea. A real bad idea," I told the empty house. "Jesus, I need a drink."

The dog hopped off the bed and placed his head on my lap, his large eyes looking up at me with concern.

"I said I *need* one." I rubbed his head with my hand. "That doesn't mean I'm running out to get one."

But God how I wanted to.

I slowly got to my feet and showered. Afterward I debated exactly how much makeup to put on. I wasn't a big makeup girl. A little eyeliner and lipstick was all I usually did when I thought of it at all. I didn't want to do more and make it look like I was trying to pretty up for Denny. I didn't want to do less and make it look like I'd neglected myself since I last saw him either. I went through the same song and dance staring at my clothes before sliding on jeans and a T-shirt like I always wore.

I knew I was being stupid because I was nervous about meeting Denny. I was also really anxious about walking into Al's Diner where all the locals hung out and where I'd downed coffee or a meal so many times before it had felt like home cooking when I lived a different life.

"Don't eat the turkey bacon. It tries real hard to be a pig but that kind of flesh never oinked," Gramps's voice said in my ear.

I grabbed a couple water bottles and tossed them in my pack, just in case I was gone longer than I thought. Then I let Wookie out to pee and filled up his bowls.

"As much as I know you'd love to see Denny, you can't come with me," I told him as I reached into the cupboard for a treat. "This I do solo."

I closed the bathroom door and as well as the doors to all the bedrooms, making sure all the windows were locked tight. Then I tossed a chew treat to Wookie, set the house alarm and locked the house firmly behind me. I glanced up at the motion-activated camera pointed in the carport and gave it a wave that was, no doubt, blocked by the spiderweb.

Clean the camera, came Garrett's texted reply.

I sent him a selfie with me sticking my tongue out

first, then I grabbed the push broom and gave the spider's residence the heave-ho.

I clicked the fob to unlock the Jeep but didn't hear the unlock sound. Maybe I hadn't locked it, which was stupid on my part. As I opened the driver's door, a high-pitched squeal left my throat like I'd seen a mouse. Or a ghost. Instead, what I saw was a bottle of wine poised precariously in the cup holder in the car's console. I dropped my pack to the ground and stood there staring at the bottle.

"What the actual hell!"

I looked all over my yard and down the drive. I spun around and around until I was completely dizzy, checking for someone nearby but the only answer was chirping sparrows.

My fingers shook as I stood a few feet away from the open car door and dialed Garrett's number. He picked up immediately.

"You okay?"

"There's a bottle of wine in my Jeep."

He paused and I could almost hear his wheels turning with questions.

"I didn't put it there," I explained. "When I went to my Jeep, it was there. In the cup holder. Just mocking me."

"How did it—"

"I don't know!" I cried. "Someone broke into my vehicle and crammed a cold bottle of Yakima Valley sauvignon blanc into my cup holder!"

I stared at it. The green bottle didn't quite fit into the holder meant for cola cans and to-go coffees. It sat there dripping with condensation and slightly tilted toward me, begging me to pick it up, unscrew the lid and guzzle it down.

"Is anyone there?" His voice was serious and business now.

"No." I blew out a breath. "Not that I can see." I was angry now. "Fat lot of good your stupid cameras did when they didn't go off to show someone breaking into my car and—"

"Look, I've called the local law. You've got that can of bear spray in your pack, right? Take it out and keep it in your hand."

I fumbled in the outside pocket of my pack and took out the can. "Got it."

"Good. I want you to go back into the house and lock your doors but first send me pictures of the Jeep. Are the windows broken? Does the door show any signs of being pried open?"

"Hang on…" I used my phone to snap pictures and send them to him, then returned to the call. "It wasn't forced open. I'm going back inside the house."

I was walking back to the house now, my legs feeling rubbery with fear. I couldn't get my key back into the dead bolt fast enough. Wookie greeted me like I'd been gone a year and my breathing came out fast.

"Take a deep breath," Garrett said in my ear. "Lock the door behind you, reset the alarm and just breathe."

I did as he said and stared out my kitchen window at the Jeep that looked somehow threatening now with the driver's door flung open as if it was waiting for a driver.

"How could that happen?"

"Did you leave the door unlocked?"

"No." Then I corrected, "I don't know. Maybe. I don't always lock it when I'm at home."

"And your spare keys are in the junk drawer?"

I crossed the kitchen and opened the drawer that held pens, tape, a couple screwdrivers and the flotsam of life. The keys were missing.

I let out a small moan.

"Your spare keys aren't there?"

"No-o-o!" I sank down to sit on the cold tile floor. Wookie came over and flopped down next to me, putting his head in my lap.

We both knew what this meant. When the house was broken into that person stole my spare keys so, not only did they have the keys for my Jeep, they also had the keys to my house. I wondered if the cameras had deterred them from coming back inside.

"You know what bothers me the most?" he asked.

"That whoever did this knows me."

"Yes."

They knew I was an alcoholic and knew my personal choice was wine. The bottle was a sarcastic taunt.

Garrett was talking but I was only thinking about that bottle balanced precariously in the cup holder and suddenly it felt silly to be so upset and afraid.

"They could've killed me."

Garrett paused in whatever he'd been saying before beginning, "Look, Julie, don't—"

"He could've just hunkered down in the back seat and killed me when I climbed in the vehicle, or hidden behind the bushes and shot me or broken into the house at night and strangled me—"

"Stop!" Garrett shouted. "You need to calm down."

"I'm perfectly calm." And I was. "They could've killed me but instead they left a bottle of wine like they're a bully making fun of me." I could feel anger replacing fear. "I'm going to chuck the bottle in the trash and go about my day. Cancel the cops."

"No! First of all, we're going to want prints off that bottle. Second, you don't know what else has been done. Maybe your Jeep was rigged and—"

"Nobody stuck a bomb in this car and rigged it to blow because there's no way they would've left me this present if that was their intention, right?" I was pleased with my own deductive reasoning. "Listen, Mr. FBI, you know I'm right."

When he didn't reply, I told him to hang on a second.

I grabbed a paper towel from the roll under the sink, disarmed the alarm and walked outside with Wookie at my side. I walked to the car, and carefully picked up the bottle of wine from the very top. Then I walked it over to the side of the house, now within range of the motion detector camera and set it down on the steps. I might have licked my lips and my fingers might have shaken just a bit as I held the bottle, but I was able to walk back to the Jeep.

I could hear Garrett's voice shouting from the phone in my pocket and when I brought it to my ear he was upset.

"You're just going to leave it there?" Garrett demanded.

"Yup. Your cop can dust it for fingerprints or take it into evidence but I've got work to do in Blaine and—"

"What are you going up there for?"

I could feel his worry creep over the phone.

"Don't get upset…" I began. I whistled for Wookie, brought him in the house and again set the alarm and locked up.

"Why would I get upset?" he demanded, his voice already going up.

"I'm meeting Denny for coffee," I replied, hurriedly adding, "Only to ask him questions about Ebba since he was the one who recommended me to her."

He was quiet and I wasn't sure if this was the jealous boyfriend kind of quiet, or the worried FBI silence.

"I'd feel better if you put off that meeting until I could drive you."

It was probably both kinds of quiet.

"I'll be fine." I took a breath and climbed inside the Jeep and started it up. "Do you want to chat with me on speaker while I drive?"

I knew he was busy. There was never a time Garrett wasn't working on one case or a dozen, but he still chatted with me on the line for over twenty minutes while I nosed the vehicle north on I-5 toward the area that used to be home but now was just throbbing pain.

He told me the officer was at the house and would check the premises and take the bottle.

"I want you coming here afterward," he told me. "You can go pack a bag, get Wookie and then come and stay with me until all this mess is sorted. You're not safe there. Not with someone having your house keys. Not with cameras and an alarm. Not without me."

I promised I'd talk to him about that later, and ended the call.

I had butterflies in my stomach at the prospect of seeing Denny. Things had ended poorly between us when my life became a vortex of doom and he'd stood on the edge of that spiral and, instead of standing by me, had chosen to cheat. I played an audible book through the speakers and comforted myself in my deep breathing and mindfulness exercises.

Big Al's was an all-American family restaurant that hugged the Canadian border. It had old-fashioned décor and you could choose to sit at one of the vinyl booths or perch on a stool at the counter. Home cooking and friendly service with a smile. Unless you were the talk of the town for the past fifteen months. Now, instead of service with a smile, the entire restaurant of locals fell silent when I walked in, and those smiles faltered and jaws dropped as I crossed the room and slipped into a corner booth.

The restaurant recovered and slowly the low-level chatter returned and the sidelong glances stopped. A waitress I didn't recognize asked me if I wanted coffee.

"Yes, and water. Please."

While she ran off to get that, I hid behind the menu as if I was going to get anything besides the grilled ham and cheese sandwich I always got at Big Al's. But maybe I should try something new. After all, I wasn't the same person as I was back when I used to frequent this place.

Denny was late but I expected nothing less. I'd ordered my grilled ham and cheese and nibbled the corners by the time he arrived. I knew without looking up from my phone the moment he walked in since the restaurant grew quiet again.

He slid into the booth across from me, tucked his thick black hair behind one ear and smiled.

"Look at you," he said with an easy smile and a tone nearing approval.

I smiled back and it was easier than I ever thought it would be. Even from across the booth I could smell the scent of the cigarillos he liked and it smelled like humbler times that gave me an unexpected ache.

"You're too skinny." He picked up half my sandwich, which was now cold, and took a large bite.

"And you're too judgey," I replied stuffing a french fry in my mouth.

"You still with that old guy?"

"He's not old."

I wanted to get the upper hand here. I didn't want this to slip into a comfortable reunion even if part of me did yearn for life before chaos. For a time when I lived in my small trailer with Wookie and worked at the gas station in town.

"Saw on your Facebook business page you're doing all that voodoo bit for a living now."

Just like that the warm fuzzy notion of coming home evaporated and I felt like he should be able to see it lift off me in a steamy vapor. Denny hadn't been there for me when things got bad, and he didn't deserve my time of day then or now. I pushed my plate toward him so he could eat my leftovers.

"Tell me about Ebba Johansson."

His eyebrows lifted and he gave me a curious look at my businesslike tone but accepted it as he chomped down on my food.

"She put herself through massage school, whatever that is, and pulled a good-sized chunk of cash out of running a bunch of those places in casinos around these parts. She has lots but I don't know how many girls rubbing people down at casinos and she gets a cut. Heard she even has people giving massages to dogs." He shook his head and laughed. "People will pay for anything these days."

"So she's just a hardworking single mom then?"

"Sure." He shrugged. "She hasn't been in the casino much these days though. Last time I saw her she just looked done. She's trying to sell the business. Guess Ava dying was too much."

"Did you know Ava?"

"Might say that." He signaled the waitress for coffee. "I did her a time or two way back when."

I straightened and could tell Denny was enjoying my startled look.

"You guys went out?"

"I wouldn't say we went out. More like we stayed in." He gave me a sly wink.

"When was this?"

He picked up a french fry and waved it in my face. "You're jealous."

"I am so *not* jealous. At all."

"Too bad." He thanked the waitress for his coffee and then took a sip.

"So when did you and Ava stay in exactly?"

"Last year sometime. I'd see her around. She'd come around the casino. She was supposed to work but most days she'd just screw the pooch, yanno. Show up late or not at all, or just show up to party, and a couple times she was there at the end of my shift so…" He lifted his mug of coffee to his lips for another drink and suddenly lowered it. "Don't be telling the cops about that. I don't need them coming around and asking me questions about Ava." His voice was low and heated.

If it was nothing but a couple rolls in the sheets I wondered why Denny was resisting telling the cops. He certainly had no problem bragging to me about sleeping with her and I bet others knew too but I didn't want to get into that with him.

"What did Ebba think of you messing around with her daughter?"

"I'm sure she didn't know about me and Ava. Not like we were a thing or anything. That girl was far too much a headache for me. High maintenance. Got on my nerves. Ebba's too, and she was pulling her hair out about her daughter most days. She shoulda just cut those apron strings and let her fly on her own but, nope, she kept trying to get her in the biz, and every time Ava showed up with her hand open, Ebba would scrape together something to give her."

I waited when the waitress came by to refill my cup.

"Guess she was trying to make a responsible young woman out of her daughter and get her to work," I said. "Seems to me if business was going well then she had more than enough to spread around to her daughter."

"She put herself on the hamster wheel, yanno?"

I didn't have a clue what he meant so I waited for him to explain after he filled his coffee with cream and sugar. "Just one of those people who work all the time and wanted Ava to be the same. I think she thought Ava was just going through a rebellious phase."

"What do you think?"

"I think Ava was never going to come and work in

the family biz. She just wanted to do her own thing, and her thing involved partying hard and hardly working."

"Anything else you can tell me that other people don't know about Ebba or Ava?"

He gave that some honest thought as he sipped from his mug. "Not really. Ebba told me she really wants to retire now. She always used to talk about living by a lake without another soul around for miles once Ava took over the company."

"Lots of people have that dream."

"The only time I ever saw her and Ava getting along is when they were sitting in one of the coffee shops having lunch and they were chatting about some cottage on a lake and living without a care in the world. They talked like it was right around the corner."

"Now that Ava's gone, it probably makes sense she doesn't want to keep working so hard."

"Who knows what's going on inside her head except she really wanted the news people to focus on you helping out with finding Ava. She was excited about that. Put some color back in her cheeks when she was beginning to look tired from all the grief, yanno?" He drummed his fingers a little on the table. "Guess she feels like if you find Ava she can bury her and it'll help her to move on."

"What do you think?"

"I think she's going to carry that anger and sadness with her forever until it drags her down into a plot next to her daughter and she'll never enjoy any cottage near a lake."

I nodded.

"Yeah, she was busy out looking for Ava with all the search parties day in and day out."

"Guess most family members do that."

"Yeah and once she heard from the coroner that all the blood found in the woods meant Ava was dead, she took a couple weeks off. I figured she'd up and walk away from everything but she randomly came back. Guess it finally hit her that Ava's not coming back but now all that money she took out of the business for the ransom is gone too. She told me she just needed to bury her daughter for closure." He nodded his chin at me. "That's when I mentioned you. Figured if you helped her find the body, maybe she'd get some peace."

I wanted to point out all the times he'd told me he didn't believe in my ability to find people. I wanted to say how he'd compared my dowsing rods to using a Ouija board and called me crazy. All the words I wanted to say stayed strangled in the back of my throat.

The waitress dropped off the bill. He didn't even make an attempt to reach for it.

"You ever meet Ronald Low? Ava's boyfriend who supposedly killed her?"

"I knew him enough to look at him but we never hung out or nothing. I did see him come around the casino with Ava a time or two. Saw Ava, Ron and Ebba all chummy a couple times too. Guess things changed."

"Guess they did." I was about to get up and then another thought occurred to me. "You ever know a guy named Wes who grew up around this area?"

"Black dude? Crooked teeth?"

I nodded.

"Sure, I knew Wes. He moved outta this area maybe

three years ago now. I heard he's got a landscaping business or something. He's a few years younger than me. Was about your grade in high school or maybe a year younger."

"Really?" I thought hard and shook my head. "I don't remember him from high school at all."

"Back then nobody called him Wes. Everyone called him Wheezy on account of his asthma."

"Oh my God! Wheezy." I rubbed the back of my neck as a strong memory jumped to the front of my mind. I'd asked Wheezy if he was okay when I heard him gasping for breath a few feet away from me. In return, he slammed me into a school locker so hard I saw stars. "He was such a dick."

"Yeah, some saw him that way I guess. I never paid him any attention."

Those who weren't bullied rarely even noticed it happening all around them.

I picked up the bill and got to my feet. "Thanks for meeting me."

"Guess that was the least I could do," he said.

"Yeah, it was." Which was a subtle reminder that he owed me so much more.

I left him sitting there in the booth and tipped heavily when I got up to the counter to pay. Once I was back in my Jeep I realized I was fine after meeting with Denny. Even though he was connected to heart-wrenching chaos from another time, I was fine.

Maybe I'm getting better, I thought, then I noticed my hands were shaking as I started up the car.

With my eyes closed I drew in a deep calming breath.

"I liked that boy well and good enough. Better than the FBI fellow. Denny knew his place."

"Shut up, Gramps!"

I screamed so loud that a woman climbing out of her car parked next to mine gave me a fearful look.

ELEVEN

I DROVE HOME with my head in a fog that didn't clear until I'd blown those old stomping grounds behind in my rearview mirror.

When I saw the highway exit for the burger place where Katie worked, I decided to take it. She'd said she would send me those secret spots that Ron liked to visit but so far I hadn't heard from her. One of the people working the counter told me that Katie didn't have a shift today but I could find her working a clothing shop at the mall. I thanked the woman for her time and got back in my car. I had no desire to go by the shopping center.

Back on the highway, I turned up the volume of my book hoping the advice for finding peace in trauma would somehow finally permeate my skull and stick. I was debating what my next step with the search for Ava would be when I saw Tracey Cook standing on the shoulder of the highway with her thumb out and her green hair blowing in the wind. I hit the brakes and angled onto the shoulder and she jogged up to meet me.

She flung open the passenger door and climbed in. "What are the chances?" Her words came out happy and breathless.

"Chances of you getting abducted by some serial

killer and tossed in a ditch somewhere?" I said. "I'd say the chances are pretty damn good."

She found that impossibly funny, dropping her over-sized purse on the ground and placing her hands on her knees as she giggled. "You are an old nasty mama in a young girl's body, yanno that?"

"I am not!" I gave her my best pissed-off glare but she only smiled back in return. "It's just not safe for you to be thumbing."

"Car is in the shop again," she explained. "I'm wanting to surprise my boyfriend on our anniversary is all."

"You should've just asked him to come get you."

"Where's the surprise in that?"

She had a point.

"Yeah but—"

"I get it." She reached over and patted my knee reassuringly. "What you see in your biz—well, you think everyone is either a murderer or setting themselves up for a killing."

"Occupational hazard," I admitted with a sigh. "Where are you going?"

"Marysville. You don't have to take me all the way unless you're heading in that direction."

I shoulder checked and then accelerated back onto the highway. "I'll take you."

I couldn't live with myself if I dropped her somewhere and she got picked up by some groper or murdered and tossed in a Dumpster.

"Fine but this depressing stuff needs to go off."

I wasn't even aware that my book on grief was still playing over the speakers. I reddened slightly but she made no other remark about it, just punched the radio stations until she found one she liked.

My peaceful although somewhat brooding drive now became a cacophony of loud music as Tracey searched for a station. At one point she found a pop artist we both liked and I even found myself singing along with her. My heart felt lighter. It was like the early days when Katie and I would drive around, windows down, bellowing along to a top hit while our hair blew in the wind.

When the radio stations all seemed to be playing commercials, Tracey hit the off button. She gave me directions to where this boyfriend worked. The area was dangerously close to a house I'd visited another time.

I finally stopped in front of a garage.

"Thanks for the lift!" she said, flinging the door open and hopping out.

"So is your guy going to give you a ride home, or what? You're not going to be thumbing back?"

"I'm sure he'll give me a ride if he can," she said, sounding less than confident as she leaned into the car to grab her purse.

"How long have you two been together?" I asked.

"It's our two-month anniversary today," she announced proudly. "There he is!"

She waved over at a skinny dark-skinned guy in oil-stained coveralls. He looked over and half waved back, not looking nearly as excited to see Tracey as she was to see him. I had a bad feeling about the entire thing but it was none of my business.

"I think that while I'm here I'm going to pop in and visit someone I know a few blocks away," I said when she went to close the passenger door. "So if you want a ride back, I'll be heading for home in an hour or so."

She nodded as if she half heard me, slammed the door shut and offered me a backward wave over her shoulder as she jogged over to her guy.

"Stupid."

It was a comment directed both at Tracey and at myself because now I had to find something to do with myself for an hour just in case she needed a ride. Unfortunately, I knew what that something would be. I angled the Jeep toward Sixth Street and slowed down. I almost rolled right past the small bungalow because the faded green wood siding I remembered was now white with bright blue trim. I pulled to the curb in front of the house, rolled down the windows to allow a breeze and turned off the Jeep.

I saw the blind slats in a small bedroom window part for someone to look out and, at the same time, the sheer curtains in the living room moved.

"Now what?"

Before long an answer came when a small middle-aged Asian woman in a tank top, cutoffs and bare feet walked out of the house and strolled purposefully toward me. I had a moment of panic when I realized she was the same woman who'd lived at the house when I visited before. It never occurred to me that my mom's ex-boyfriend, Ted, might still live here with his girlfriend.

"Enough of the watching us!" she yelled, waving her hands at me as she got closer to the curb. "Enough already! We told you everything we know!" She came right up to the passenger door shouting about a right to privacy.

"Okay, I'm leaving," I told her, nervously starting up the car.

"Wait a second." She put her hands on the window and leaned inside. I froze. "I recognize you. You're not a cop or fed. You're Molly's girl, right? You came here last year looking for her."

"Yes."

"Well, that's different then. Fine. You can come in. Thought you were a cop. Or fed. Sick of those creepers hanging around here and sticking their noses where they don't belong and going through our trash. Jesus!"

She walked back up the sidewalk and looked over to give me a hurry-up wave. I didn't want to go inside. Except I did. Desperately. So I rolled up my windows, locked up the Jeep and followed her.

Last time I was in this house I'd been following a lead in Garrett's files about the last known location of my mother, and it brought me here to this Marysville address. It was here that this woman had been shacking up with Ted. When I came here over a year ago, Ted told me my mom had gone out for smokes and beer and never come back. They'd discovered her car and it looked like Mom had just walked away or drowned in the nearby river.

I stepped inside the house now and stopped short. Last year the house had been littered with beer bottles, debris and the aroma of overwhelming neglect. It was now pristine. Same old furniture and threadbare carpet but every area had been scrubbed within an inch of its life, and the reek of pine cleaner and furniture polish stung my eyes.

"Ted doesn't live here anymore," she told me. "I kicked his sorry ass out a couple months ago when cops first started coming around. He kept spending the rent money on booze and drugs. I don't need that kind of headache."

"Oh. Well, I'm sorry to bother you. I dropped a friend off a few blocks away and just thought I'd drive by here. I don't know why. I'll just go." I turned to leave but she stopped me.

"Don't go. Come on inside. Sit down. Want some iced tea? I make it fresh myself."

I did still have an hour to kill. "Um. Sure. Thanks."

I kicked off my shoes and walked into the living room, taking a seat on the sofa probably in the exact same place I sat all those months ago except I didn't have to look for a stain-free place to park my butt this time. There were a number of table fans but they only swirled the hot air around and did little to cool the small room. Suddenly, a plump white cat startled me when it jumped onto my lap and began to rub up against me. I stroked its back and was rewarded with loud purring.

"Well, look at that," the woman remarked when she returned with our drinks. "Fluffy likes you. She belongs to my friend, who's visiting. Fluffy doesn't like many people so this is a good sign. I never trust a person if animals don't like them."

She put my glass down on top of a coaster on the coffee table in front of me and took a seat in a chair next to the sofa.

"I feel the same way," I told her honestly but didn't tell her I was more of a dog person.

Fluffy the cat jumped off my lap and went to the opposite corner of the sofa to perform an elaborate genital bathing ritual.

"My friend got her at the shelter. Can you believe someone just threw her away because they didn't want her anymore? Who does that kind of thing?"

Well, my mother had done that to me.

I picked up the glass of iced tea and took a sip. It was extremely sweet but I was thirsty and the cold felt good against my throat. When I put it back down on the table, I made certain to place it back on the coaster.

"I'll be back in a second." She picked up the cat and went down the hall, where she quickly disappeared into a bedroom. I could hear the murmur of voices and then she returned to the living room and sat back down in the chair next to me. "You probably want more information on your mom. I wish I could tell you more about her but, well, not much else I can add to what you were told by Ted last time you came by here."

She fanned herself with a newspaper and took a long drink of her tea before putting the glass down.

"You were saying that officers have been coming around the house recently?"

"Yes, the police came by and the feds too. After they made that big drug bust a few months ago, I guess Ted's name came up and your mom's too, so everyone wanted to check if they were here. Nobody's here. Obviously." She laughed and rolled her eyes. "First time they showed up it was with a search warrant. They looked over the entire house and even brought in a couple of drug-sniffing dogs. Fluffy didn't appreciate that much." She chuckled. "I told them nobody here but me and I'd already kicked Ted out of here but they kept coming around. I didn't mind at first because they're just doing their job but I wish they'd believe me that Ted isn't coming back."

I couldn't help but wonder if one of the federal agents over here had been Garrett.

"Now just because your mom's name came up that doesn't mean she's alive or anything and, if she is, you may not want to find her anyway. I know Ted told you she walked outta here and never came back. Her car was found but no sign of her. She was in a bad way, you know. All that booze and drugs—well, I'm sure she's the same now if she's alive, and maybe it even caught up to her by now."

I didn't tell her about Molly's name coming up at a drug house and that Garrett had shown me a recent picture of her. I got the impression this woman wanted to protect me.

"It's not like Ted was any kind of a ringleader, you understand. He wasn't that smart but I'm sure he had his grimy fingers involved in that shakedown some-how. Probably just buying dope there and maybe sell-ing a time or two, which is why I told him to hit the curb. I guess the officers are looking for anyone with connections to that big drug bust and they won't rest until they tie it up in a neat bow." She pulled a tissue from the front pocket of her shorts and dabbed at the sweat on her forehead. "Gawd, it's hot these days."

"Super hot," I agreed. An oscillating fan turned and teased me with a short burst of air and then turned away. "So you heard my mom's name come up when the officers were coming around?" I probed.

"Yeah. Sure." She picked up her glass and drank a little more. "Guess they arrested a lot of those people and now they're looking for others, and your mom's name was part of the group they're looking for. That shocked me and I told them she was either dead or near dead and they were wasting their time looking for her. One of the cops said maybe she was alive and she only left him because he was an asshole." She laughed quite loudly at the idea. "Ted was definitely an ass-hole at times."

"When the officers and agents came by, did they say anything else about Molly?"

She shook her head. "Nope. Her name was on a list of a few people they missed when they did that big takedown of a lot of drug houses. It's not like they're searching high and low for her or Ted. It was just their names because maybe someone at one of those houses ratted them out or something. Maybe the officers fig-ured if they found them they could get information on more drug houses." She fanned herself more with the newspaper, lifting her hair and trying to move the air around her damp neck. "Sorry I don't have any more information for you."

"That's okay. I really didn't expect you would."

"It would be best to forget all about your mother. And Ted." She leaned toward me. "You can help people and you can point them in the right direction but you can't make them better. Addiction is a horrible thing."

"Yeah, it really is."

My phone chirped and I pulled it out of my purse.

It was a text from Tracey asking if I could come back and get her. That was fast. I replied that I'd be there in a few minutes.

"Thanks so much for the tea and for taking the time to talk to me." I realized that I never even asked her name but didn't see a reason to ask for it now. I wouldn't be back. Still, I dug a business card out of my purse and handed it to her. "I know it's a long shot, but if my mom ever does come around, maybe you could tell her I'm looking for her."

"Of course. Don't expect that'll happen. But sure." She tossed the card to the table dismissively. I was already at the door slipping my feet into my sneakers when she said, "Just a sec." She disappeared down the hall and returned a minute later. "I have something for you."

She walked over to a potted plant in the corner, lifted up the pot and picked up a small bag from underneath. She brought it over, opened it up and pulled out a long chain with a gold band strung on it like a pendant.

"I found this hidden there under my fern when I first moved in here with Ted. I just left it there in case your momma ever came back for it." She took the pendant and held it out to me. "I never mentioned it to Ted in case he decided to pawn the thing, which is probably why your mom woulda hid it there in the first place."

My fingers shook a little as I took the necklace from her. "How do you know it belonged to my mom?"

"Looks like it was your dad's." Then, ever so coolly, as if this wasn't a life-defining moment, she picked the simple gold band from the palm of my hand and held it between her fingers, tilting it so I could see there was engraving inside.

I plucked the band from her hand and held it closer so I could read the inscription.

U + me 4ever xo Molly.

"Thank you." The words came out a hoarse whisper as tears burned my eyes.

"Glad you like it. I don't have no use for it, of course."

I slipped the necklace over my head and gave her a quick hug. She smiled, obviously proud of the emotion it brought on.

"If your mom ever comes around you can be sure I'll pass along your business card."

"Thank you," I repeated and headed out the door.

I walked back to my Jeep with one hand still clutching the ring around my neck. Once inside the car, I started it up and rolled down the windows all the while gripping the ring in a tight fist. It was the first time I'd ever had proof that my father existed beyond my being the result of his sperm donation. I sat in the car a while, my head and chest filled with emotion.

"Let's talk about your dad," Dr. Chen suggested.

"No."

"It might help you to grieve."

"No need to grieve someone I never even met."

Holding evidence of my father's existence in the world seemed to shift everything in my head. He'd lived, loved my mother, and died a soldier after I was born. Maybe he'd even held me in his arms and loved me too.

I let the tears flow down my face, surprised by their

intensity. The scorching yearning for a drink to bury all that emotion was incredibly intense. I considered calling Dr. Chen or Garrett but then my phone chirped a message from Tracey. She was sitting at a bus stop a block down from the garage and would wait for me there. I carefully tucked the pendant inside my T-shirt. I'd gripped it so long and so hard that the gold was warm and comforting against my chest as I steered away from the curb.

I found Tracey red-eyed and sniffling about half a block away from the garage where I'd dropped her.

She opened the door, wordlessly climbed inside and buckled her seat belt.

"I take it that the anniversary celebrations didn't go as planned?"

She shook her head and hiccupped as she tried to hold in a sob.

"I'm sorry about that. Are you hungry? Want to stop for burgers up the road before we head home?"

"I need a drink." Her voice hitched on the words. "A lot of drinks."

Damn, it would be so-o-o easy to pull into a pub and spend the day there even though I knew one day would turn into many. "I'm going to just take you home."

She didn't reply and, instead, sat sullen and sulky in the passenger seat. In spite of her refusal, I went through a burger drive-through and got us both milk shakes.

"Thanks," she said with a sigh after sipping on her shake.

"You're welcome. Wanna talk about what happened?" I asked. "Sometimes talking helps."

At least that's what everyone always says, especially if they can charge you a ton of money to listen.

"We broke up." She sniffed. "Apparently, he thinks I'm too needy. What does that mean anyway?"

It means you feel you have to celebrate a two-month anniversary. "I'm sorry. Is there anything I can do?"

She shook her head and concentrated on her milk shake while I steered out of Marysville and back toward home.

"You know what you could do? You could let me help you with your investigation," she said eagerly.

"Um…" I struggled to find the polite way to say no way.

"I need a distraction and maybe having someone else listen to all the clues about Ava would help you too! You know what they say, a second pair of eyes and all that."

"In this case there have already been a lot of eyes. Cop eyes. FBI eyes. Search party eyes and all that too."

"So another pair won't hurt one bit."

I looked at her sideways and was torn between wanting to blow her off and wanting to make her feel better. "I need to go home and take Wookie for a walk."

"Oka-a-ay, well, I can wait for you in the car or something while you do that and then we can get to work."

I found myself nodding in agreement, and a few minutes later I snapped Wookie's leash on his collar and jogged down the road with him while Tracey sat in my vehicle listening to music at a decibel that would loosen her fillings. The ring on the chain around my neck had come out of my T-shirt and bobbed against my chest as a light thumping reminder of both my own abandonment and the spark of a chance maybe someone at one time loved me when I was still Delma Arsenault.

I tried to push thoughts of my mom and dad out of my head as my feet rhythmically hit the gravel and Wookie kept pace beside me. I breathed in the clean country air and thought about nothing but my feet on the ground and the warm air swirling around me. On the jog back, my concentration turned to Ava Johansson. The pulsing beat of my feet on the road cleared my mind and helped me sort through what I knew. So many things about the Ava case felt like a tangled mess of knots and I couldn't seem to untie them in my head. Maybe Tracey was right and talking it through with someone else would help. Normally I'd work through something like this with Garrett but sometimes his analytical FBI brain got in the way of creative thinking.

When Wookie and I turned the corner of the tree-lined street back onto my driveway I stopped short.

"Son of a—"

My Jeep was gone.

I tore inside the house looking for my cell phone on the counter in order to call police. Snatching it up, I immediately noticed a text from Tracey.

Gone for beer. Back soon.

"Oh goddamn," I cried out, slamming the phone onto the counter.

I took a quick, cooling shower to clear my head and clean my sweaty body. She'd be at least a half hour since it took that long to get to town and back. I knew that Tracey was back when Wookie started barking his head off.

"Relax." I patted Wookie's head. "I'm pretty sure she's crazy but the harmless kind of crazy. At least I hope so."

With a sigh I grabbed a Coke from the fridge and met her outside.

"Don't do that again," I told her.

"What?" Tracey asked as she reached into the back seat for her purchases.

"Don't take my car without asking."

She straightened with a look of surprise and proudly held up two sacks. "But I bought enough for both of us. I figured, you know, investigating would go better with a couple cold ones."

"Yeah, well, I don't…" I cleared my throat. "I don't drink."

"Oh-h-h." She slowly put the sacks down on the ground. "You should've said something."

"I just did." I nodded at the bags. "That doesn't mean you can't." I raised my Coke. "I'm good." I pointed to the back of the house. "I've got a picnic table out back where we can sit to talk about the case."

"Well then I'll have a Coke too. If you don't mind."

I wanted to tell her to grab her beer because it didn't bother me if she drank but, honestly, I didn't know if I was strong enough to watch someone drink on my own property without feeling the bite of temptation at every sip she took.

She fell into step beside me as I walked to the back of the house and then, abruptly, she linked her arm in mine. "We're going to be like Sherlock and Dr. Watson, right?"

"Oh I doubt that very much." I laughed at the idea. "Probably more like Laurel and Hardy." I bumped her hip with mine.

"Or Thelma and Louise," she said.

"Don't they both die?"

We both burst out laughing.

The faded picnic table was under the shade of a huge cedar tree only a few feet from the back patio door. Tracey took a seat at the table while I went inside and snagged her a Coke. I made a couple trips, grabbing my laptop and also the box of Ron's belongings. I figured that, if nothing else, Tracey could busy herself going through the box while I answered emails. At least, that was the plan.

Unfortunately, Tracey's plan was to rant and rage about her now ex-boyfriend, and when she grew tired of that, she asked me a million questions about Garrett. When I didn't give in to satisfy her curiosity about our relationship, she started asking questions about dowsing.

"I don't know why I'm able to find people using dowsing rods. I just can." I clicked open another email.

"Okay, so why don't you do that divining thing where you hang a crystal on a string and ask questions? Isn't that a kind of dowsing?"

I looked at her from over the screen of my laptop and answered her patiently. "Pendulum dowsing doesn't work for me."

"But how do you know if you never—"

"I've tried it!" The words came out on a shout. So

much for patience. "Look, it worked for me once but, since then, I've tried it many, many times on practically every case but I've never had so much as a tremor. So I'm sticking to what works and not wasting any more of my time on pendulum dowsing."

She finished off her can of Coke with a gulp and a loud belch and then put it down. "Why do you think it worked that one time?"

"I'm not really sure." I blew out a hot breath. "Maybe it was just one of those things. A fluke. Or maybe it was because I was personally connected to that particular situation."

"Oh-h-h." She nodded and looked at me with wide eyes. "That was the case in the news. The one about you and your friend and your grandfather and—"

"I don't want to talk about it." My voice came out low and soft with a little beg on it. "Want another Coke?"

"Yeah, and you got anything to eat? I could use a sandwich or something."

"Sure."

My own stomach was also growling. I went inside and my phone beeped. A text message from Garrett saying he was glad I was having fun with my new friend.

Ugh. The cameras.

I replied with a thumbs-up emoji.

Was I having fun? I thought about that while I put together a couple grilled cheese sandwiches. Maybe this wasn't the kind of club and partying kind of fun I used to have with Katie. It was definitely more relaxed and casual with Tracey. There was something to be said for that, and I had to admit I liked Tracey. She was different. An oddball. But then so was I so it made me more able to relax around her.

Wookie tried to come with me when I walked back outside balancing a couple plates.

"Sorry, boy, you have to stay here." I closed the patio door behind me and left Wookie staring at us with sad eyes.

Tracey was sitting cross-legged on the ground next to the picnic table. She'd opened the box of Ron's stuff and was spreading the various books and random packages and other things out on the grass next to the table. I put her sandwich on the ground next to her but she didn't even look up.

I sat back down at the table, scrolling through emails. The one thing missing from my inbox was an email from Ebba. She hadn't called, texted or emailed me again to ask about my plans to find Ava. It felt out of character for her to give me space, even though I appreciated the time. I sent her an email telling her the truth. I was spending the day doing more research on her case and hoped to follow that up with action soon.

I ate my sandwich as I looked at messages for media requests and people wanting help finding their loved ones. A mother in Australia and an aunt in Alaska both got a form regret email in response. The locations were just too far to go. I replied to one in California and one in Idaho asking for more information. Maybe Garrett and I could book a B&B somewhere for a weekend. I could find a body and then we could hole up in a hotel room, order room service and make love night and day like we once did. The idea made me smile.

Sitting outside at the picnic table with my laptop had been a great idea. A light, grass-scented breeze chased the heat away and had me daydreaming of time away with my guy. When Tracey spoke, it startled me. "I'm sorry, what did you say?"

"I was just looking through the yearbook. Funny how I can look at faces and not even remember the girl I sat next to in a class for an entire year."

"Wait. You went to that high school?" I pointed at the book in her hand. "That one where Ron and I went?"

"Sure but only for a year." She held up the book and pointed to the thumbnail-sized picture of herself.

"We're the same age so we would've been in the same grade?" I frowned. "Did we know each other?"

"I had some surgeries in eighth grade so I was behind a year," she admitted, tossing the yearbook to the grass. "I wasn't there long enough to get to know anyone really. Except maybe Wes."

"Abel's grandson?"

"Yeah. We went out a few times back then but he had a bit of a mean streak."

"How do you mean?"

"Well, he liked to play practical jokes on people. One time he brought a box of cream-filled donuts to school except he'd replaced all the filling with mayonnaise."

"Ew-w-w." I shuddered. "That's nasty."

"Yeah, that was gross and, at the time, I kind of laughed but then when a teacher gave him a really bad grade he made it his mission to get revenge on her, and eventually she just up and quit."

"What did he do?"

"He started with stupid stuff…petroleum jelly on her classroom door, dowsing her car with hot sauce. Silly things that everyone still thought were funny but then someone gave Wes her home address and next thing there was a rumor going around that he'd broken in and poisoned an aquarium filled with exotic fish."

"Wow. Do you think it really was Wes?"

"I wouldn't put it past him. When I told him I didn't want to go out anymore, he left a long message on my home answering machine talking about how great I was at giving BJs. Of course he knew my mom and dad would hear the message before I did." She shook her head. "So, yeah, the guy is a big dick."

"Abel tried to convince me to go out with him," I said.

"Jesus. Good thing you got yourself a hunky FBI guy to tend to your needs."

"A very good thing."

We laughed.

I went back to looking at my laptop and a few minutes later Tracey started talking again.

"You know, I was just wondering if all these comments Ron made in his hiking books might help," Tracey said.

I got up from the table and joined her on the grass. She was bent with her legs in a W shape and grunted when she rearranged her body to allow me next to her. She held open a book and pointed at scribbled notes in red ink in the margin. I took the trail book from her and began reading Ron's handwritten notes. Mostly, Ron seemed to rate the trails with various one-word comments throughout the pages: *hard, steep, long, rocky, wet* and the occasional trail rated a few stars next to the description.

"It would take me a lifetime to check every trail for Ava's body." I put down that book and picked up another.

"Yeah, too bad there wasn't a way to narrow it down."

"Yeah. Like if he wrote a description that said: this would be a great place to dump a body."

We laughed until we snorted.

I flipped through the pages of another hiking book, pausing wherever Ron wrote comments. Toward the end of the book, just as I was about to toss it to the ground with the others, I stopped on a page that described hiking in Oak Lake.

A paragraph describing the relatively short trail had been circled. On the side of the page in red ink was a large heart, and written inside the heart was *Ava + Ron forever.*

I got chills.

TWELVE

WITHIN A FEW MINUTES I'd tracked the location of the trail on the map on my phone.

"Oak Lake is about an hour away. It sounds so familiar," I said to myself as I looked at the area on my screen. "Why does it sound like a place I should know?"

"You hike, right? Maybe you've hiked there," Tracey chimed in.

"Nah, I don't think so."

The trail itself didn't seem like the type of place Ron would go for a hike. It wouldn't be a challenge at all for him.

"It's rated as an easy day hike in a cottage-like area," I said. "It's not the type of trail Ron would do on his own for a challenge but maybe it was a place the two of them enjoyed. Joon Kim told me Ava wasn't much of an outdoorsy person but she tried hard to be like that for Ron. She could've suggested an easier hike just so the two of them could have something to do as a couple."

"I think we need to do a field trip and check it out."

"We?"

"Of course. You need backup."

I shook my head. "I don't need backup."

"Your superhero sidekick."

"You're going to be the Robin to my Batman?" I smiled.

"Navigator then. Who doesn't like someone riding shotgun who can tell them when to turn so they don't have to take their eyes off the road."

I wanted to tell her that was what the navigation system in my car was for but the look on her face was so hopeful that I couldn't stand it. "We'll see…"

Another hiking book caught my eye and I grabbed it off the grass. *Best Hiking Trails of the World.* The book was hardcover and looked expensive. A page in the center had a corner folded at the beginning of a chapter titled "Trekking in Argentina," and across the top of the page was the same loopy handwriting as in the other trail book: *Soon this will be us!* There were lots of Xs and Os after it.

"They were planning a trip." I was talking to myself but Tracey snagged the book from my hands to read the note.

"Or just dreaming of traveling. I buy travel books all the time but I never go anywhere."

She had a point. I'd just been dreaming about going to a bed-and-breakfast with Garrett. Didn't mean it would happen even though I wished it would.

When she tossed the book back onto the grass, a receipt slipped out and I picked it up.

"If they'd broken up a couple months before she was kidnapped, why would she be buying him a book and writing a note like that?" I held up the receipt for the book that was dated about a week before Ava's kidnapping.

"She wouldn't."

"Exactly." I used my phone to take a picture of the page.

Tracey reached for the foil packs that had come out

of the box along with the books and a few knickknacks. "What are these?"

I started to tell her that they were something medical to do with Ron's condition but she'd already torn a package open and dumped the contents on the ground.

"Weird. So he was stockpiling his own phlebotomy kits?" She pointed to the tourniquet, alcohol pads, needles and gauze pads. Everything you needed for drawing blood.

"His dad told me he had a medical condition where his body made too much iron. Hemochromatosis. I looked it up later and one of the treatments is to go for regular blood draws. Ron was a young guy and got regular treatment for it. Got blood drawn every so often and that took care of it."

"But he wasn't just drawing his own blood at home himself, right?"

"Why not? Maybe he got sick of going somewhere to have it done if he could do it himself." I shrugged. "No different than someone with diabetes learning to give themselves shots, right?"

"I guess, but then what would he do with the all the blood? Just dump it down the sink?" Tracey visibly shuddered.

"Or dump it in the woods," I murmured. I pulled out my phone and dialed Garrett.

"Everything okay?" he asked.

"Yeah. Tell me when they found all that blood on the ground that's how they knew Ava was dead, right?"

"Yes, that's why she was presumed dead."

"Presumed."

"Sure. No body so we can only deduce that she's dead."

"What if it wasn't her blood?"

"It was definitely her blood. The lab tested it and confirmed."

"Oh." I chewed my lower lip as I thought. "What if someone took her blood and dumped it there? Or she even drew her own blood?"

"First of all, she would've had to draw a lot of blood. Not just a couple tubes full like you have done when going for a blood test. Why go to that extreme to disappear? It wasn't like she had a life she needed to run from but if she wanted to walk away, she could've picked up and done that at any time and nobody would've blinked an eye besides maybe her mother."

He had a point.

"Okay, I'll talk to you later."

"I thought I'd swing by with a couple steaks around six and we could break in your barbecue," he said.

I glanced over at the covered stainless cooker sitting behind me on my patio gathering dust. "That sounds nice but make it a bit later. Around seven o'clock. I've got some errands to do."

"I love you."

"Love you too." After I ended the call I explained what Garrett said and then returned to looking through the books on the grass. I didn't find any more hidden notes so I went back to answering emails on my laptop. Tracey sprawled out on the grass and appeared to doze for a few minutes while I worked. When she woke up I told her I had some errands to do. She glanced at her phone and said the garage called to say they were still waiting on a part for her car.

"Do you mind driving me home?"

I agreed to do that and we packed up the box of Ron's stuff and climbed into the car. Tracey lived in the basement apartment of a small older two-level house in town.

"You know where I live now so you can just come over anytime," she said as I pulled to the curb. "Or, you know, text me so we can do coffee or tea or burgers or even just hang since you don't drink and I don't need to drink either so…"

She hopped out and mouthed *text me* as she offered me a wave and a smile.

Once she was inside her place I punched an address into the navigation system. It was the cottagey area at Oak Lake mentioned in Ron's book. I'd never frequented the area before but it was only an hour each way so I'd be back in plenty of time for dinner with Garrett.

I stopped for gas and checked my phone before hitting the road again. There was a message from Katie saying that she had come up with a list of places Ron used to go and she believed they could all be areas that would be useful in my investigation. She didn't include the list, instead, she told me which nights she was free to go to dinner and named the steak house she preferred.

"Katie at her best." I just shook my head.

Part of me felt bad for my old friend because she lost so much after last year. She'd nearly been killed because she was connected to me and then she lost her mom and her home. Although the fact that she had to grow up and get a job or two to survive like the rest of the world might actually be a good thing.

As I drove up to the lake area I thought about Tracey and how easy things were with her. My only other true experience with friendship had been my friendship with Katie. Being with Katie had always been a tumultuous whirlwind of activity and, at the end of the day, Katie did what was best for her. Tracey wasn't like that. She was easygoing and made me feel interesting. I was cautiously optimistic about the idea of having a friend.

Dr. Chen would be so proud of me.

The Oak Lake area had one corner store with a gas station, an ice cream shop and a small commercial building with a combination of insurance and housing sales. I decided to stop for an ice cream before I headed out for a look-see around the lake. The woman serving up soft-serve behind the counter looked as old as the town. After I paid her for my cone, I showed her Ron's picture on my cell phone.

"Do you ever remember seeing this guy around here?"

She took readers out of her pocket and slid them up her nose before she glanced at the picture. "Ronald Low. The guy who killed that nice Ava girl. Haven't seen him lately on account of he's dead but then you know that already because you're that weird girl who found him."

She was a helluva lot smarter than I gave her credit for and she watched a lot of news. I took a long lick of my ice cream cone.

"So before Ron turned up dead, or even before Ava went missing, any chance you saw just him or even the two of them together out here? I understand he enjoyed hiking up this way."

"Nope, never saw either of them up this way but of course saw her mom from time to time." She motioned for me to step aside so she could take the order of two boys behind me.

After she'd served them I walked back up to the counter. "Ebba Johansson? You've seen her around here?"

"Well, sure, but not lately. Not since her daughter was killed. Who feels like coming out to their lake cottage after that? Always said she'd retire here but who knows what'll happen now."

"I didn't know she had a place out here…" I stared out the window as if I could see the cottage or the lake from where I stood, but access to the lake was still a half mile away and the other side of the street was only dense bush and tall cedars. "When was the last time you saw her?"

"Not sure. I heard rumor she was trying to sell that massage business of hers and maybe she'll sell this place too. Can't say I blame her. Your only kid dies. What else you got to live for, right? She should get a pretty penny for the cottage. All the small lakeside cabins out that way are selling off and they're being replaced with McMansions. Guess our lake is the next hot spot to buy real estate. Who woulda thought, right?"

All kinds of thoughts started spinning through my head. I looked out the window and then gave another lick to my cone. "So how far is Ebba's cottage from here?"

"The creek overflowed this spring and took out most of the road out that way so the road is closed for repairs. If you're up for the walk, it's about a mile by trail. You start off to your right when you're in the parking lot at the boat launch. You'll pass a couple other small cottages that are going to get torn down and rebuilt too. Ms. Johansson's is the third one on that side of the lake. A small white house with gray shutters." She tilted her head at me. "Not that you're going to find anyone or anything up that way on account of the road's closed and nobody's living in the other cottages. Don't know why you'd bother. Ebba's too busy grieving so she ain't been around."

"Maybe I'll just enjoy the walk around the lake then."

She offered me a derisive snort.

After I thanked her for her time I returned to my vehicle. The heat of the day had the ice cream racing to cover my fingers. I did some fast lick-slurp maneuvers so that not a drop was wasted. I drove through town to the boat launch's empty lot and parked facing the lake. It was a beautiful view. The lake was so calm and clear it acted like a mirror to the pines that surrounded it. I reached for my phone and took a picture of the view. I went to send the photo to Garrett along with a text of my location before heading on my hike but there was no cell range. Guess that would have to wait. I reached in the back seat for my pack only to find it wasn't there.

"Shit."

I popped the trunk to look but knew it would be empty. I'd left my pack in the kitchen with my dowsing rods and a few water bottles and had completely neglected to grab it when I left to drop off Tracey. Oh well, it wasn't like I was climbing Mount Baker. Even by Ron's hiking book notations this trail was rated easy and considered just a stroll around the lake without any inclines or challenging terrain.

I checked my phone for the time. It was an hour to get back home and a mile each way to check out this cottage. Even if I meandered a bit and took in the view I'd be back in plenty of time to be with Garrett feasting on barbecued steaks by seven. It was a nice leisurely one-mile stroll so it wasn't like I needed a pack full of water bottles and granola bars but it would've been helpful to have my rods. Especially because it was as likely a place as any for Ava's body to be dumped. Maybe even a more than likely location.

"I'll just have to make my own."

I didn't want to be hauling my purse around on the trail so I stuffed it under the back seat and locked up. I stuck my phone and keys in my pockets and set out to the edge of the boat launch parking area where a visible trail disappeared after a few feet into the bush. It didn't take me long to find a forked branch growing out of a tree that lined the trail. With apologies to the tree, I broke it off and cleared it of leaves and shoots. It had been a long time since I'd used old-school divining rods, and just holding the Y-shaped branch took me back to that first time.

"If you have the knack, they'll help you find water," Gramps told me.

Neither one of us had counted on rods helping me find dead people instead.

Even with sweat pooling in my armpits from the heat, that early memory iced my veins.

With a shudder I held the Y arms of the branch in

each hand, leaving the stick part pointing in the direction I was headed. The minute I stepped farther down the shade of the trail I felt my body relax a little. I walked with the rod out front and breathed deep the fishy scent of the lake and piney smell of the giant cedars around me. The path was weed-choked and hard-packed dirt and obviously hadn't been used a whole lot but it wound scenically, following the bend in the lake.

I thought about everything I knew about Ava and Ebba and knew something was entirely off about the ransom murder thing. Ron had never felt like a likely suspect. Maybe Ebba killed her daughter and faked the ransom note. I don't think Ebba hated her daughter, but it could've been done in an argument. I knew from my own experience that family relationships were complicated and seldom how they appeared. She could've killed Ava in a fit of rage. And if she killed Ava, maybe she killed Ron to cover it up? But then she leveraged her business to get the ransom and called me in to find Ava's body? What would the purpose of that be? If she was the killer, why wouldn't she just lay low and hope Ava's body was never found?

I paused as I came upon the first cottage, which had a massive wraparound porch with a perfect view of the lake, but the entire building leaned precariously to one side. The new owners would no doubt level it but they'd have themselves a great location.

An annoying fly buzzed the sweat around my upper lip and I swatted it away and wished I'd thought to buy a water bottle from the ice cream shop before going on this jaunt. I picked up my pace, rod out in front of me, just wanting to get this over with. As I walked another

idea occurred to me. Ava could've sent the ransom to
her mother to get the money. Her note inside Ron's hiking trail book sounded like she was excited to travel
with him. Maybe he wasn't quite as excited about her
and she killed him in the caves and then sent Mommy
a letter to try and get out of town forever. I'm sure she
could've faked her own death somehow with all that
blood but I wasn't sure. From everything everyone told
me, the relationship could've been a one-way street.
She loved him and Ron was just not that into her. If
she had faked her own death, hiding out at the cottage
until she could make her escape seemed pretty likely.

The second cottage was only a couple hundred
yards or so from the first and was in roughly the same
shape. The land had been cleared behind and I could
see clearly to the road that would've been the regular
access to these houses had it not been closed. Windows of the cottage were boarded, the door hung off
its hinges, and some development sign was displayed
prominently in back facing the road. I thought I felt
a tremor in the branch in my hand and I paused and
stared hard at it for a couple minutes.

"If you're going to do something, just do it," I grumbled.

I tried stepping a few feet right and then left but
the rod remained still. Some dowsers had better luck
with a tree branch but my copper divining rods had
always been more in tune to my skill. Still, I hoped
this branch would give me an indication if Ava's body
was around these parts somewhere. I never thought to
ask, but I'm sure Garrett would tell me the police had

done a thorough search of this area once they found out Ebba owned land here.

At one point I paused to take in the view of the lake. I let the branch dangle from one hand as my other went to touch the wedding band still around my neck. Although it might seem weird, it felt comforting to have this token of my parents' ill-fated match around my neck. I checked my phone but still no signal so I marched on with a mosquito chomping my right ankle and some gnats tickling my ears.

Dense shrubs briefly swallowed the trail, leaving me to wonder if I'd somehow lost my way, but when I pushed through I could see the small white cottage with the gray shutters just off to my right. I took a picture of it with my phone. It was just a simple building but my heart thudded painfully as I approached it. Warily I pushed away branches from my face until I got to the house's yard and then began stomping through the knee-high weeds.

A movement in the grass to my left nearly caused me to scream but it was only a cute brown bunny getting away from me. I breathed a sigh of relief and hoped I wouldn't pick up a tick or step on a snake in this tall grass as I trudged forward. The branch didn't move at all and I was both disappointed and relieved. If Ron killed Ava at the state park a hundred miles from here, it felt ridiculous to think he'd drive her all the way here to dump her body and if Ebba killed her own daughter she wasn't likely to have brought the body here either.

I stopped walking once I got to the wooden stairs of the cottage. The place looked quaint but unused and badly in need of paint. The curtains were all drawn tightly closed with nobody enjoying the sparkling lake view but me. I sat down for minute, putting my self-made dowsing rod on the step beside me, and looked out to admire Ebba's view. It was pretty damn awesome. The sound was a cacophony of birdcalls and honeybees and the smell was of lake water and pine. If you were going to retire and get away from it all, this would've been a good way to do that.

Turning back to face the cottage, I took in the faded wood siding. It really would be a great place to get away from it all. I hoped if Ebba had sold it that the new owners wouldn't tear the place down and build what the ice cream lady had called a McMansion. Sure, it wasn't in perfect shape but, unlike the other two that were beyond salvage, this one just needed a little TLC. A slap of paint and a few boards replaced and it would be good as new.

I left the branch on the stairs and walked toward the door. The steps moaned softly as I walked up. I thought I heard muffled crying but when I strained to listen, a murder of crows cawed and cackled in the blackberry bushes nearby. I reached for the screen door and it creaked loudly on rusted hinges. I expected to find the inside door locked but the handle turned easily.

"Hello?" I called out.

Once inside the dim cottage, my eyes strained to adjust to the darkness.

"What are you doing here?" a woman's voice sniffed.

"Ebba?" I squinted my eyes and turned in the direction of her voice.

"You were expecting maybe Ron's ghost?" She hiccupped loudly and then belched. I was about to ask her if she'd been drinking but the stench of wine wafted over to me just as the question formed on my lips.

"Sorry, I didn't mean to just walk in." Finally my eyes adjusted to the hazy lighting. "I didn't expect to find anyone here."

All the furniture was covered in white sheets. Ebba Johansson sat on an overstuffed chair in the corner. There was a bottle of wine between her knees and no glass in sight.

"I could say the same about you." Her words were slurred and her lipstick smeared. "Never thought I'd see you here either."

She pointed a manicured finger at me, then lifted the wine bottle to her lips to drink. After she guzzled what was left inside she let the bottle just drop to the floor where it toppled over on its side next to a couple of full bottles.

"Sit down. Let's chat."

She nodded toward the sofa next to her chair. I hesitated at first but then walked over and sat down. Dust lifted off the covers as I landed on the couch.

"I guess this is a pretty peaceful place to get away from it all," I said. "The view is amazing."

"Mortgaged to the hilt but, hey, what do I care? Worked my ass off to buy it so I'm hanging on to it a little longer." She lifted her chin proudly and then tilted her head at me. "Why are you here? Shouldn't you be out stomping around Washington State with your rods looking for my poor daughter?"

An odd smile played on her lips at the end of that statement.

"Just thought this might be as good a place as any

to have a look," I told her. "Did Ava ever come out here with you?"

"Once or twice on her own with some guys. Maybe even with Ron. She'd party here and leave a mess. She never wanted to come out here just to relax with me."

When she got to the last couple words her voice hitched and she began to sob. I let her cry. She'd lost her daughter. Sure she was sitting in a cottage in the woods by herself and getting drunk but who was more entitled to do that than someone who'd lost their kid to a violent death? It was unbearably hot and stuffy in the house.

I pulled my damp T-shirt away from my chest and blew air onto the pendant nestled in my cleavage while Ebba cried. I wanted to reach over and comfort her but I didn't know how. I wasn't exactly raised knowing how to show affection. If I ever cried, I was given a reason to.

After a few minutes, Ebba blew out a long breath and then she picked up her purse from the floor. She dug inside and took out a fistful of tissue and blew her nose noisily.

"Seems stupid, you coming out here," she snapped at me. "You know what? I'm going to let you go. You are free." She waved an unsteady hand at me. "Consider yourself off the clock. I don't need you anymore."

"If that's what you want."

"Why are you here anyway?" she barked.

"Like I said, I thought this would be as good a place as any to come and look. I saw a note from Ava about this place in a book that was with Ron's belongings."

I explained about the hiking book and Ava's notation about this location and being with Ron forever.

Ebba looked bewildered. "She gave him a book?"

"Yeah, I know they'd broken up, so it seemed kind of an odd thing to do especially since the receipt I found said she bought him the book after they were supposedly not together anymore. Anyway, the message from Ava made me wonder if maybe they'd visited here and, you know, maybe Ron had…well, dumped her here."

"That stupid, idiotic child." Ebba shook her head angrily and left me to wonder who was the stupid one, Ava or Ron, and why. "Stupid. Stupid. Stupid," she spat.

"That's not why you came." Suddenly she fixed me with an angry glare. "You don't believe Ron dumped her here. Why the hell would he kill her all the way a hundred miles away and then drive her a-a-a-l-l-l the way over here…halfway across the state to dump her body?"

"I was asking myself the same thing and—"

"Do you think I'm a moron?"

I looked at her and didn't reply. I knew better than to reason with an angry drunk. Even whenever that angry, unreasonable lush was myself.

"Who came with you?" she asked. "You got your FBI boyfriend and half the state wasting time looking for Ava out here? Can a grieving mother get no peace at all?"

"Nobody else came so you're good." I glanced at my phone. Still no signal. I got to my feet. "How about you give me a call tomorrow and we can talk some more when you're not—"

"Drunk?" She laughed but there was no humor in it, just sadness. "God, it's like Satan's kitchen in here."

She reached up and tugged at her hairline and next thing I knew she was bald as a cue ball and a wig was dropped on the floor on top of the empty wine bottle. I could only stare.

"Cancer," she said as she rubbed the top of her head. "Doesn't that suck? Worked my ass off so I could retire here and leave the business to that stupid daughter of mine and now it's all gone."

"I am so very sorry." And I meant it. "I didn't know."

"Nobody knows. Except Ava." She sighed, reached for another bottle of wine and unscrewed the top. "Whatever. No use in pretending anymore, right? What for? The insurance company finally paid out for Ava, so…" She raised the bottle to me before taking a drink. "Might as well celebrate. This is what it was all for." She waved a hand to encompass the room. "Just so I could die here, looking at the lake and not in my stupid apartment."

I didn't know what to say to that but I was hot and tired and didn't want to just sit here smelling the wine and watching Ebba get drunk.

"Do you have any food here? Can I make you a sandwich or something?" I got to my feet. "I'm meeting my boyfriend for dinner so I have to get going."

"Sit. Down," Ebba yelled.

I remained standing. Then she got up and slammed the wine bottle down on the table in front of me.

"Drink," she ordered.

"You're on your own there," I said.

Ebba reached in her purse and pulled out a huge silver revolver and pointed the gun directly at me.

"Sit down and have a goddamn drink."

THIRTEEN

I SLOWLY LOWERED myself back onto the sofa without taking my eyes off the gun.

"You're depressed about Ava and being sick and all," I began in a soft, reasonable tone. "But this isn't the answer. Put the gun away and let's talk."

"About what?" She plunked herself back down in the chair but kept the gun pointed at me. "You know the truth. Don't even pretend you don't."

I blinked at her. "Truth about what?"

"That Ava isn't really dead. That we faked it for the insurance money."

"I—I didn't know that…" Jesus! I rubbed the sweat at the back of my neck. "Then why hire me to find her body if you knew she wasn't dead?"

"Because, you idiot, the insurance company was dragging their feet. They wanted to wait until there was an actual body before they paid me but I don't have that kind of time. Doc said I've got maybe six months left if I'm lucky. So when Denny suggested I call you up I figured I might as well. Getting you to look for Ava with all the media in the world watching was perfect. Distraught mom is willing to go to any extreme measures and will even hire some kook to find her daughter's body. It hurried things along. I told the papers how expensive it was to hire you and I'd lost all that money gathering the ransom so it made the insurance company look bad they hadn't paid out. So a few days ago they finally cut me a check."

"I don't get it." I pinched the bridge of my nose. "If you're dying, why did you need to fake Ava's death? And who killed Ron?"

"Poor ol' Ron was just collateral damage." Ebba belched loudly. "'Scuse me." Then wiped her lips with the back of her hand, smearing lipstick across her cheek.

"Wait? Did Ava kill Ron?"

Or was I sitting here with a murderer and nobody even knew where I was? My stomach began to ache.

She didn't answer but I wanted to keep her talking. If I could get her to keep talking and keep drinking maybe I'd get lucky and she'd pass out. Or at least drop the gun.

"What about all the blood? Was it Ron's blood left at the scene?"

"Of course not." Ebba rolled her eyes. "CSI people check DNA and such. We're not stupid. We watch the crime shows. Ron had that weird blood condition. Too much iron. He had to get blood taken as a way to keep him healthy. He had a nurse come to the house to do it and sometimes Ava was there and she watched the nurse do it. That's what gave her the idea. She took a few of the phlebotomy packages off the nurse's bag when she was busy."

"So it was Ava's idea."

"Yes, her idea was that she'd fake her death. I tried to sell my business when I got sick but the market wasn't giving much. Ava figured rightly that in a few months she was going to be left high and dry. I could leverage the business to get a hundred thousand for the ransom and give that cash to her. Then I'd get the insurance money and split it with her and then she and Ron could go off to South America and live happily ever after once I was cold and stiff in the ground."

"Oh and Ron was okay with that? He was okay leaving his mom, dad and brother behind and making the world think he kidnapped and killed Ava?"

"That wasn't the original plan," Ebba admitted. "Ava was going to fake her death and just leave blood in her apartment. She figured she'd take off and then send for Ron but I knew it would be more believable if there was a ransom note and a fall guy."

"So you wrote the note on Ron's computer and mailed it to yourself, and then you killed him."

My hands were clutched into tight fists at my side. She was old, sick and drunk. I could totally take her if I could keep her talking long enough that she relaxed with the gun.

"Yeah, I followed him down to those godforsaken Bat Caves. Almost broke my frigg'n neck!" She pursed her lips angrily. "He sent Ava a message to meet him at the caves so they could talk. I met him with my trusty friend instead." She indicated the gun that was still pointed at me. "I got the ransom note printed off his computer and told Ava that Ron and I had it all arranged that he would fly to South America and meet her there. They were to have no contact and she was supposed to lay low for a couple months until the insurance paid out. I'd get half the insurance money to help me die in peace and she'd get the other half to add to the hundred thousand she already got from the ransom. She'd run away to be with him once I was dead. Except, of course, she didn't know he was already dead. I knew she'd cry over that but she'd meet someone else. Even though she claimed to love Ron, she would've met another loser just like him in a heartbeat. When Ron didn't show up in South America, she'd just think she got blown off and hook up with someone new."

"And so where is she?"

"I don't know!" Ebba wailed. "She was supposed to come here and leave me a note under my mattress of a place we could meet so we could at least say goodbye. Maybe have one last day or two together but I've been checking for weeks and no note.

"Now she's probably pissed at me because by now she will have heard that you found Ron's body and she probably figured out that I killed him." She rubbed her eyes and lowered the gun briefly before leveling it back at me. "All I wanted was for you to make a show of looking for Ava's body and, of course, there was no Ava's body so it was just for show to pressure the insurance company. So you screwed everything up finding Ron. Thanks a ton, missy!"

I licked my lips nervously. "So maybe Ava will show up here and the two of you can run off together. I'll just leave and, if you like, I can keep pretending to look for her, you know, so the journalists think I'm still on the search for Ava's body for you." I was rambling and trying to keep her talking and thinking about anything except killing me.

"Too late for that because you know everything." She narrowed her eyes at me. "This is how it's going to play out. You're going to drink that bottle of wine in front of you and then you're going to drink this other one next to me."

"I'm not going to—"

"Shut up!" Ebba raised the gun and closed one eye as if taking aim. "You are going to drink that wine and then, as soon as the sun sets, I'm going to paddle you out to the middle of the lake in our canoe and drop you over the side." She smiled a sickening saccharine grin. "The water is cold mountain runoff and it's very deep with a deceptive undertow. It'll be over in less than a couple minutes. Everyone knows you're a drunk and so they'll all assume you fell in while looking for Ava."

She got up and walked over to stick the gun right between my eyes. "Hand me your phone and your keys."

The barrel of the gun pressed against my forehead as my fingers fumbled in my pocket.

Please don't let her finger slip.

I tossed the keys onto the table and then dropped the phone on the floor, hoping she'd look away long enough that I could overpower her. She only laughed and kicked the phone away from my reach then walked backward and squatted to pick it up. For a woman who'd drunk a lot of wine, she was very much in control. Far more than I was going to be if I drank the bottles she was insisting.

"I could just leave and close your case," I said quickly. "The cops aren't going to figure out that you killed Ron and I sure won't tell them. It's not like it'll make him undead for everyone to know. None of my business, right? I'm happy to let sleeping dogs lie."

Ebba rolled her eyes at me as she unscrewed the

cap off the bottle of wine. She thrust it into my hands. "Bottoms up."

She sat down on the coffee table so close that our knees touched. If she shot me that would blow her story. If I had a gunshot wound then people wouldn't believe I drowned in a drunken stupor.

As if reading my mind she said, "If I have to shoot you, I will." She reached over and tapped the bottle with the gun. "It just means I'll have to wrap your fingers around the grip after you're dead so your fingerprints are all over the gun and people will think it was a suicide. You broke in here and found the gun and wine I keep here. You're crazy and you're a drunk. Everyone knows that, so it would be no biggie."

Three hundred thirty-four.

"I've been sober for three hundred thirty-four days."

"Well, hurray for you but now's the time to end things on a high note. Get it? A hi-i-igh note?" She giggled and then burped loudly before leveling the muzzle of the gun at my head. "Drink."

I looked down at the bottle in my hands. It was a cheap merlot. Not that I was a fussy drunk. Tentatively I lifted it to my lips. Maybe after being sober this long and so many months of therapy my body would physically reject the alcohol. Although it wasn't a pretty plan, if I projectile vomited all over Ebba there was a small chance it would cause her to falter and allow me to gain the upper hand.

The first sip of wine passed my lips like a welcomed lover. It was closely followed by a longer, deeper swallow. Almost immediately a rush of warmth spread from my belly to my extremities. I lowered the bottle and wiped my lips with the back of my hand.

"You really don't need to do this, Ebba." My voice was soft and reasonable and gentle like I was talking to a small child. "You love your daughter and, surely, you don't want her to see you spend your last days in a jail cell."

She chuckled softly and shook her head. "Ava couldn't care less about me."

I thought about growing up without a mother and tossed out to grandparents who weren't fit to raise a rat and then I got angry. "She loves you. Obviously. How could she not? You've worked hard. Given her a place to live. A future."

"Stop talking!" Ebba yelled.

She grabbed the wine bottle by the bottom and lifted it to my mouth, tipping it upward so that it poured into my mouth, and I was swallowing and choking and gasping and fighting her until it was nearly gone. I gagged and coughed and it took me a few minutes to catch my breath.

"You don't get it!" Ebba was furious now. "Ava's dad took off and left me to raise her. It was just the two of us. I was never what you'd call maternal. Sure, I put her in the best daycare centers and after-school programs but I worked long hours. I was determined to build something with my life. By the time I really paused and took a look at my daughter, she was already a train wreck."

The effect of the wine was hitting me hard and fast. I could feel the edges of the world growing blurry. I didn't have the resistance I used to have when two bottles or more would be a daily occurrence.

"She's young," I said, my words coming out slurred. "There is still a lot of time to make things good with Ava."

Which was an idiotic thing to say but then the stupid, drunk part of me was bound to bubble up.

"There is no time. I'm dying and there's no way that girl is going to get her shit together before I'm long gone. Everything else is leveraged to the hilt and I sold all my massage holdings to cover medical costs. The money from her own life insurance policy is all she'll get and, let me tell you, she positively salivated at the idea of getting that money and the ransom cash to start a new life fa-a-ar away from her dying mother."

"How is she getting the money? She can't exactly walk into the bank and withdraw it since she's supposed to be dead and all."

"I'm not an idiot, you know." She looked exasperated at having to explain things to me. "Everything is available for a price in this world. Set her up with fake ID and already transferred almost all the money into an account for her. All I've got left is enough to live on for the next few months. Here. Alone. In peace."

It seemed a dreadful way to go. I watched her unscrew the cap from another bottle of wine.

"So if you set it up so that she could access the money and leave the country, why were you expecting her here?"

"We had a deal." Ebba's voice grew softer and she had a faraway look to her eyes. "The deal was that she could get the money and a fresh life but she had to stop here to say goodbye to me. She agreed. She said she'd come spend a few hours, maybe even a day or two with me." She blinked back tears and then her voice got hard. "But I guess she changed her mind. She got what she wanted." She pushed the second bottle of wine into my hands. "Drink."

I didn't fight her now. The first bottle had already weakened me and as I drank, Ebba sobered up. Wine no longer felt like my enemy, and if I was going to die, honestly, I'd rather be hammered when it happened. The part of me that could reason with Ebba was being washed over and diluted by alcohol. The angry drunk part of me was there, though, and she was not going to get me into a canoe and try to drown me without me kicking up one helluva drunken brawl.

The sun was going down. I knew Garrett would be frantic but I was stupid and hadn't told him where I was going, and I'd left him no trail of breadcrumbs to find me. I needed to do this on my own. My best bet would be to break into a run as Ebba brought me out of the house toward the canoe. How much running can a drunken girl do when chased by a gun-wielding woman with nothing to lose? Hopefully, whatever I could muster would be enough.

After a few drinks from the second bottle of wine I purposely knocked it to the floor. Ebba reacted by slamming the revolver into my cheekbone with such force that I felt it shatter. The immediate swelling under my right eye left me vision impaired on that side. Not exactly a help considering my need to take flight.

Next, she nonchalantly picked up her wig and plopped it on her head like a jaunty beret.

"Let's go."

Ebba got to her feet and motioned with the gun for me to go ahead. I walked toward the front door, where she ordered me to stop. I tried to glance over my shoulder to see what she was doing and only caught a glimpse of her pulling something from a basket on the floor near the door.

"I'm not much of a pet person but Ava begged for a dog. Of course, she couldn't care for it any better than she could work a full-time job. She let the dog get out of the yard last year and it got hit by a car."

"I'm sorry," I mumbled, wondering why the trip down memory lane.

Abruptly I felt a cold, thick chain slide over my head and then a hard tug of the collar yanked me backward and had me coughing and choking. She'd put a dog's choke collar and leash around my neck.

"In case you get any smart ideas to take off before we're in the lake," she explained.

I felt my plans to escape slip through my fingers. As we headed through the front door I tried to find my footing on the steps in the dark. I tripped only to be yanked back by Ebba, causing another gasping fit as I clawed at my neck to loosen the chain.

"Slowly," she ordered. "The canoe's on the shore directly in front of the house. Maybe fifty feet. Don't try anything. I know this land like the back of my hand."

Except I was the one in front leading the way and I could hardly see anything beyond what was right in front of my face. I thought about the scrabble of shrubbery that had obscured a lot of the house from the trail. We were in bush now and I knew from seeing the area in daylight that the trees and shrubbery thinned as we got closer to the lake, and the last few feet would be sandy shoreline. I needed to try to break loose before we were in an area where she'd have a clearer shot at me.

"Just keep going and don't stop," Ebba said.

"There are lots of low branches," I pointed out.

I had one hand up around my neck, my fingers tucked between the chain and my throat to guard it from being pulled tight. A cool breeze licked off the lake and helped clear my wine-soaked brain. It had clouded over and the moon and stars were hidden, so there was little light at all. With me walking in front, Ebba couldn't see what was directly in front of me. When we pushed through some tree branches I pulled one away and then warned her before it swung and hit her in the face.

"Branch," I called out.

I felt a slight pull to the collar as Ebba stepped to the side to avoid a twig in the face. I didn't want to take the chance she'd get thwacked by a tree limb and shoot me when startled.

"You know, I'm really going to enjoy living out my final days here." Ebba sighed. "Sure it would've been nice to have Ava here with me, but she might decide to come around once she stops being all pissy about Ron." She huffed a little as we walked. "In fact, I bet she hasn't even left the country to get the money yet. She's probably just waiting for things to calm down and I'm betting she'll want to spend some time here with me before she leaves."

She was rambling and going on about how peaceful

it was around here and how proud she was that she'd managed to work hard enough to buy the cottage. I wanted to point out that all that hard work had cost her a relationship with her daughter, who'd turned her back on her now that she was dying. I kept my mouth shut because it wasn't going to win me any points while the woman held a gun pointed at my back.

"Branch," I announced.

When I felt the collar shift as Ebba sidestepped right, I deftly whirled and reached behind me with my right hand to grab the leash. I tugged her toward me with a furiously hard yank and, with my left hand, pulled the collar over my head. She let out an *oomph* when she slammed into me.

In a deft move that defied the wine in my system, I brought one leg behind both of hers and simultaneously pushed her chest with both my hands. She was off her feet and landing hard on her back in the time it took me to break free. I could hear her scrambling to her feet and screeching in rage as she struggled to come after me, but I was younger, faster and, sadly, had a lot of experience escaping people meaning to do me harm.

The temptation was to run back in the direction I'd come but I had no keys for my Jeep and that would be exactly the direction Ebba would assume I was going. Instead I took a sharp left at one point hoping that the sound of her own footsteps as she ran after me would cover up the stomping of mine going through brush off the trail. I knew from looking in Ron's trail book that a creek fed the lake, and a quarter mile north along its banks was a small community of older creekside cottages. I'm sure there was a separate road unaffected by the spring water that would access that community. Maybe I'd get lucky and find someone home there who could help me or a car driving by.

The clouds began to roll in, and for the first time in weeks it would be a starless night. I tried to move quietly through the thick brush but whenever I slowed my pace I could hear Ebba's footsteps also crunching on twigs. The wine made me feel clumsy and slow, and for an older sick person, Ebba seemed to be keeping up because whenever I'd pause I could hear her thrashing through the bushes.

Abruptly I was in a clearing, and to my left was a walking bridge that crossed over the creek. I could see more cottages on the other side and some had lights on but I stopped short. The bridge was at least fifty feet long and in the wide open. I'd be a clear target if I began walking across and Ebba caught up. The bushes were rustling nearby and she would soon be on top of me.

Instead of crossing over I decided to duck underneath the bridge. Thick blackberry brambles with long thorns poked and scratched at me but also made a perfect cover. I sat there, my bum on the damp creek bed and my arms wrapped around my knees. I curled my lips over my teeth, fearful that Ebba would hear them chattering. Footsteps sounded approaching the bridge. She was coming. I held my breath as the sound of her feet could be heard on the wood planks over my head and then they stopped there.

"Goddamn little bitch," Ebba muttered.

She stomped her feet directly above my head before walking forward on the bridge a few feet and then changing her mind and coming back. My heart pounded so hard that I was sure she'd be able to hear it even as I could hear the sound of her footsteps walking away.

After what felt like an hour I thought about breaking free from my hiding spot but I couldn't bring myself to do it. I debated waiting until daylight. It would make it so much easier to see where I was going but it would also make it easier for Ebba to see me and put a bullet through my chest. Hours went by and there were two other times I heard Ebba's footsteps nearby and at one point she crossed the walking bridge only to return quickly on a run as if she realized I hadn't made it across. She wasn't giving up.

Mosquitos snacked on my skin as the temperature dropped, and the first cool breeze in days began to raise goose bumps on my body. Frogs and crickets serenaded me as I strained my ears to hear the sound of feet in the bush. I was listening so hard that I was sure I was beginning to hear things. With my hands on my knees I took deep breaths and calmed my drilling heart and then forced myself to listen again. Voices. Male voices. And they were coming closer. I slowly made my way out of my thorny hideaway and crouched low as I moved around to the bridge side. I hunkered down behind a bush and stared down the road to my right. A glow of flashlights moved side-to-side scanning the road and ditches as a group of three men walked purposely in my direction. The stride and gait of one of those men was achingly familiar. I bolted from the bushes.

"It's me! Julie!" I called and my voice broke into a tearful cry.

Garrett ran to meet me and had me fully engulfed in his arms. My swollen cheek was being crushed against his chest but it didn't matter at all. Nothing else mattered.

"It's Ebba," I sobbed. "She killed Ron."

Garrett and the other two officers talked in hushed plans about circling the area. Suddenly the sound of a shot rang out, and I felt a sharp searing pain in my thigh. Garrett dragged me back into the woods where he searched for my wound with a flashlight and told me it wasn't bad.

"You're fine," he said. "You're okay."

He squeezed me tight against him and I sobbed quietly against his chest, breathing in the goodness of him. Over the next few minutes we heard the other officers searching and more gunfire sounded. Garrett covered my body with his and pushed me to lie flat in a bed of damp leaves. I shook violently against him and knew he could smell the wine on me.

"She made me drink. It wasn't on purpose. I didn't mean to—"

"Hush," he murmured into my neck. "It's okay. I'm here. You're okay. I've got you."

And the weight of his body on mine and his calming voice in my ear stripped the terror that shook my bones. We lay like that for what felt like an eternity. The sun was teasing the horizon by the time the officers came to us and announced they had Ebba in custody. I did not want Garrett to let me go.

THE WOUND IN my leg only required a couple of stitches but Garrett still insisted I spend a couple nights in the hospital for my mental health. He contacted Dr. Chen and told her what had happened and the next morning she came to visit me in the hospital. The overwhelming sense that I'd failed by drinking was a dark cloud of despair over me. Sure, I was forced to drink the wine but my body betrayed me by hoping someone held a gun to my head on a daily basis so I could have more. I reached for the pendant around my neck and clutched my father's wedding band for reassurance.

"And so you start over. Today is day one," Dr. Chen said gently. "Life is always about starting again and not giving up."

"I can do that. I can start counting again."

"Of course you can." She placed a hand on my arm. "You're a lot stronger than you think."

I didn't feel strong swathed in a hospital gown with my backside exposed.

Garrett brought Tracey to visit me in the hospital and they both stood at my bedside.

"She was the reason we were able to get to you as quickly as we did," Garrett explained. "When you were late and didn't answer your phone, I contacted the grocery store and got her number. She told me about the hiking book and the lake. We knew Ebba had a cottage there."

"Your old man here did all the real work," Tracey said. "I just told them where I thought you might be and he went into all hero mode."

"Thanks so much," I told her. "Guess you're my sidekick after all. We'll have to think of a nickname for you. Maybe something like Deputy Green Sprout."

She snorted. "No thanks."

Garrett stepped out of the room to take a phone call, and once he was gone Tracey drew her splinted fingers through her green hair in a nervous gesture.

"There's something else I need to tell you and you won't be thanking me for that. On the way here, your man talked to me about everything that happened to you. The break-in with your stolen laptop and your tires slashed and then he mentioned someone putting a bottle of wine in your car and how it freaked you out. That's what made me realize I mighta saw something that's important."

She took a breath and the suspense was killing me.

"Spit it out already," I told her.

"Okay, okay." She held her hands up. "So one time I came by to visit you and your dog was nutso in the window and I could hear him from the road. I slowed my car down as I drove by and saw this woman in your driveway. She opened your Jeep and stuck a bottle of wine in there. I figured it was a present from a friend, like a birthday gift or something, right? So I kept on driving."

"Woman? It was Ebba Johansson, wasn't it?"

"Nah, I saw Ebba's face on the news and it wasn't her. This gal was younger. She was about our age with a cheap blond dye job and driving an old brown four-door sedan."

"Oh my God." I exhaled loudly in disbelief. "Katie! How did she…and why would she?" Words failed me as I was slapped with a dose of disbelief and betrayal. She'd hurt me before and now, given a tiny window of opportunity, she'd lashed out again.

"This Katie a friend of yours?" Tracey asked.

"No. Definitely not. She's no Deputy Green Sprout."
I took her hand and squeezed.

Garrett came back into the room then and I filled
him in on what Tracey told me and he just kept shaking his head in disbelief. "I'm going to her place right
now and—"

I stopped him with a raise of my hand. "You're not
going to her place. I am."

I was discharged in the early afternoon after Dr.
Chen paid me a visit and pronounced me mentally
healthy enough to go out into the world. Garrett had
taken the time to discreetly place some calls. He found
out Katie wasn't working at her mall job or her fast-
food place today and an officer had recently driven by
her house and seen her vehicle in the driveway.

We dropped Tracey off at home on our way.

"You sure you don't need me to come along and slap
this ex-friend for you?" she asked as I walked her to
her door. "I'm stronger than I look."

"I'm sure you are, Sprout, but I gotta do this on my
own," I told her.

"Okay. Shoot me a text and let me know how it all
went."

I nodded and then, abruptly, I leaned in and hugged
her. "Thanks for everything."

"Aw-w-w. It's what friends do for friends," she replied, hugging me back.

I returned to Garrett's sedan and once we were close
to Katie's I began to feel more confident. "I'd like to
confront her by myself."

"Not a chance," he replied.

"But—"

"No. You don't know what she's capable of."

We pulled into the driveway of a dilapidated old house with a weed-choked yard and Garrett walked beside me to the door. Even as I rapped my knuckles against the peeling paint part of me wished she wasn't going to be home, but she answered almost immediately.

"Oh hey-y-y."

Katie stood there in a ratty bathrobe and looked from me to Garrett and back again. "I'd invite you in but, as you can see, I'm about to get in the shower, so-o-o…"

I pushed my way past her into the living room. There on the coffee table was my laptop. A ball of fury in my gut had me putting fists on my hips and raising my voice.

"So you drugged Wookie just for a stupid frigg'n laptop?"

"That's not yours!" she protested. She ran to the coffee table and closed the lid on the laptop. "It's mine. You're not the only one that can afford a newer computer! I work two goddamn jobs, you know!"

She stood there straightening her bathrobe and attempting to look at me with righteous indignation but she only looked weak and pathetic. I was finally seeing Katie for the person she really was.

"It's mine and not only did you steal from me, you put a bottle of wine in my Jeep. Why? Because you thought that would bring me down?" I shook my head. "Don't even try to deny it because it was all on camera." I hooked a thumb in the direction of Garrett. "He had cameras installed everywhere on my property."

"And the cameras at the shopping center showed you were the one who slashed her tires," Garrett piped up. "You popped the trunk and then climbed inside and got her address from the insurance papers in the glove box."

"You think you're such hot stuff," Katie yelled, running her fingers through her greasy bottled blond hair. "If it wasn't for me you woulda had no one growing up! No one! I was your only frick'n friend. When my life went to shit last year because of *you*, you were nowhere to be found. Too busy living in your new house, driving your new Jeep and screwing your FBI boyfriend. You owe me, Delma." She drew out my old name on her tongue as a taunt, and then sneered. "You owe me big-time." She tucked hair behind her ears. "So what ya gonna do now?" She stuck her arms out, wrists up toward Garrett. "If you're here to arrest me, just do it already."

"I'm not going to have you arrested. You say I owe you? Now we're even," I said quietly. "Just stay away from me and mine, you got that? Stay away. Forever."

I stomped out of the house in a whirl of anger that was mostly all tears and raw hurt.

Garrett joined me in the car a few minutes later.

"You won't be hearing from her again. I guarantee it." He turned and kissed my tear-stained cheek. "You okay?"

I nodded. "Just take me home, please."

WOOKIE GREETED ME like I'd been gone a year. He'd been well cared for by Garrett in my absence but he needed to give me a hundred licks and needed two hundred head pats to make everything right again. It was my pleasure to give him all the attention he needed and I didn't get annoyed with him when he climbed in bed with Garrett and me for a snuggle that night.

The next day I insisted on a road trip with Garrett.

When he parked in the boat launch parking lot near the spot I'd left my Jeep before, he asked, "Why are we here?"

I could hear the anxiety in his voice as he covered it with an exasperated sigh. Maybe part of him thought I was some masochist wanting to relive the terror.

"Just humor me." I hoisted my pack from the back seat of his car. "If nothing else, it's a beautiful day for a walk around the lake and it's a very easy hike. So easy—" I elbowed him in the ribs "—even a soft federal agent like yourself can handle it."

He mumbled something under his breath about not being soft and I giggled. I smiled sweetly as he insisted on carrying my pack after I'd retrieved my dowsing rods.

He leaned forward and kissed me chastely on the nose. I wrapped my arms around his neck and brought my mouth to his kissing him deeply until we were both breathless.

"Have you ever done it in the woods before?" I breathed against his mouth.

"Certainly not while someone was poking the back of my head with dowsing rods."

I laughed and we trudged down the trail. "Yeah, so as you know I forgot my pack that day and made myself a divining rod out of a branch." I walked ahead holding the rods out in front of me. "Using a branch isn't exactly my thing. Sure, that's how I learned but it isn't as…well, the vibe isn't as strong." I glanced over my shoulder. "Does that make sense?"

"Nothing you do makes sense but carry on."

"Right well, I remember there was a spot where I felt the branch offer a tremor. Barely a shake but it was…something."

"And what was it?"

"That's the thing." I glanced back. "I was determined to get to Ebba's cottage and thought I had more than enough time to check the trail a little more thoroughly on my trip back to the car."

"But, of course, you didn't."

"Nope. Things got a little crazy," I said in the understatement of the decade.

It felt good walking the trail with Garrett. We paused at one point to smile at a squirrel who'd stopped half up a tree to glare and chatter at us.

"Do you remember where it was that you felt the branch move?" Garrett asked.

I stopped and looked around.

"I thought it was before this point but I could be wrong," I told him. "I know it was near one of the other cottages before Ebba's place." We'd already passed one of those houses. "Let's go as far as Ebba's before we turn around and head back."

I didn't want to go that far. I didn't want to see the small white house with the gray shutters that looked so innocent. I concentrated on the trail and the beautiful summer day. The air was thick with the smell of cedar trees and lake water and even the gnats who buzzed my face didn't dampen my feeling that all was right with the world. Until it wasn't.

The rods both pulled right and I stopped in my tracks and nodded. "This way."

We turned and walked through thick shrubs.

The bush opened onto tall knee-high grass that swayed in the breeze and parted as we walked only to close around and disappear around our feet. I followed the rods slowly and deliberately, allowing them to lead me like they had countless times before, knowing that in the end there'd be a body.

When the rods pulled right again I followed and when they crossed in an X pattern it was under a giant monkey tree where the grass was nearly waist high. At the sight of pink high-tops I stopped cold.

FOURTEEN

GARRETT MOVED AROUND ME to take a closer look.

"It's Ava," Garrett confirmed over his shoulder.

"Did her mother kill her?"

"She's been here a while. I don't see any visible sign of being shot, and Ebba confessed to everything but never once mentioned anything but concern about Ava. Then again, who knows? I think we'll have to wait for the coroner to rule on cause of death."

I turned away from Ava's body to view the tranquil lake that peeked between the trees and bush we'd just traipsed through. This peaceful lakeside community was about to be forever tainted.

We stayed with the body until others arrived and then walked back to Garrett's car in silence. Once buckled up and headed back, he thanked me for helping them find the body. I didn't want to think of Ava dying however long ago in that field. And I didn't want to believe her own mother had killed her in a fit of maniacal rage.

"Could we get ice cream?" I asked, wanting and needing at least one thing to be that simple.

On the drive home from the lake with ice cream cones in our hands I casually mentioned to Garrett about changing my name.

"I started using my middle name partly because I didn't want the name my mother gave me and also because that was the name my grandparents called me. I figured they were the ones raising me."

I took a long lick from my cone knowing that saying my grandparents raised me was a huge understatement. I'd survived in spite of that upbringing.

"So you're thinking about going back to being Delma?" Garrett asked.

"Maybe," I admitted. "I'm going to give it some thought."

Even though Garrett was in the middle of his own investigations he managed to wrangle some time off. We spent a lot of time in bed and, when not in bed, Garrett spent a lot of time cooking. We had Tracey over for steak so that Garrett could finally use the new barbecue. Even though the sirloins were too well-done for my liking, we enjoyed each other's company.

"You two are kind of made for each other," Tracey remarked. "Sure you're lot different but you're also the same, you know?"

"I'm not at a-a-all like him." I elbowed Garrett in the ribs.

"And I'm sure not at all like her," Garrett protested, feigning insult. "She's crazy."

"Yeah, but you're both the good kind of crazy."

Then she sliced up a birthday cake she'd brought from the store even though it was nobody's birthday, and before the end of the evening I'd agreed to attend the next stitch and bitch with other women my age in the community.

THE NEXT MORNING Garrett told me the coroner report had come in on Ava Johansson's cause of death.

"Blood infection. She was septic."

"But how?" I frowned.

"She did a bunch of blood withdrawals and stored her blood to fake her own death but she wasn't careful with the needles. Coroner figured she gave herself a raging infection and it killed her. I'm guessing she was on her way to meet up with Ebba at the cottage when the infection did her in."

"That's so sad."

He shrugged. "I think it's more sad that all she wanted from her mother was cash. Her mother is dying and all she wanted was to get as much money as she could so she could take off once her mom was dead."

"Well, maybe in the end she was trying to meet her mother and spend time with her. I'd like to think that."

He nodded. "They did find a key for the cottage that she wore around her neck."

"I'm sure Ebba will go to her grave thinking her daughter was on her way to see her," I said. "And I'm sure that might bring her more comfort than thinking her daughter flew off to South America without saying goodbye."

"Ebba went off the deep end and almost killed you," Garrett said, his eyes hard. "I really don't care to bring her comfort in her dying days."

"Point taken." I leaned in and kissed him. I thought about the key to the cottage around Ava's neck and my own hand went to the wedding band around mine. It was time to try something I'd been avoiding.

"I want to try and find my mother."

Garrett watched as I removed the pendant from around my neck.

"I don't think this is such a good idea because—"

"I just want to try," I interrupted him. "I *need* to do this."

He'd watched me discover bodies using my divining rods but he'd never watched me pendulum dowse before. It wasn't something I did regularly. It had helped me once when Katie's life was in danger, but it never worked on a single case since. When I researched the topic I realized it might only work if I have a strong attachment to the person I needed to find. I looked at the wedding ring on the gold chain in my hand. Was there still enough attachment to a mother who'd tossed me to wolves?

I was about to find out.

Holding the chain up above the kitchen table, I stilled the band with my hand and waited until it no longer moved.

"Show me your yes," I whispered.

The ring began to swing ever so slowly in a pendulum fashion from left to right, east to west, in a deliberate sway. I stopped the movement with my free hand and waited again for it to become motionless.

"Show me your no," I whispered.

The ring swung north away from me and then south toward me, back and forth, back and forth, gaining momentum with every sway.

"Thank you," I said and, again, stopped it with my hand.

I drew in a deep breath and exhaled loudly. Garrett's eyes were on me and Wookie had taken up residence on my feet. I had all the love and support I ever needed but I still needed to know.

"Is my mother, Molly Arsenault, dead?"

The ring swung on the chain up and down giving me a vigorous *no* answer. I felt tears burn my eyes.

I stopped it from moving and took in another deep breath.

"Is she still in Washington State?"

Again, the ring began to move and this time it swung left to right to show a positive answer.

I turned to Garrett. "Could you tell me the names of all the cities where that big drug bust happened?"

"Well, sure, but are you going to ask that thing about every city and then every street in that city?" He rubbed the back of his neck nervously. This flew in the face of every kind of hard fact a federal agent relied on and I knew it was a lot for him to swallow.

"If I have to, I will."

He nodded and got up to retrieve his phone. When he got back, he tapped a couple minutes and then rattled off a few town names.

"Wait a second, did you say Marysville?"

He glanced at the list. "Yes, there was a known drug house just a few blocks down from where that Ted guy used to live with your mother."

I held up the ring on the chain again.

"Is my mother in Marysville?"

Immediately, the answer was a wild swing from left to right. The answer was yes.

A few minutes later we were on the road. I was jittery and anxious in the passenger seat of Garrett's sedan. He was silent and stoic as he drove down the highway. A half hour later we pulled up in front of the white bungalow with bright blue trim.

"You ready?" Garrett asked.

"Give me a second."

I closed my eyes and focused my thoughts on my breathing to relax my anxiety, then I ran my hand across the worn denim of my jeans. Feeling the texture so I could focus on the moment and not on my thumping heart. I looked over at the house and saw Fluffy the cat sitting in a window staring at me, and a memory hit me so hard it knocked the breath out of my lungs.

"You okay?" Garrett placed a hand on my leg.

"I remember." I swallowed thickly. "I remember living in an apartment. It was dirty. I slept on a mattress on the floor and there were cats. Two of them...white and fluffy. Mom always had cats."

It was the first time I'd ever remembered anything of my life before the day that my mother dropped me at my grandparents' place.

"You don't have to do this," Garrett said quickly.

"Yes, I do. If I don't do it right now, I never will."

I swung the passenger door open and climbed out. Garrett was at my side in a heartbeat and we walked together up to the front door. I didn't even have to knock before it was opened by the same woman, Ted's old girlfriend.

She looked from me to Garrett. "I figured you'd be back."

"I never got your name."

"Jia," she replied, stepping aside to let us in.

I didn't wait for permission and I didn't take off my shoes either. I just walked down the hall toward the bedroom. Jia and Garrett both followed but nobody tried to stop me. I flung the door open and there sit-

ting in an overstuffed chair that almost swallowed her
sat my mother with Fluffy on her lap.

A low moan escaped my throat as I froze in the
doorway. My mother got to her feet, placed the cat on
the ground and took a tentative step toward me.

"Delma?" she asked, pushing a strand of her waist-
long hair behind her ear with a frail hand.

"Yes," I murmured.

She opened her arms wide and I went to her. She
was all jagged bone and cocaine withered. As I pressed
her against me I felt like I could crush her with too
strong a hug so I only lay my head on her shoulder and
let my tears dampen her stained T-shirt.

She patted my back and whispered, "I'm so sorry,
Delma. I'm so very sorry."

A few minutes later we were all sitting in Jia's living room. Iced teas in our hands while Molly Arsenault
told the tale that was every addict's story. She chatted
about addiction and recovery and more addiction. She
talked about the lifestyle that brought her from one bad
relationship to another and one flophouse to another.

"I did come back for you after I went to rehab but
my mom told me you'd been adopted out," she whispered, her deep set eyes meeting mine.

"I know."

"Your grandma and gramps…"

"I know." I put a hand on her knee. "I know." I
didn't want to talk about the past and didn't want the
quicksand to swallow me if we talked about Grandma
and Gramps.

"How did you end up here?" Garrett asked her.

"After my last round in rehab I came back here to

see if Ted would put me up but, thankfully, Jia has a heart of gold and didn't put me out on the street."

"I figured she needed a break," Jia said and then added apologetically to me, "I didn't tell you she was here when you came to visit because she asked me not to."

I looked hard at my mother, taking in her emaciated form that looked so much older than her late forties. "How sick are you?"

"Well, I got the Hep C and my liver is shot." She wrung her bony hands nervously. "I don't have too long left so that's why I asked Jia not to tell you I was here. Didn't think you'd care to meet me now when it's too late."

"Better late than never," I replied and wondered inside if that was true.

We didn't stay much longer. There was a lot of exchanging of information. Mom didn't have a phone but she got my number and Garrett's and we got Jia's number as well. When we were leaving I saw Garrett slip a wad of bills into Jia's hands and tell her it was to help with groceries. It was a kindness that made me love him even more.

A couple days later we packed up my mother's one bag and her cat, Fluffy, and brought them both back to my house. Wookie was enthralled with my mother but less than impressed by her furry companion. That dislike between the fur-kids was mutual and there was a lot of woofing and a scratched nose before a tense truce happened.

Garrett went back to his own place because he had lots of work to do but I suspected he just wanted to give me time with my mother. I appreciated having her in my house, but we were polite strangers afraid to say anything much for the first couple of days. Her skin and eyes were leaning more and more toward a sickly yellow, and there was hardly anything she could eat that would stay down.

"Would you like some chicken noodle soup?" I asked.

"That would be nice," she replied. "Thank you."

She sat at the kitchen table wrapped in my thick housecoat, her hands gripping a cup of coffee as if for the warmth even though the house was too warm for me.

I brought her the soup and Wookie sauntered over and sat next to her. He placed his large head in her lap and she obliged him by stroking the top of his head with one hand and spooning soup into her mouth with the other.

"Wookie is a funny name for a dog," Molly mused. "Like those characters from *Star Wars*, right?"

"I didn't name him. I got Wookie from a friend and since he already answered to the name I didn't think I could change it."

She ate a little more soup and then put her spoon down and turned to me.

"Your dad loved *Star Wars*. I used to watch the movies a lot because they made me think of him." She closed her eyes and a faraway smile played on her lips. "One time you and me were staying at a crummy flea-bag motel and a couple next door were fighting real loud and you were scared. I made us some microwave popcorn and got a couple Cokes from the vending machine and we—"

"You turned the TV up real loud so I couldn't hear the fighting and we watched *Star Wars* and ate popcorn in the bed." The memory washed over me and took the air out of my lungs. I gasped as a flashback brought me the smell of microwave popcorn and the feel of thin motel sheets and the heady recollection of her arm around my shoulder and my head nestled into the crook of her arm. I blinked back tears as I finished. "I dumped some of the popcorn in the bed and you said it didn't matter because spills happen when you're having a party and we were going to party all night."

"Can't believe you remember that." She smiled and reached to give my hand a brief squeeze. This was the second time I ever remembered anything besides the back of her head as she drove away leaving me with my grandparents.

"It was only a day or two afterward when I made the call to get into rehab." She gave my fingers a brief squeeze before letting them go. "I left you at the farm because I had nowhere else to keep you while I went away, but I came back. Your grandma said you were adopted out and I hated it but knew it was for the best because who needs an addict for a mom, right?"

Over the next few weeks she told me stories of when I was little and told me things about my dad like how he snorted when he laughed and cried during movies. We didn't talk about the bad. My grandparents. We let the dead lie where they couldn't hurt either of us anymore.

FIFTEEN

WE BURIED MY MOM on a rainy Friday morning. Her plot was at a small, peaceful cemetery near my home, far away from the place where her own mother and father were laid to rest.

Garrett and I both took some well-needed time off then. We rented a cottage on the Oregon coast that was okay with a large, energized Rottweiler and a fuzzy white cat that were still getting used to each other.

We slept until noon and Garrett cooked and fattened me up on big morning breakfasts of omelets and hash brown potatoes and late evening cookouts on a deck overlooking the ocean. We'd end our days wrapped in each other's arms listening to the sound of the waves crashing against the beach.

Forty-nine days without a drink.

Starting over seemed to be part of life.

One evening on the deck, snuggled on a porch swing, Garrett asked me, "So you've decided then, to change your first name back to Delma?"

"Yes, I think I have." I snuggled in closer against a cool breeze drifting in off the ocean. "What do you think of that idea? Think you can get used to calling me Delma?"

"Sure, I could do that but…" He shrugged.

"What? You don't like it, do you?" I sat up and

frowned. It would be nice to go back to the name my mother gave me.

"I think," he said, pulling me tight against him, "you should consider changing your last name as well. To Pierce."

It was a suggestion that ended in a kiss that was long and slow and made me breathless.

"You want me to be your wife."

"I do. More than anything," he answered, trying to kiss me again.

"Garrett…" I lightly pushed him away. "We've had this conversation before. I want to be with you. I love how we are together but…" I sighed. "You want normal. I don't do normal."

"I don't want normal." He took both my hands in his, turned them upward and kissed my wrists. "I want you."

"That's what you say, but…"

"No buts." He pulled me tight against his chest. "I want this. I want us waking up together and going to sleep together."

Just then we heard Fluffy hiss and Wookie yelp like he'd been struck and we both laughed.

"And I want that." Garrett pointed a finger in the direction of our fur-children. "I don't just want it some of the time. I want it every day."

And I could feel in my heart I wanted that closeness too but I also didn't feel that pressing need to take another person's name.

"I want that too but…marriage…" I licked my lips nervously as I chose my words. "Could we try you moving in? I know it's a long commute into Seattle but Wookie needs the acres to run and, well, so do I. Or…" I sat up straighter and looked him in the eyes. "Or maybe I could sell the house and we could pick out a new place. Together. Somewhere closer to Seattle for you, but still far enough away for me. I know it's not marriage but, can we try that first?"

He pulled me close again and kissed the top of my head. "Yeah, baby, we can try that first."

Shortly after that time away, we went house hunting together and we found an older home with good bones that wasn't too far a commute. I moved first, making room in the closet for dark suits and pressed shirts and the spare room became an office where Garrett spent a lot of time when he wasn't in the field. As for my own work, I took a hiatus from finding the dead. My head and my heart needed time away from the turmoil of discovering bodies.

One thing I knew was true: there would always be more skeletons waiting to find their way home.

* * * * *

To purchase and enjoy more books by Wendy Roberts, please visit Wendy Roberts's website here: www.wendyroberts.com/books

Turn the page for an excerpt from Grounds to Kill *by Wendy Roberts, now available at all participating e-retailers.*

ACKNOWLEDGMENTS

THIS BOOK IS made possible by the tireless work of my editor, Deborah Nemeth, and the wonderful crew at Carina. I owe them much wine and chocolate!

Thanks, as always, to my agent, Melissa Jeglinski, for her support.

ONE

THERE'S A SUPERSTITION that says if the palm of your hand is itchy you'll soon be receiving money. If that were true, I'd be a gazillionaire instead of an underpaid barista. Instinctively, I felt my itchy hand might one day bring me luck. So far, nada.

I rubbed my burning palm on the countertop while I concentrated on whipping up a large café mocha, no sugar, no whip, extra-dry, half-skim, half-whole milk, with chocolate syrup.

"Watch your back, Jen." My coworker, Mitch, squeezed behind me to get to the cooler for more milk.

Mitch was tall and muscular with golden hair and eyes like hot espresso. When Mitch worked, Merlot's Café saw a fifty percent increase in female clientele. The estrogen-enriched customers flocked to flirt with him. They tended to hang around too long and talk too much, but I didn't mind. Mitch's hundred-watt smiles had a direct correlation to how the tip jar overflowed, and we shared gratuities. I reaped the benefits without having to sell my own soul with plunging necklines and pushup bras.

My palm was itching even more, so I snagged a wooden stir stick and scraped it roughly against my hand.

"Eczema acting up?" Mitch asked, raising his eyebrows.

I merely shrugged. No sense in complicating our working relationship by telling him I was crazy.

Mitch took a woman's coffee order, then elbowed me good-naturedly.

"Hey, look." He indicated outside the coffee shop with his chin. "It's your pal, Mr. Stinky."

He chuckled, but I didn't. My teeth clenched as I glanced out the coffee shop's window. A disheveled homeless man took up his usual sloppy stance on the sidewalk across the street.

"He's not my friend."

I took an order for a medium, extra-dry café mocha with raspberry syrup.

"You say he's not your friend but I doubt you've bought anyone else on the planet as many coffees as that guy."

Mitch was bent at the waist restocking the pastry case and looked up at me with a smarmy grin. He was trying to be funny so I resisted the temptation to send him flying into the lemon scones.

"Admit it," Mitch chided as he got to his feet. "As far as coffee dates go, you and Mr. Stinky are on a roll."

"Right. You caught me." I tucked a wayward strand of brown hair back into my loose ponytail.

Normally, working with Mitch was a coaster ride of wit made even more fun because he was so easy on the eyes. But it was only halfway through my shift and my feet already hurt in my new espadrilles. Don't mess with a girl with sore feet.

"Oh you li-i-ike him," Mitch teased. He elbowed me in the ribs as he passed.

"You got me. I'm a pushover for skinny fifty-year-olds that smell like a Dumpster."

"Fifty? You think he's fifty?" Mitch straightened, tilted his head and stared out the window. "I'd say a hard sixty."

A bouffant-blonde regular stepped up to the counter in thigh-high boots and an impossibly tight blue dress.

"What do you think, Molly?" Mitch asked her. "How old do you think Mr. Stinky is? Jen says fifty and I'm going with early sixties."

"Who?" she asked, looking confused.

"The homeless dude who's been sitting across the street every day the last month or so." When Molly continued to offer him a blank stare, Mitch added, "You walk by him every morning to get your tea."

Molly glanced quickly over her shoulder.

"He's there every day?" She frowned and blinked long false eyelashes. "I never noticed."

I poured Molly her usual peppermint tea, but the steam rising came from between my ears, not from the small vent at the top of the plastic lid. Pushing Mitch aside, I thrust the cup into Molly's hand and took her two dollars. I gave her a quarter in change, and she deposited it into the tip jar. Great, I could plan my trip to Hawaii now.

"Thanks, Mitch." Molly fluttered her eyelashes.

Once Molly was out the door with her tea, I picked up a rag and began energetically wiping down the counter and pastry case.

Merlot's Café was just one of thousands of independent coffee shops in Seattle. I'd been whipping up java there for nearly two years. It was located on the main floor of an old, five-story brown brick office building on James Street halfway between Yesler and Second in

Pioneer Square. The place was owned by a seldom-seen
owner named Mervin Lo. Here at Merlot's we served
fair trade, shade grown, organic coffee usually with
a smile. The inside was long and narrow with lots of
exposed brick, a wide glass pastry case, half a dozen
tables and counters with bar stools at the front windows. The walls were lined with framed black-and-
white photos from long-ago Seattle when vegetable
stands stood where Pike Place sprawls today.

"Amazing that she could walk by every day and not
even see him," I snarled under my breath. "Obviously
her dresses are too tight and have cut off circulation to
the gray matter beneath her dyed roots."

"Nothing amazing about it, Jen. Hundreds of people walk down the streets of Seattle every day and I
bet most of those don't give the homeless a second
thought." He stood next to me and nudged my shoulder good-naturedly. "C'mon, even you must've had
times when you crossed the street to avoid a panhan-
dler or pretended not to hear the guy asking you for
spare change."

"Whatever. Just drop it."

My gaze cut sideways to the guy across the street.
It was starting to rain. My throat constricted. You'd
think if you chose to be homeless, you'd at least have
the sense to thumb a ride south until you hit the California sun instead of hanging out in Seattle. The burning itch in my palm ramped up a notch and I rubbed
my hand against my blue-jean-clad thigh.

Mitch caught me staring across the street and said,
"I told you when he started coming round a few weeks
ago that if you feed him he'd keep coming back." He

paused. "They're kind of like cats, and for him…" he nodded across the street "…coffee is like tuna."

"Shut up!" I slammed my palm on the counter, somewhat for emphasis but also to help relieve the itch. The half dozen customers in Merlot's looked up from their newspapers and laptops to regard me curiously.

We served the last of the customers in a long line and I picked up a pen in my left hand to offer my itchy palm some solace. I doodled on the thick pad left near the register.

"How come you write with your right hand, but you always doodle with your left?" Mitch asked.

"Guess I'm just talented." I winked.

I wiped the already clean counter and Mitch went off to make small talk with a petite brunette. After a minute, I began to feel restless.

"It's slow." I two-pointed my rag into a nearby sink. "I'm going on my break."

Mitch wisely kept any snarky comments to himself when I poured a large black coffee in a to-go cup, snagged a bran muffin from the basket containing the day-olds and headed out the door.

As I crossed the street, I observed Mr. Stinky was still getting organized. He finished a smoke and ground it under his toe as I walked over. Placing a twelve-inch square piece of cardboard on the damp sidewalk, he sat down, crisscrossing his legs clad in dirty blue jeans. He had on a denim jacket and leaned his back against the gray concrete slab of the parking garage behind him. In a death grip in his left hand he held the orange Jan-Sport backpack containing all his worldly possessions.

His eyes looked dead ahead at Merlot's, and he

didn't acknowledge me in any way as I dodged traffic and risked becoming the victim to an angry Prius driver. Once I was right in front of him, I crouched down to eye level. The stench of him brought tears to my eyes. At least I told myself it was the smell.

A curl of steam rose from the vented lid of the hot coffee that I placed on the concrete sidewalk. He took the muffin from my outstretched hand and unzipped his backpack using a small yellow compass dangling from the center pocket zipper pull. He placed the muffin gingerly inside next to the oatmeal bar I gave him yesterday and the cinnamon roll from who knows when. Then he reached deeper to the bottom of the pack and pulled out two things—his usual worn paper coffee cup with "change please" scrawled in black Sharpie and a lost dog flyer. He placed the cup in front of him and handed me the sheet.

I sighed, barely glancing at it.

"Right. Lost black lab. Got it. You've given me the same paper every day for a month. You know that you don't have a dog, right?"

I ran an impatient hand through my hair, tugged out the ponytail then scrunched up my hair and pulled the elastic around it tighter than before.

"Look, you gotta find somewhere else to hang out." I dug in my pocket for a folded index card. "I've made a list of all the shelters and soup kitchens in the area. The one up on Third even has a daytime program. You could, you know, be inside all day. No more sitting in the rain. Wouldn't that be nice? Plus, they'd feed you so, um, yeah…wouldn't that be good?"

I held out the card but he continued to look straight

ahead. Not *at* me but *through* me. For a minute we stayed like that. Him staring. Me holding out the list. I'm sure he could've easily done this all day but I had a life. The rain ramped up from mist to drizzle and pasted my hair to my head and made my mascara run but did nothing to wash away his eau de toilette. Finally, with a small exasperated sigh, I tucked the card into his donation cup along with a twenty I couldn't afford.

I was about to get to my feet then changed my mind and leaned in to snap my fingers in front of his face to try to get his attention. His gray eyes flicked to my face then away.

"I don't get it." I threw up my hands in exasperation. "Why do you come here every day if you don't even want to talk to me?"

He reached out a grubby hand and tapped the lost dog flyer I still held in my left hand.

"The dog? There is no dog!" I crumpled the sheet and tossed it at him angrily. It bounced off his stained jacket and landed in his lap.

"You can't keep coming here." My voice hitched. I placed a hand on his shoulder. "Sorry, Dad, but you just can't."

Don't miss
Grounds to Kill *by Wendy Roberts.*
Available now wherever
Carina Press ebooks are sold.
www.CarinaPress.com

ABOUT THE AUTHOR

WENDY ROBERTS IS an armchair sleuth, fan of all things mysterious but a huge chicken at heart. Her mind is often in a secretive cloak-and-dagger world of intrigue while her physical presence is usually at home feeding feral cats and a demanding guinea pig. Wendy resides in Vancouver, Canada, where she happily writes about murder and is always at work on her next novel.

You can find Wendy on the web here:

Website: www.WendyRoberts.com

Twitter: www.Twitter.com/AuthorWendy

Instagram: @WendyRoberts_Author

Facebook: www.Facebook.com/WendyRoberts-Author

Get 4 FREE REWARDS!

We'll send you 2 FREE Books plus 2 FREE Mystery Gifts.

Harlequin Intrigue® books feature heroes and heroines that confront and survive danger while finding themselves irresistibly drawn to one another.

FREE
Value Over
$20

Get 4 FREE REWARDS!

We'll send you 2 FREE Books plus 2 FREE Mystery Gifts.

Harlequin® Romantic Suspense books feature heart-racing sensuality and the promise of a sweeping romance set against the backdrop of suspense.

FREE
Value Over
$20

Get 4 FREE REWARDS!

We'll send you 2 FREE Books plus 2 FREE Mystery Gifts.

Love Inspired® Suspense books feature Christian characters facing challenges to their faith... and lives.

FREE Value Over $20

YES! Please send me 2 FREE Love Inspired® Suspense novels and my 2 FREE mystery gifts (gifts are worth about $10 retail). After receiving them, if I don't wish to receive any more books, I can return the shipping statement marked "cancel." If I don't cancel, I will receive 4 brand-new novels every month and be billed just $5.24 each for the regular-print edition or $5.74 each for the larger-print edition in the U.S., or $5.74 each for the regular-print edition or $6.24 each for the larger-print edition in Canada. That's a savings of at least 13% off the cover price. It's quite a bargain! Shipping and handling is just 50¢ per book in the U.S. and 75¢ per book in Canada.* I understand that accepting the 2 free books and gifts places me under no obligation to buy anything. I can always return a shipment and cancel at any time. The free books and gifts are mine to keep no matter what I decide.

Choose one: ☐ **Love Inspired® Suspense** ☐ **Love Inspired® Suspense**
                 Regular-Print   **Larger-Print**
                 (153/353 IDN GMY5)   (107/307 IDN GMY5)

Name (please print)

Address   Apt. #

City   State/Province   Zip/Postal Code

Mail to the **Reader Service:**
IN U.S.A.: P.O. Box 1341, Buffalo, NY 14240-8531
IN CANADA: P.O. Box 603, Fort Erie, Ontario L2A 5X3

Want to try 2 free books from another series? Call **1-800-873-8635** or visit www.ReaderService.com.

LIS19R